MERRY GO ROUND

SARAH TOLL

Wrate's Publishing

First published in 2020 by Wrate's Publishing

ISBN 978-1-8380128-8-5

Copyright © 2020 by Sarah Toll

Edited and typeset by Wrate's Editing Services

www.wrateseditingservices.co.uk

A CIP catalogue record for this book is available from the British Library.

For the real Lily. Whilst I might have saved you, you most definitely rescued me. I hope we meet one day so that I can thank you.

Chapter 1
DECEMBER 2017

It was a filthy night in October the last time Nathaniel Deighton died. His car, wet with rain, slithered as though it were a freshly caught mackerel, coming to rest in the bowels of a black embankment, with its wheels spinning and its belly facing the moonlit night. Nat's Humpty-Dumpty head, pressed against the driver's window, was smashed by the force of the crash, his right eye bulging to twice its normal size and reflecting the terror he must have felt, as the tarry scented and bitter, scorching air filled his lungs and snuffed the life out of his bloodied body.

Time and time again I'd imagined the scene in slow motion. I could hear the roar of the engine as the car left the tarmac, catching air; the endless cracking and grating as it ploughed through bushes and gorged up mud until it came to rest in that dank-smelling darkness. And I wished, I wished that the pant-shitting terror I could see in his eye was because of his impending day of judgement, but I knew it was really because he would no longer be able to cause carnage with every bat of those strawberry blond eyelashes.

And then, as though by way of a miraculous reincarnation, he was back after having ghosted me for nearly two months. Exhausted by the insane imaginings that kept me awake for nights on end and scouring the internet for news of men killed in car crashes or found dead in their beds, my resistance was low. The relief of knowing he wasn't dead was enough to welcome him back into my bed, where he could fuck me senseless. And that was our lives pretty much. We'd live together like man and wife for a few weeks and then he'd vanish. I'd panic, imagining him to be dead or in prison – he was fond of the wrong side of the law – or worse still, off with another easy lay. Then he'd get back in touch, be nice and we'd carry on as though nothing had happened.

On the day he made the call, he was driving. My heart sank as soon as I heard the echoing sound of his voice over his hands-free system. Calling whilst driving was one of his favourite distraction techniques. If the conversation became too sensitive for him, he would interrupt and proclaim all kinds of near-miss incidents that would take him away from what we were saying. That, or he would get bored and invent a call that he 'must just make', before hanging up, sometimes not calling back for several days, and at other times not at all.

I could tell from the moment he said, 'Hi, Hotpants' in his too-excited way that he was out of control. At the best of times he was energetic and ebullient, but on that day, on December 11th 2017, as Bounds Green basked in a lemony, winter sunshine, I could sense straightaway something big was about to smash into me. I waited for it. I sat in the too-hot coffee shop amid the delicious smell of roasted coffee and buttery croissants and the low hubbub of flushed menopausals and too-smooth salesperson sorts, and I waited for it, as the cloying chai latté I'd not long finished sat like a

2

brick in my stomach. Without him having to say anything, I knew I would not be spending Christmas with Nat.

He lied easily. He insisted he was calling me from his office, despite the mic of his car picking up the rush of the world passing by and the synthetic fading and surging sound of his voice. I ignored his mendacity. There was no sign of the gentle Liverpudlian inflection that inhabited his voice when he was at ease and relaxed – all I could hear was the clipped and clear enunciation of his very best business voice. He sounded maniacal when he was like that. The trick was to wait for him to run out of steam, then he would engage with me and we would have a proper, two-sided conversation. To pass the time between his banal and ridiculous ramblings – a conversation he was having without me – and finally getting to the point, I stabbed a spoon into my empty cup and stared through the window of the coffeehouse at a woman at the bus stop. Her hair was purple and tied high in a messy knot on the top of her head, pinned in place with a geisha-like hair stick. I drifted off at the bit where he started recounting stories of internal politics and the fuckwits he was working with and refused to allow him to draw me in on what underwear I had on or whether I had used my vibrator the night before. I'd heard it all before, you see.

As pieces of me were whittled away by Nat's prattling, the purple-haired woman exhaled white puffs of vapour into the air and stamped from one foot to the other with impatience. I watched her take something from her bag; she didn't put the strap over her shoulder properly and the soft leather hung open. Skewed and twisted, it gaped open-mouthed at me. I was sickened by Nat's torrent of nonsense. He was ugly when he was like this. But then something different happened. The line was quiet for the first time in five or six minutes.

'So, Lily, you're OK, then? Happy enough?'

His apparent concern wasn't what I was expecting, and it

3

took a second or two to get my answer out. I noticed a lump in my throat, where the expectation of grave news had lodged. It ached as I stammered out a reply that sounded as though I was uncertain whether I was all right or not. He ignored my response.

'Listen, I had a bit of unexpected news last night; it was a bit of a shock really, and well . . .'

And there it was, only it was far worse than I could have imagined. The wrecking ball slammed into my back as I sat in the coffee shop staring at the woman with her purple hair and condensed breath and her bloody bag with the grimacing, zippered mouth in danger of spewing its contents. The smell of roasted coffee and buttery croissants suddenly sickened me.

'I just thought you should know . . . Lily . . . you still there?'

I was still listening and somehow, in my response, I managed to find words that were way too generous. Even after the worst kind of hurt I still couldn't tell him what I was thinking. I made my excuses and ended the call. Before I could even begin to take in what he had told me, I rang him back and said that if things didn't work out for him, or if he needed anything in the future, then he could call me. It felt brave and the right thing to do. I reassured him that he would be OK. He said 'cheerio' and rushed away before I had closed the call. I stared at the phone's blank screen in disbelief.

Chapter 2

Before making my way to the office, I spoke to the purple-haired woman and pointed out her gaping bag. She sucked her teeth disdainfully, suggesting I'd rifled through it first. She dismissed me with a flick of that purple head, as she turned her attention to the overdue bus. I was more hurt by her dismissiveness than I was by Nat's callousness. It was as though she had taken her hair stick and poked me through the chest with it. I struggled to walk along the pavement. I felt giddy and my legs moved as if I were drunk. The leaden chai threatened to make a reappearance.

For some ridiculous reason, I made it to work and stayed there. My professional, British upper lip remained loyally stiff as I dragged myself from one end of the day to the other. I made it through conference calls, meetings with my staff and, finally, the crammed underground, where genitals and reeking bodies were thrust into my personal space. I made it past the small row of shops in front of my building and almost to the foot of the toilet before I spewed every ounce of myself in the general direction of the bowl.

'You're such a filthy cow, Lily!'

5

Mya towered above me, her naturally hollow cheeks sucked further inwards with disgust. She slunk out of the bathroom but was waiting for me in the lounge. The reflection of her resting bitch face in the large mirror over the fire demanded an explanation, so I recounted the telephone conversation I'd had with Nat. I hadn't tasted the words. I hadn't tested them to see how they felt as they rolled off my tongue – and they stuck. They were thick and bitter and tasted of bile. With each discordant syllable, acrid juices that tasted of treachery swirled around my teeth and gums. It was as though I were talking about a different Nat, someone who was cold and unloving and cruel.

'Well, you had it coming, Lily, although, to be honest, it turns out he was more of a fucker than even I could have imagined.'

'Thanks, Mya, that's so helpful.'

'Better to have been fucked up by a psycho than be–'

'Mya! He may be a lot of things, but a psychopath isn't one of them. I can't believe . . . I just, it's–'

Tears came, which was better than the vomiting, but my bottom lip rolled over and my chin wobbled. I felt impotent, as I fiddled with the ring on the little finger of my left hand. I simply could not believe that finally it was over. I'd imagined it often enough and was convinced the only thing that would take him away was death or prison. I hadn't considered that he would go because he was a monumental liar.

'Please don't tell me you're going to mope around pining for him?'

I couldn't answer Mya because I knew I would be lying to her, to myself.

'You're fucking useless!'

She threw the words at me and, as she walked away, I watched her tall, thin frame and striking black hair meld into the darkness of the hall. Sometimes I hated her so much, but right then I wished she had stayed and thrashed me with her callous honesty.

In the following weeks, I took time off work and wandered around aimlessly in a state of shock and bereavement. It was as though I had some form of PTSD: I would get flashbacks of him, I'd see his face, hear his voice, his favourite music. I saw him in everything I did and everywhere I went. The spectre of Nathaniel was ubiquitous.

My job became intolerable, even without the distraction and devastation of Nat. I had gone from being determined and devoted to the work I did, to being disengaged and disheartened by the false promises of my boss. I had been at the bank since leaving college and had worked hard, striving for one qualification after the other, as though certificates were some kind of life belt that would keep me afloat and save me from drowning like my mother.

———

You could say I am an orphan. My father decamped the moment his sperm left his body and before my mother could pull up her drawers, but his absence was not half so punishing as my mother's presence. It would have been kinder to all had his seed been sprayed into a piece of toilet tissue or an old sock, but it wasn't, and I was born to a wraith of a mother, who, in her middle-class way, referred to herself as a social drinker. I suspect my grandfather, a Rolls Royce engineer, had left her his savings as well as the semi in Waltham Cross where I grew up. Having tried employment a couple of times, she gave up because it 'didn't agree' with her and gathered up the lost and lonely instead. A waif here, a stray there, people whose vacuous souls were also filled with booze, who consoled their wounded spirits with likeminded folk. Our home was always buzzing, choked up with cigarette smoke puffed from the lungs of people who outwardly appeared respectable but, in reality, were drifters. They would sit around offering to bring me presents, precious promises that were never realised. Whenever our doorbell rang, there was always a Picasso-esque composition of hope and disappointment standing on the doorstep.

Along with the house, we'd been bequeathed Uncle Tom. He was the man who lived next door; always ready with a trick or a joke that would have me giggling, even though half the time I didn't understand the whistles and slurs of his toothless chatter. What I did understand was that the warmth of his hand clasped tightly around mine, as we walked across to the ice cream man, meant safety. I knew I could trust him from the smile in his eyes, his pear drops smell, his braces and slippers and the fact he always wore a tie. When he died, he did so with dignity, something that, I came to learn later, wasn't always the case. Uncle Tom had simply fallen asleep in his favourite chair, which he kept in the shed, surrounded by nuts and bolts and sawn bits of wood, twine and bottles of wine he'd brewed from the rhubarb that grew wild in a pile at the end of his garden. He was the epitome of goodness to me and I lived to achieve some of the peace and goodness that ran through his veins. That was, until I met Nat. Aside from Uncle Tom, my life was filled with hypothetical beings who had left me with a deep-seated confusion about how to *be* in the world. I was mystified by people and life, as if I were on the outside watching it all happen to others. It was little wonder I had no idea how to cope with people and their idiosyncrasies, especially multifaceted people like Nat.

———

My mother's determination not to conform formed my determination to have my own home with my own bits of sawn wood and balls of string, just like Uncle Tom. I started out as an admin clerk but ended up as a manager in the people development team. My most recent boss checked on every decision I made, questioned each plan I put forward and hounded me for documents, budgets and training schedules for projects that would never see the light of day. My last hope was a project instigated by the CEO, who wanted to invest twenty-five million in a programme of staff development led by a team of organisational psychologists. He hired an independent team of consultants to help navigate the complex seas of procurement and contract management, and along with them came Nat.

The first time I met him was during a programme board meeting. It was more than just eyes across a table, it was an intention on his part. He knew what he wanted, he knew he would get it, and he knew what it would cost me. I only know that now. During the meeting, I tabled some concerns and he leapt in with an offer of help followed swiftly with an invite to a 'one-on-one' meeting, where he proceeded to woo me with his knowledge and approach to people development, his expertise in NLP and his desire to take me under his wing and develop my skills.

He soon learned the challenges I faced and worked with me to evolve and progress, which got me recognised by the programme's senior team and, on his insistence, I was seconded to be the lead for staff advocacy. All too soon his six months was up, and time rushed us towards the end of his contract via my bedroom and the start of his ghosting behaviours. To add insult to injury, when the programme began failing, just after he'd left, I was the one who bore the brunt. I had put my head above the parapet out of greed for greater recognition and a nudge up a rung of the ladder, only to find myself as the scapegoat.

———

The whole thing with Nathaniel in December consumed me and was the final straw in the misery that had become my job, so I bunked off as much as I could and by the time the inevitable HR review meeting was scheduled, I had typed up my letter of resignation. I'd spent four months getting paid for living in a sickening state. I couldn't bear to look around me and I hated everyone. My emotions were so strong that I became quite fearful – for my safety and that of others – of being out and about. London was closing in on me; I felt stifled and oppressed and my time was filled with hatred and self-loathing. I barely ate and did so much exercise my body permanently hurt. I realised I was abusing myself, but I couldn't stop. Mental anguish was no reason to keep crying. I had to hurt physically – really, really hurt.

It all stopped at a yoga class one night. The teacher, Steve, asked us to set an intention of being kind to ourselves in our practice, which included being gentle with our bodies, as well as with our minds and spirits. As soon as he'd framed the session, I felt a massive connection with what I was being asked to do, but I panicked, as it struck me I was frightened to do it. As the class progressed, I realised that this gentleness was something I needed to do, or else I'd be lost and would remain in purgatory. During the final meditation, I cried, but not out of despair. It was as though something had been released from within me.

That night was the first night I slept properly in months, and the next day I was finally able to begin working on a plan. I'd known from a young age that a traditional married life wasn't for me, but I'd still worked, saved hard and put my life on hold, until that day after my yoga class, when I decided to run away from the life I had always known.

I'd always wanted to live by the sea, as I loved the wildness of the coast, the spontaneity offered by the elements and its variable weather; the lingering sea frets, horizontal rain and translucent sun. I reasoned that a change of scenery and pace, of air and light would be healing for my jaded spirit. And so, I rented out my tiny flat, stored my belongings and found myself a troupe to join, which turned out to be a live-in cleaning job at some holiday cottages on a small farmstead in Welcombe. It was a place that had a foot in both Devon and Cornwall, as it straddled the county boundaries. To make it a more appealing proposition for the owner, Mrs Enys, I found myself agreeing to her suggestion that I might like to take on the additional duties of laundering the bed linen and towels, too.

The interview for the job took place in a small café in Bideford, which was nowhere near the farm complex that was to be my home. It struck me I was being naïve and foolish by not seeing the place I would be living and working in before starting the job, but I didn't care as long as it would secure my escape from the city I was convinced was holding me hostage in the world of Nat. Besides, Mrs Enys had business to attend to in Bideford and made no secret of the fact that we were there because it suited her. I judged from her stern appearance and manner of speaking that she was a conscientious businesswoman, and although rather formidable there was something about her direct nature that appealed to me and I liked her instantly.

When she offered me the job at Tregellas Farm, I accepted it without hesitation, after which life became a seesaw of conflict about whether it was the right thing to do or not. The loss of Nat had crushed me. It had inverted my world, plunging me headlong into a life filled with a constant, morbid undertone, as I grieved in a way I had never known before. Mya was being her usual trite self, arguing with pleasure at my expense, switching sides and changing her stance on the situation in an effort to confound me further. She reckoned her behaviour would help me to make peace with the decision and be confident that it was right for me, but I felt mouse-like to her cattish torment. On good days, I was able to remain positive by reassuring myself that moving away wasn't forever. The first let on my flat was only for twelve months, so at worst this could be my chance to have an adventurous year off. Even if it was a complete disaster, it couldn't be any worse than my life in Bounds Green without Nat. On bad days, I was terrified at the thought of what I had let myself in for. I had no idea what it would be like living in Welcombe and had only seen pictures of Tregellas online. But truth be told, I didn't have the energy to be worried about that kind of detail. From the images I had seen of the area and the description of it as 'a remote and energetic place', I reckoned it would be just what I needed.

The farm's website described each of the cottages as 'home-from-home living spaces', and the fact they were nicely fitted out and were named after notable locals made them sound both appealing and quaint. My plan was to work hard during the mornings and spend the afternoons and evenings escaping to the beaches and surrounding countryside, in which I was certain I would be able to finally repair and recover. The farmstead itself was nothing more than a stone's throw from the coastal footpath, which would be perfect for getting me out and about.

Whereas Bounds Green was crowded and suffocating, the population of Welcombe was small, with only around two hundred permanent residents living in the whole area. The thought of such seclusion was a worry for me. In London, my own isolation was something I had control over and could break if compelled to do so, but it appeared I would have little choice in the matter on the farm, and I was all too aware of what lay in wait if the space was too quiet. I already knew that given the opportunity I would obsessively pick away at the harm Nat had caused me during the rollercoaster era of a relationship that was as malevolent as it was glorious. I would allow myself to wallow in a haven of despair. In my solitude, I would fester uninterrupted in the exhausting darkness of being alone with my thoughts of him. This haven wasn't somewhere new to me. I'd been there before and knew it well. Being in that bleak place would be as though I had returned home to the semi in Waltham Cross. In no time at all, I would be back in the bosom of the maleficent friend and nursemaid who had tended to me as a child, the same one who had held me tight and whispered to me that nothing would ever be all right. I found isolation a compelling and unassuming place in which to retreat, but I also had to believe it could be a place of healing.

Chapter 3
JUNE 2018

The late afternoon sunshine spilled through the dirty windows of the train that whisked me through the Wiltshire countryside. I turned to stare through closed lids at the burning rays, forcing myself to face the sun's searing gaze. Mya was fast asleep, slumped against the window and dead to the world. She would sleep for the whole journey now, which I resented, although it made things easier. On days of great importance, such as today, she tended to be riotous and mischievous, but the chaos of recent months had at last caught up with her. Once in Devon, I figured she would stay awhile, at least until I had settled in. But as I allowed the warm rays to kindle a hint of hope within me, I still needed to convince myself that running away was the right thing to do. The greater part of me did not approve of leaving Nathaniel in London, or wherever he was. Each time I recalled that terrible telephone call I wished I could hate him. His frenzied exhilaration and his thrilled voice continued to echo in my ears. 'I thought you should know' played on a continuous loop in my brain. Goosebumps stippled my fair skin, as his presence sidled in and draped itself around my shoulders like a moth-eaten old fox fur.

'You look as though you need this?' A cup of something hot was being offered by a striking-looking woman standing in front of me. 'Forgive the intrusion, but I was sitting across the carriage there. I noticed you crying earlier and then you dozed. I wondered if you might appreciate a coffee. I reckoned it'd brighten you up.'

'Oh, OK, thanks. Thank you.'

'I'm Diana, mind if I join you?' The woman gave me no opportunity to object and, as she sat down, she ruffled her spiky, silver hair and brushed imagined particles from her dark jeans and silk blouse. 'Obviously, I'm not sure how you take it,' she said, pointing to the coffee, 'there's no milk but a ton of sugar. Nothing beats a hot, sweet drink to perk one up, aside from a good brandy, that is.'

I attempted to sip at the liquorice-coloured liquid, whilst she carried on with her non-stop chatting. As she spoke, she made grand gestures with her willowy arms and my gaze followed the streaks of turquoise embedded in her silver bangles, which jingled around her wrists.

'And you, are you travelling as far as Exeter?' she asked.

'Yep. I'm running away to live on a farm by the sea.'

As I told her my plans to take time out from a life that was too full, I tried to sound excited. I stopped talking and stared ahead, at a piece of chewing gum stuck above the bin, before describing my bright, handsome lover with his slightly corpulent belly and enigmatic style. I told her that despite his bravado he was in fact quite uncertain of his place in the world, which made him sound vulnerable, which was probably the case. I told her that he had made me brave and that I had achieved so much whilst with him. However, when the time came, I couldn't bear to tell her the truth about our lives together, nor how our relationship had ended, so I told her that despite being very much in love, the demands of his business meant we couldn't be together and that we had parted amicably but broken hearted. The lie to my benevolent stranger was barefaced. She didn't deserve it and I'm not sure she bought it.

'Ah, that explains the sadness–' she faced me with her hand to her chest and flushed with embarrassment '–if you don't mind me saying?'

'No, I don't mind. I know I look awful; I *feel* bloody awful, but that's why I'm running away.' She nodded in a way that suggested she had experience of my pain. 'I can't stand this constant moping around, so it's better if I leave.'

Diana placed a nut-brown hand on my bony knee, tapping out a hit-and-miss rhythm as she gazed out of the window. She radiated poise and dignity and a healthfulness I envied. As she considered what I had said, we swayed in unison with the motion of the train, and the moment of wordlessness between us was soothing.

She sighed before speaking. 'I see it from a different angle. You're not running away you're running towards a brand-new life. Bravo to you!' She clapped her hands together in front of her chest, as though in a fleeting moment of prayer, and turned to look at me. 'How old are you?'

'I'm 35.'

'And what do–did you do for a living?'

I was uncertain as to where things were going but was intrigued by her interest in me. 'I worked in banking; I managed projects around staff development and change. But I'd had enough. I'd done it for years, so it wasn't hard to leave.'

'Well, I reckon it'll be perfect. It's serendipity – a wonderful opportunity to take all you know and bring about change in *you*! Fancy that, 35 and reinventing yourself–' she paused '–don't let him rule your world; you may as well stay in London if you allow that to happen.'

She was right. I needed to be purposeful, self-sufficient, strong like her. It's not as though I could depend on Mya to keep me safe, but I could run towards something new and unsullied.

Maintaining her ambiguous and intense gaze with me, Diana rested the side of her head on the back of the shabby bench seat of the train, as though our conversation had depleted her in some way. I liked what she had to say. As well as moving away from something, I was moving towards something new. Mya stirred in her seat and I prayed she would remain silent and leave me in the kindness Diana had gifted me. I fiddled with the ring on the little finger of my left hand. I had worn it for years after buying it at a craft fair as a teenager, and somehow it had become a connection to my inner strength; it was my anchor for those moments when I felt vulnerable or afraid and, on rare occasions, when the vibration of something good was rising within me. In that moment with Diana, the energy of possibility surged through me, and as I spun it around more quickly, confidence welled up inside of me, working its way from the butterfly feeling in my stomach until it erupted into a gentle smile upon my out-of-practice lips.

Seeing the glimmer of hope, Diana smiled back at me. 'You have a pretty smile. I *hope* things work out for you and perhaps then you'll be able to smile a little more often. Make the most of this opportunity. Open your heart to love and life, you never know where it'll come from, but believe in your life, your love, your work and your longings – you'll be fine.'

'But how can I believe? How do I become open to love?' I thought I'd asked the question in my head, but without hesitation, Diana answered it for me. 'You just need to relax and go for it.' And with a sympathetic sigh she closed the conversation. She stood up, then asked if she could hug me before she moved back to her seat across the carriage.

After my initial reservation, I wished that she would have stayed and completed the journey with me. I observed her out of the corner of my eye. She sat with great poise and dignity in her seat and turned her head in dismissal to watch closely as the world whipped past the window. Her closure on our interaction left me feeling perplexed, but greatly comforted by our meeting. The feel of her light hug was lasting and although the whole interaction had been a little strange, her kindness and words comforted me.

Chapter 4

For the remainder of the journey, I zoned in and out of a meditative state. As I stared back at my reflection in the darkening grey of the window, I pondered my conversation with Diana and mulled over the proposition of a new life. I looked at Mya in her peaceful sleep and was grateful that she hadn't butted in and monopolised the conversation. The frisson of excitement remained. However, I couldn't ignore the gargantuan struggle that lay ahead. And before long, after being so buoyed by Diana, I noticed that in my own company I had descended into doom and gloom once again. As I began waking myself from my contemplation, I became aware that the engine noise of the train had changed; we were approaching Exeter.

'We're here,' I said to Mya, but she feigned sleep and ignored me. 'Mya. Come on. We're here. You need to move it, lady.'

The gentle thrum was different and the clang it now made was reverberating throughout the carriage. In my head, the noise sounded like a weary blacksmith hammering upon a rod of iron somewhere at the back of the train. The tune he bashed out was the mechanical, metallic utterance of the word 'friend' over and over again. Of all the things I wanted, more than anything else in the world, I wanted my friends. The discordant chime of metal upon metal as the train slowed toward its destination somehow reminded me of how detestable I had become. I had banished my own friends when I chose my sordid life with Nat over them. They should have been part of my reinvention, and had I listened to them in the first place, I might never have needed to make it.

By the time the train had called to a halt, the sun had faded and dusk was edging twilight along. The next bit of the journey was to be by road, in a car I'd bought from a neighbour's brother. He lived in Exmouth but happened to be visiting Bounds Green just after I had been offered the job at Tregellas. Call it serendipity or synchronicity, but the car appeared in my universe just at the right moment in time. It was a 1973 Beetle in a gorgeous, spangly red. I'm sure I paid over the odds for it, but it felt right to go ahead with the purchase. The seller, Mark, seemed a nice enough guy and promised to deliver the car to Exeter St David's and leave it in the car park ready for my arrival. But as passengers rallied and doors opened, an icy chill tapped me on the shoulder and I involuntarily shuddered. I had believed this Mark guy was an honest man. I'd taken him at his word that the car would be where he promised it would be, and that he would have left the spare key behind the petrol filler and hadn't just disappeared in a puff of exhaust smoke with a wedge of my money.

As we disembarked, Diana briefly nodded, but didn't engage with me any further. I followed her along the platform with gratitude and a slight infatuation and, as I came out of the station, I sniffed the faintly moist evening air, surprised at how warm it was. Meanwhile, Mya skulked along behind me like a moody teenager.

'You know he's legged it with your dosh, don't you?'

'I'm not listening, Mya, just give it a rest.'

'Just sayin''

'Enough!'

The furrow in my cold, sweaty brow grabbed the knot in my stomach and ran away with it as soon as I saw the old Beetle parked under the orange glow of the car park light. I ran my fingers over the mouse-shaped keyring Nathaniel had bought for me. On it was a long, thin key. Ancient and smooth, it had been worn into a sliver of itself with the passing of time, but it was quite literally the key to the heart of my new love.

'See, I told you,' I whispered to Mya.

I squeezed the mouse for reassurance while marching as confidently as I possibly could towards the car. I made for the back of Bertie, smiling. I had loved the car as soon as I had spotted 'his' red, sparkly paintwork, and seeing him again made me glad. I put the key into the lock, turned the chrome handle and opened the boot of the car. I then laughed out loud at the oily engine, as it sniggered out of the darkness at me.

'Twat,' muttered Mya.

But then we giggled and, in some small way, I was delighted at my capacity to laugh at myself. Nonetheless, feeling a bit of an idiot, I remembered that the boot was at the front of the car and after loading my suitcase, I finally jumped into the driving seat and took a big breath in. The car smelled of warm vinyl and petrol. It was intoxicating, and I sniffed the air several times just to take my fill. Everything about the car smelt and felt ancient. There were no carpets, no modern-day flourishes – just a hunk of metal and plastic. He was rustic, authentic and all mine. Mya had clambered into the back and was sitting lengthways with her long legs hitched up at the knee and her back against the side. I could tell she was intent on achieving sleep again, unwilling to indulge me in sharing a moment or two of contentment.

I fumbled to find the ignition keyhole and eventually had to look to insert the fragile key into its well-worn slot. I remember how reluctant I was to turn it, scared that it might twist or snap, and then, as I pressed the accelerator, Bertie roared into life. Ahhhh, the noise, the power, the smell – it was wonderful. I played for a few moments, revving the noisy engine quite hard just to engage with the thrum it made, smiling broadly as it growled in response to my right foot. I gently touched the thin metal indicators, idly flicking them up and then down. The tick-on tick-off noise they made was strangely irritating. It was hollow sounding and didn't befit the testosterone-fuelled persona I had bestowed upon my sturdy Bertie. I quickly kicked off my shoes so that I could feel the pedals beneath my feet. The brittle rubber pads that covered the chrome pedals were coarse and ticklish under the soft skin on my soles, but they felt robust and I liked the sense of connection they gave me to the car. I clapped my hands with glee – we were going to be great friends. I settled myself into the car and checked the map to ensure I knew the roads I would need. On the passenger seat next to me, I placed a torch, my shoes and the map. 'Ready, then?' I asked Mya.

'As I'll ever be,' she managed to respond before resting her head on the back of the car seat. I promptly stalled the car. The lurch sent everything flying off the passenger seat and into the footwell, and Mya slammed into the back of my seat.

'For fuck's sake, you moron!' she howled. 'What the actual fuck are you playing at?'

Her dark eyes glared at me in the rear-view mirror. Embarrassed, I recovered the map from the floor and restarted the engine. As Bertie roared into life once more, I shifted the gear and lifted the clutch pedal. We were off.

Once on the A30, I started to get to know the little car. I

became used to the weight and the feel of him as he responded to the will of my hands and feet. Soon I could gauge the play in the steering wheel, how far it would move before Bertie reacted, how he responded under my touch. It was like getting to know a new lover. What did he like, how did he like to be handled? The pedals under my bare toes soon took on an air of familiarity. I began speeding up and down through the gears, negotiating the twists and turns and the ups and downs of the partially lit road, as we wound our way across the Devonshire countryside.

Unused to driving, I hadn't really appreciated how long the journey would be, and after forty minutes or so, I could feel my excitement waning and I began to get fidgety. I tried listening to the radio, but it interfered with the sound of Bertie's heart beating away behind me, so I turned it off. I began to imagine my new world of clifftop walks, brazen winds and nestling down with hot chocolate on weather-whipped beaches. It wasn't long before I noticed my spirit rising and falling, soaring in time with the hills I descended and climbed, all the time being drawn in, becoming tighter and tighter with the landscape that beckoned me onwards. I barely moved a muscle as the road steered us this way and that. Bertie hunkered down, hugging the tarmac passing below. It was almost as though he knew intuitively where to go and which way to turn, as he propelled us towards the sea.

Chapter 5

Whilst my imagination was full of encouraging thoughts of an idyllic existence by the sea, Nathaniel and thoughts of our experiences together were ever present. As I sped along in the little car through unlit sections of road, interspersed occasionally with tiny hamlets, I became consumed once again by what I was about to embark upon. I realised I was going to be living my part of a dream we had tentatively batted between us. Nat had wanted to buy a home in Spain, while I had a hankering for a life down by the sea in the Southwest of England. Generally, these were post-coital ramblings, as Nathaniel couldn't even be pinned down to a home together in London, let alone anywhere else in the world. We'd playfully argue about who had the best plan and which one would be most achievable.

We'd argued more vociferously about what names we would give our children. Both of us liked Imogen, or simply Immi, for a girl, but boys' names had been warfare. I'd wanted Tom after Uncle Tom, Nat, however, had wanted Jack, just because it was a boyish-sounding name; he was adamant and wouldn't be moved on it. The narky silences that lingered after what started as playful debates were agony. He would mope and sulk around, as though bored and restless, before vanishing for a chunk of time. Whilst he was gone, I would pick over each sentence, searching for a morsel of hope, like a seagull foraging for food in a landfill site. We both needed to learn that difference didn't have to be harmful.

My friends had used the word harmful when talking about Nat, and although accurate, I preferred to ignore its presence in our conversations. But, as I whizzed along, I contemplated the word. *Harmful: causing or likely to cause harm.* The very essence of its meaning bothered me and as I threaded my way along the ribbon of black tarmac, instead of slowing down, I pressed down my bare foot onto the accelerator harder.

I grasped the large Bakelite steering wheel and although I focused intently on the road ahead, I saw little but the bushes and hedges passing by at the speed of lightning. My best friend Lou's words sprung to mind: *'He's got a bloody nerve, Lily . . . He's an accomplished liar . . . All I hear are cover stories from you . . . Please, just bin him before he does you any real harm.'*

The last time I had spoken to her, nearly a year ago, her imploring tone had frightened me, because the words she spoke were truer than I cared to admit. After that, it had been easier not to talk with her than to suffer the indignity I felt when we chatted. I missed her desperately, but not desperately enough to tell her I was moving to the seaside, nor to reveal just how much of an accomplished liar Nat was, or how harmful he had turned out to be.

The twists and turns in the road came faster and faster, sucking me into their blackness as the road began to blur. How the hell did I let this all happen? Why did he do this to me? Why should *I* be the one running away? Suddenly, the road vanished. Panicking, I blinked rapidly to regain focus, as I slammed down a gear and hit the brakes. The road plummeted away down and sharply to the left and, swerving fiercely from side to side, I slewed around the bend. Bertie spun around and bounced from wheel to wheel, teetering on the brink of rolling over, but without quite enough impetus, he remained upright.

By the time the car came to rest it was diagonal across the centre of the road, its headlights dimly lighting the hedge. I thought of the slippery mackerel car crash I'd envisioned Nathaniel dying in and buried my face in my hands. In the silence that followed, I breathed heavily. Mya said nothing, but I heard her lean forward. I could sense her icy hands resting upon my shoulders and she squeezed them gently. 'You're OK, Lily,' she offered with unusual kindness.

I couldn't take my hands from my face. There were no tears, but my body was consumed with shivers that grew in intensity as the shock of such a close call began to register. I sat for some time before gathering myself together enough to start the car and drive to the left-hand side of the road, where I remained stationary for a few minutes longer.

'So, d'you reckon we'll make it as far as Welcombe?' Mya asked, and although I couldn't see her face in the mirror, I could hear a gentle smile in her words.

Setting off again, I gingerly made my way along those first few feet of road. I noticed a fine tremor in my hands before I hooked them, claw-like, around the steering wheel. I travelled cautiously, almost too slowly. Before long, I came across the village of Kilkhampton and, recognising the name, knew I was not so very far away from Welcombe. I turned from the A39 into a pitch-black lane. Bertie's lights weren't so good in the complete darkness and I only had a vague idea of where I was headed, so I carried on in the blind hope that I was in the right place. I drove past a sign for the community shop and then for The Old Smithy Inn, the local watering hole.

'Nearly there, I reckon,' I said to Mya. Her silence made me uncertain if she was asleep again or didn't care.

I continued carefully and was soon descending the steepest hill I had ever driven down. The pull of the car and the pitch of the engine chafed and gnawed away at my nerves. I sat forwards in the driver's seat and peered over the steering wheel, hoping and praying that I wouldn't make a mistake that would result in me plunging off a cliff edge, leaving no trace that I had ever been there.

Eventually, I came to a fork in the road. There were no road signs to guide me, so I decided to take the left-hand lane on the basis that it was slightly wider than the lane to the right. However, I had only driven a few metres when the road descended further still into the darkness. I crawled along. The lane became little more than rough ground. The stones and boulders were large enough to make Bertie's wheels bobble and pitch around wildly. It was as though a gigantic, road-eating monster had taken vast bites out of the very ground in front of me, creating chasms that were large enough to dip into but not so large as to swallow me whole. This was a road I should not have been on.

'You ploughing or driving, asshole?' I could see her head bobbing around in the mirror. Mya didn't look at me but stared out of the window. 'We're gonna die ugly, so gonna die!'

'Shut up, for God's sake, this is . . . fucking hell . . .' I couldn't speak and concentrate on keeping Bertie heading in the right direction at the same time. I lurched down the ludicrous fairground ride of a road, until eventually I came to a grassed area that I roughly parked Bertie on. I pressed the heels of my hands into my eyes as I tried to repress the inevitable tears that were now desperate to break free. The shock of nearly crashing and the godawful hill I'd just risked had released all kinds of devils, who ridiculed and tormented me as they darted about my head like a million midges. I slumped behind the wheel; the journey from my life in Bounds Green to this pit of despair had taken little more than five or six hours, and yet I felt as though I had been hauling myself along for days getting nowhere. It was agonising. The journey itself was a metaphor for the drawn-out process of escaping from a life filled with Nat. Like a fly trying to escape a web, I was bound in silk, trapped in a lacework of lies spun by Nathaniel Deighton. He was relentlessly holding me, saving me up to devour later. I wondered why I had ever been involved with him and his repeated assaults on me. They weren't physical, but his mental and emotional treatment of me was cruel and callous. Unlike the fly, though, I had been a willing hostage; my alliance with my captor enabled me to embrace his skewed view of the world. In the blackness, I realised I had done little more than pack up all my fears and uncertainties and drag them along with me. I couldn't do it. I couldn't make the change and must've been crazy to think I could. No matter what Diana had said, it wasn't as simple as running away and starting again. She and my mum and Nat and Lou could all just fuck off.

Chapter 6

I stared despairingly at the uninviting moonscape of threadbare grass and dusty granite and concentrated on bringing my breath to my energy centre until I felt calmer. Then I realised I could hear the sea crashing away in front of me.

'Hey, Mya, we found the sea!'

Wiping my cheeks and chin of tears, I strained over the steering wheel, but I couldn't see anything other than a vast expanse of white stars against a black velvety backdrop. For a long while, I stared calmly into the darkness. I wanted to stay put and to be lost in that moment forever. If my life had come to an end at that point, I would have been OK with it.

I knew I had to face it, but at that time I didn't have the strength to reconcile all I had been through with Nat. I hadn't had any contact with him since he had told me his news in December, and for the first time in our history, I was confident I would never hear from him again. Contact with him had never been easy or conventional and my reaction to his abandonment – to his rejection each time – was, without fail, an all-consuming desperation that left me baffled. And yet I accepted it without question. This time, however, was different; this time, his death was as real as it was ever going to get. I hadn't even experienced such a prolonged or desperate reaction when my mother eventually killed herself when I was 18. Until then, the only death I'd known had been that of Uncle Tom's. I was a child, probably 7 or 8, when he slipped away. I remember crying, sad at the thought of no more ice-cream chats together, but OK, too, because he was always happy in his beloved shed and going to sleep was a safe thing to do. Whereas my mother's demise was traumatic, I didn't cry and couldn't think of anything positive I would miss. I knew I should have felt grief, but I just couldn't. Instead I felt guilty, guilty at the overriding sense of relief the news of her death brought.

I say my mother killed herself, but it wasn't as though she had committed suicide. Her gullet had ruptured one evening at a so-called friend's house, and she had gagged and drowned in her own blood. The friend had left it for two days before contacting me to tell me she had passed away. I was never a priority and in her demise I became an afterthought, or at least a priority for the wrong reason. The man felt I had some responsibility towards the restoration of his Berber carpet and numerous pieces of Ercol furniture, which had been sprayed in my mother's blood as she'd coughed and spluttered to death. It was down to me to sort out, or to send money so that a cleaner could do it. I went and cleaned up the carnage myself. It was as though from beyond the grave my mother had arranged one final humiliating task for me to fulfil, one final chance to rescue her.

I had always rescued her. My mother could spend time being reasonably settled, but then some small deed would knock her off her axis, her world would start to fall apart, and she would create some trauma from which she needed to be rescued. I'd step in, get her back on her feet, we'd get close and then she'd go off on her next 'adventure', as she liked to describe her benders, leaving me wondering, quite literally on the last occasion, what the bloody hell had happened and having to pick up my life again. Like Nat's, her life had also been one crazy carnival ride that had both astounded and employed me. The similarities between her and Nat were startling, but I ignored them.

———

The blackness of the night seeped into the spaces around me and snuggled me in. Like a ginormous duvet, it held me close and began to make me feel safe. And in this safe space, I realised that Nat had to slip into my past and become part of my history, just like my mother had done. But in all honesty, the flawed and primeval me wanted his attention and affection.

It was marginally less terrifying going up what I subsequently called The Hill of Death, and, having had the experience of coming down, I realised that if he didn't slip and slide, Bertie would be able to tolerate the bashing he was taking. I took it as steady as I could, searching fruitlessly for a sign, anything that might indicate the whereabouts of Tregellas Farm. I had no idea what I would do once I reached the summit. It was far too late to start scouting around for a phone box to call Mrs Enys from, and anyhow, she would think me hopeless if she received a call from me so late at night and would no doubt wonder why on earth she had hired such a pathetic creature. I had relinquished my work mobile and hadn't thought about replacing it – after all, I had no one to call – but I hadn't given a thought to how it might be useful to have some form of contact with the outside world. I approached the top of the hill, grateful for the fact I was still alive, and continued to drive around in the loop of lanes, passing the community shop and Old Smithy Inn three times.

Upon approaching the Hill of Death for the third time, I found myself blinking hard in uncertainty, as in front of me at the crossroads a small light appeared from the turning on the right. Trying not to panic, I focused on what was approaching out of the darkness and, as I did so, a man walking alongside his bicycle came into view. He stopped walking and stood stock-still about six feet in front of me, staring directly at me. I pulled Bertie to a halt. From a distance, I could see that he was tall, broad shouldered and dishevelled. I needed help, but it was impossible to tell if he was an angel or the devil in disguise.

'Mya,' I hissed.

The man remained rooted to the spot in the middle of the lane, staring into Bertie's headlights and waiting for me. So, with my heart in my mouth, I rolled Bertie forward as far as I could and called out to him through the open window. 'I'm looking for Tregallas Farm . . .'

He remained stationary and made no attempt to move or answer me. I called out 'Hello?' to him, but still no response.

I sat for a while and neither of us moved. I gripped the steering wheel; my mind scampered along in various directions until it froze. I just didn't know what to do. In London, I considered myself streetwise, but I had no idea how to handle this situation. The guy wasn't menacing, but he was standing very still, staring at me unswervingly. I couldn't drive anywhere without running him down, but he obviously couldn't hear me over the noise of the engine. Reluctantly, I realised he wasn't going to come to me. I was going to have to leave the sanctuary of my car and approach him, yet the thought terrified me.

'Mya. Please, we have a . . . er . . . we have a *situation.*'

I reached out for my shoes, but they had been thrown into the passenger stepwell when I had stalled the car in the car park. I was a little uneasy about taking my eyes off the stranger, but I had to retrieve my shoes. I bent over and scrabbled around in the dark to find them and, once located, sat back up again. As I did so, I jumped from my seat and screamed loudly, as the man was now standing alongside the car, his face looming through the window. He jumped as high as me when I screamed, reeling backwards and away from me and falling over his bicycle.

'Jesus Christ, you made me jump!' I yelled at him. 'What the hell do you think you're doing creeping up on me like that?'

I grabbed the torch and leaned out of the window, from where I could see he was on the ground. His limbs and the bike were an entwined mess; the front wheel twisted right round, the handlebars facing the wrong way and the leg of his jeans taught against one of the pedals. He groaned but didn't move, as his level of consciousness continued its cycle ride off into the distance.

'Are you OK?'

No reply. I tried to open the driver's door, but the man was so close to Bertie there wasn't enough room.

'I said, are you OK?' Another moan. 'Hello! Can you hear me?'

'Arrrgghhhhhhh! Of course I can hear you!'

The creature let out a mournful growl and in one fell swoop disengaged himself from under the bike and somehow managed to leap up. Panting, he untangled his bike and stood staring back at me through the window, all bloodshot eyes and wild-mouthed. He was inches away from me. 'What. Do you think. You are doin'?'

I recoiled . . . beer, a very strong smell of beer. 'Well, I was looking for Tregellas Farm until you freaked the living daylights out of me!'

'Well, then,' the man yelled. 'Why were you sitting in the lane? Not moving, not going anywhere, blinding me until I was, until I was–'

'Because I couldn't find the lane to take me to Tregellas Farm!'

I noticed I was yelling too. Then the man started weaving about in front of me. I couldn't be certain if it was because of the accident or because he was very drunk. I contemplated driving off.

'Why didn't you say so. Come on, then, this way . . .' And with that he turned and walked away. I reasoned that all I could do was follow and, as the man was so very drunk, I didn't think he would be that much of a threat. He walked away from the car and I watched his dusty and scruffy back as he pushed his bike ahead of me. Once he was a reasonable distance away, I slipped Bertie into first gear and made after him.

'Well, now, he's charming. You sure he's not going to lure you to his cave and then pick your bones clean?'

'Enough, Mya!'

I heard her take a sharp intake of breath and the squeak of the vinyl as she sat forward to whisper in my ear. 'Suppose they're all like that round here? Suppose he's like the mayor or something and is one of the educated ones? Oh god, that would be fantastic. They're all ten-thumbed swede munchers and he's the pick of the bunch.' She laughed at me.

'Mya, shut the fuck up!' I began to wish she was still fast asleep in the back.

'Swede. Munch. Ooo-arrr. Cider, my luverly? Hahahaa, you lucky girl.'

'Mya, enough!' I shouted. She hated it when I yelled, but it

34

was often the only way I could get her to shut up and leave me alone.

The man walked around to the left and into the unmade road with the monster potholes. When he reached the point at which tarmac became gravel, he pointed to the right and to the entrance to another lane, which, although concealed, was now obvious. My concentration had been so focused on navigating the terror of the unmade road, it wasn't surprising I hadn't seen it. This 'new' tarmacked lane also dropped steeply down, so my concerns about being consumed by voracious gullies had been justified.

After a short distance, the man moved to the side of the road and unsteadily waved me past. I acknowledged him with a tentative nod and a wave of thanks as I drove by and followed the winding lane downwards and into a secluded valley, where the little farmstead nestled.

Chapter 7

I pulled into a gravel courtyard around which stood three large converted barns.

Apparently, Mrs Enys had left the key to my accommodation in the porch of the main building, which was the reception area for paying guests. Fortunately, considering my recent failure at finding the farm, this was well signposted from the yard. I turned Bertie off and breathed a dizzying sigh of relief that I was now home. Grabbing my torch, I made my way over to the dimly lit porch and found an envelope with my name on it. Inside was an old iron key and a crudely printed map of directions to the cottage, which was set way back from those settled around the edges of the courtyard. The route to Hawker's Hut was highlighted in thick, luminous green pen. Feeling audacious and yet nervous at the same time, I held the map and caressed the cold, iron key. I momentarily dwelt upon what was to come and wondered how it might be influenced by those who had held the key before me. Who else had walked the ancient ground of Tregellas Farm, and what magic had they created for themselves?

Turning the diagram upside down so that I could make sense of it, I followed the bright green lines into an inner courtyard. The crunch of gravel under my feet reverberated around the yard, bouncing off the stone walls. I didn't want to spook or disturb anyone and yet the quieter I tried to be, the noisier I thought I sounded. Eventually, however, I located the hut, which was recessed back against the end of another, larger barn. My success at finding my new dwelling was redemptive. At last I had done something right, and there I stood face to face with the ancient-looking front door. Taking a deep breath, I purposefully put the key in the lock and went to turn it, but it was stuck solid and wouldn't budge. I stepped nearer to the door and was shining my torch directly upon the lock when footsteps on the gravel behind and a quiet 'ahem' made me jump. Spinning around, I quickly flashed my torch into the blackness; the glowing beam picked out the wretched drunk guy again, only now with no bike he was free to raise both hands to shield his eyes.

'You found it, then?'

He seemed to have sobered up, or at least got his words under control a little.

'Yes . . . yes, thank you. I'm just having a bit of trouble with the lock.'

We both whispered loudly. I had no idea why I told him I was struggling again and was immediately embarrassed by how inept I was.

'Ah-ha,' he uttered as he did a sideways shuffle. 'Erm, any chance you can drop the light a little. S'too bright?'

'Oh god, yes, sorry – sorry!' and with that I lowered the torch so that the beam shone across the vacant space between us.

'Would you like me to have a look, or will you be . . ?'

Without giving me time to tell him to go away and leave

me alone, he stepped into the light and walked straight towards me.

I was peeved with him for making me jump again – although I was perhaps more irked that he had found me in need of his help once more. So, without waiting for him to arrive by my side, I turned back to the door determined to gain entry without his help. I pulled the latch so that the lock and clasp were better aligned, but try as I might, the lock failed to release. I tried repeatedly and was about to proclaim my inability to manage a simple lock and key when it sprung free.

'Ah, you're in!' He stopped moving quite quickly but was already way too close for my liking.

'Yes, thank you, and thanks for your help this evening . . . and, sorry for running you over . . . and for blinding you . . .' I trailed off with little else to say. I felt like a bumbling idiot who had lost control of her senses, who had lost control of everything.

'You're all right, then; night, then.'

The man backed away from me before turning and disappearing into the courtyard. Through his scruffy, baggy clothes it was possible to see that he was healthful; his thick dark hair suggested he was probably around my age, but his weathered face and drunken state made him look worn and tired.

'OK, g'night,' I said to the darkness.

———

The fusty smell that emanated from within the dark little hut wasn't welcoming. I fumbled for a light and once it was on, I could see that Hawker's Hut was tiny, uninspired and not the cosy place I had imagined it to be. My flat in London was on the small side too, but I'd lived there for more than ten years and in that time, it had become a comfortable home filled with giant beanbags, statement walls and sassy pieces of upcycled furniture that made it feel French somehow. My expectations weren't high for my new home, but I was disheartened and disappointed as I stepped from tiny room to tiny room; three paces here, two there and I had covered the whole of the ground floor. There was nothing more than a small double bedroom, a bathroom and a studio flat arrangement for cooking and living. In the tiny hall, a large, smoky mirror magnified the dingy aura in its patinaed reflection, as well as a flight of open, wooden stairs that led to what was once some kind of hayloft with a very low ceiling and two futon beds. The saving graces of the hut were the exposed beams and ancient, whitewashed stone walls, which suggested the shabby building held sketchy secrets of lambing and the ungainly fumblings between the randy farm hands and dairymaids of yesteryear.

I sighed heavily as I stood in the hall and stared into the 'master' bedroom, which was where the fustiness was at its strongest – it smelled like the inside of an old bin.

'Holy-fucking-macker-oly! *That* is rannk!' The appalled look on Mya's face summed things up perfectly.

Chapter 8

I inhaled. I smelled – in fact, I stank! After a night of
sleeping in my clothes, my blouse was stuck to me, my
jeans irritated and I felt filthy, so I decided to get up and see
what my new world held for me. I stood up but the room
darkened, and I felt a little faint.

As I wandered out to the yard to find Bertie, I consciously
breathed in the fresh morning air; it lifted my spirits and
tranquillity flowed into my lungs with each gulp I swallowed.
With it came a wave of wholesomeness that tiptoed over me
as I headed towards the car. Bertie's sparkling red coat
reminded me of Dorothy's ruby shoes in *The Wizard of Oz*. I
smiled. In the light of a new day, my situation felt surreal. The
swing between uncertainty and unwavering confidence made
my head spin. At that moment in time, I had a strong sense
that Diana was right – I *could* do it; I *could* make this dream
come true and at last find inner peace. And yet, a few hours
ago, I was wondering what on earth I had let myself in for.

I yanked my case out of Bertie's boot and, as I did so, I
noticed Mrs Enys in her garden, accompanied by two border
collies. A black and white one was chomping on a stick, but

the larger one – the colour of a faded grey sweatshirt – was sitting to attention and staring towards the morning sun, as though in meditation. He was magnificent and I was hopeful I'd get to know him well. I offered my new boss a cheery wave and called out a tentative 'morning'. I wasn't due to start work until Monday, but she knew my arrival date and shouldn't have been surprised to see me. However, she completely blanked me. I walked towards her garden and tried again in case she hadn't heard me.

'Morning . . . Mrs Enys. Isn't it beautiful here. A stunning morning.' I stayed some feet away, as though waiting to be invited into the headmaster's office.

She eventually stopped looking at something on the floor and granted me a response. 'It is. You were late arriving, you had trouble finding the place?'

How did she know? I felt as though she was testing me, and I couldn't be sure if she was making a statement or asking a question.

'Erm, yes, a little. I couldn't find the lane down to the farm. I think I was a bit tired and was looking too hard. The lanes are a bit confusing and the hills, wow, so steep, especially in the dark. How are you? Aren't your dogs lovely! The grey one is so unusual.'

In perfect timing, just as I made mention of the animals, she yelled fiercely at the black and white one, who had scampered its way down the garden to look at me through the gate. She called it 'Dog' at the top of her voice and with a yelp it ran towards her and sat at her heel with its head down, apparently ashamed at its lack of constraint.

'Working dogs. They know their place and what to do. The roads are all right once you know them, plenty of visitors get here OK.'

I wished I hadn't mentioned the lanes, as I felt Mrs Enys was pointing out that everybody else in the world could manage to find their way to the farm except me. The useless feeling returned, and my spirits plunged as I gazed at the gravel under my feet, much in the way Mrs Enys had been doing until I'd foolishly interrupted her. The conversation dried to a cringeworthy drought, and I didn't know whether to press her further or to just walk back to the car and carry on with my unpacking. Flustered by the interaction, I bumbled on regardless, in the hope that the conversation would at least reach a satisfactory conclusion rather than just die mid-air.

'I'm just unpacking my stuff then I thought I'd go for a walk. You know, take a look around the coastal paths. Do you get out much?'

'Sometimes, I'm mostly working, though.'

And with that and a quick 'heeere' to the dogs, she was back in her house with the door firmly closed behind her. I was flabbergasted, there was no engaging her at all. She clearly didn't want to stand and chat, and I reasoned she was probably a very busy woman, but still, I found the fact that she didn't want to enter into even a little chit-chat unfathomable.

I clumsily wheeled my case over the gravelly yard back to Hawker's Hut feeling much less cheery than I had been on the way out to the car. I tried to convince myself that I was mistaken about Mrs Enys's apparent rejection of me, but her body language and cool dismissal seemed to suggest otherwise. I had clearly done something terribly wrong already, and I wondered how on earth she knew I was late arriving the night before. However, I figured my transgression, whatever that might be, must be far worse than just showing up in the dead of night.

Back at the hut, there was no sign of Mya, so I opened my case and set about restoring my sense of self. I put my coffee pot on the hob to brew and felt happy to see my turquoise mug, which was as round as a ball and the perfect size to fit in my hands. I threw clothes and shoes into the wardrobe and unpacked the five books I'd brought with me and the framed picture of me and my girlfriends. But the love and happiness in their eyes were too much to bear, so I put it back in my case along with my laptop. I took my crystals from their nest of tissue paper in an old Fly London shoebox: an amethyst geode the size of a duck egg, which, in its deepest crevices, was as dark as an aubergine. It immediately began to settle my soul. Then came a tiger's eye, hematite, rose quartz, jade and fifteen other gems that had remained the only constants in my life. The oldest and most treasured was a macadamia nut-sized pebble from Uncle Tom's back garden. He had given it to me as a child, telling me to hold it whenever I felt frightened, and it had never let me down. Its caramel coat, now slightly shiny, was soothing and cool in the palm of my hand and I took a moment to enjoy its reassurance. I placed the stone and the rest of the gems on their wooden tray and muttered a few words of intention that they would protect me and bring abundance into my world. I ignored the fact they should have been cleansed under a full moon and arranged with care and attention. As I placed my laughing Buddha statue amongst the crystals, I caught his eye and he seemed less than pleased with my feeble attempt at spirituality.

By the time the coffee had percolated, I had tucked my case into the eaves of the loft room and wafted smoke from healing white sage into every corner of the rancid hut, in the hope of clearing the smell and changing the low vibration. I'd run a bath, too, but the bathroom felt cold and was a little damp to be in, so once naked except for an impressive display of goosebumps, I stepped quickly into a deep and scorching hot tub. My feet felt as though they were burning but somehow the pain felt good. I wouldn't allow myself to add cold water to the mix. I slowly edged myself deeper and deeper into the water until my body pressed the length of the enamel bath, the swirling steam dancing around in the cool air.

Nat and I had loved bathing together, sitting one behind the other and gently soaping and stroking every inch of bare flesh, as we laughed and teased one another. After he had gone, the whole ritual of bathing had become a much too painful process to endure, so I became used to showering. With only the old tub to wallow in at Tregellas, I had no alternative, and in the dizzying heat, I resolved that bathing was something I would make a pleasure again.

———

The last time Nat had come to stay with me, one Saturday in March 2017, he arrived at my flat with a bottle of wine, a smile that stretched from ear to ear and an insatiable appetite for me.

'You smell tasty. I love it when you've just bathed and you're all pink.'

As I stood preparing a salad, he gently nuzzled my neck. I could feel his erection pressing into my back, and the tone of his voice and his presence had me melting into him.

'I like to smell nice for you, bec . . .' Without allowing me to finish what I was saying, Nat turned me around and picked me up. My legs were wrapped around his waist and, as he held me just a little too tight for comfort, he began making his way to the bedroom. He walked cautiously and moved his mouth to mine, his lips gently seeking out the warm, damp lining of my cheeks; licking me from inside to out, tantalising me with promises of where else his tongue might go. He spent ages touching and stroking every inch and orifice of me until I was pleading with him for more. Eventually, he pinned me down with the weight of his body, taking great delight in mine. A frenzied burst of thrusting signalled that his climax was near and, with one gigantic grunt, he collapsed breathless and sweating onto me. The intensity and passion of those few minutes set the tone for the night until, exhausted, we nuzzled together and fell into the sleep of the satiated.

The following morning, I was full of happiness and energy when I awoke to the smell of mushrooms on toast cooking and Nat singing away in my kitchen.

'Come on, Sexy Pants, it's on the table!'

Knowing full well what he was referring to, but being my puerile, pushy self, I replied sleepily in jest, 'What's on the table, Nat?'

'Me and my great sausage, come and get a mouthful.'

And with that, giggling excitedly, I leapt out of bed, pulled on a soft, old hoodie that came down to my knees and made my way into the kitchen.

'See you've dressed for the occasion, then. Nice of you to make the effort!'

'Eh?' I sidled up to him. 'I've just got up, I'm still asleep really.'

'And that means you can't get washed and dressed, does it?'

'Wha . . . But you just called me in to come and get breakfast, and I thought–'

He said nothing, just looked at me and right through me. His stony stare suggested he had just stepped in some stinking mess I had shat all over the floor. He was appalled by me.

By the Monday morning, Nat had his business head on and at 6:30, he left to travel to a meeting in Staffordshire, for the final chat about a director role that was based up there. It was a job he was keen to do and one that would bring him to London at least twice a month, giving us time together and, most importantly for him, pay the large sums of money he needed to keep the bank from his door. He messaged that night to say he was tired and had driven back to Oxford, which is where his own home was, but he didn't tell me whether the meeting had been a success or not. Then I heard nothing from him for three weeks.

His retreats were something that had become a frequent occurrence, yet they were something I could never get used to. With each of those silences, I was filled with a rising, disproportionate sense of loss. The terror of being without Nat in itself was bad enough but was made worse by the real probability that if he *had* died, no one would know about me. There would be no knock at my door at 3am by the traffic police to tell me of his death. The truth was that our relationship was ugly, but I kept that nugget of shameful information safely stored away in a box in my head, where I could ignore it.

I could cope with the fact that he needed to take time for himself. After all, everyone needs space, but I could never reconcile the warm and loving Nat with the cold-hearted person he became when he needed to escape; the man who wouldn't even send a quick message to say he was OK and that he was thinking of me. It felt as though he was punishing me for something I might or might not have done and even after two years, I didn't know how to respond to his periodic silences. I was never sure whether I should text, email or call him. Instead, I would scour the papers and obituary columns while waiting patiently for him to return, full of his usual excuses: that technology and a million-and-one other things had *supposedly* failed us, that he'd been 'uber busy' or had simply been too tired to be in touch. No matter how hurt or angry I felt, I didn't have the courage to say to Nat that he was wrong to ignore me.

On this occasion, his silence made a resounding boom. One minute we had been making love and enjoying each other, both excited about his potential new role, and the next he was gone, vanished into the ether. Eventually, around August time, I started getting the chatty, 'hey, how're you doing?' type emails. They were warm and friendly missives full of apologies. He explained that he was now settled in and enjoying his role and he asked if he could call me. Stupidly, I told him there was no reason he shouldn't call, so before long we were talking on the phone for a couple of hours a day and I was back in the destructive cycle of life with Nathaniel Deighton.

I spent three months keeping him at arm's length, trying my very best to hold onto some self-respect and integrity, but all too soon there was a plan for him to come and see me and we set the date for December 15th. I was so excited at the thought of seeing him and silently hoped that we would spend some time together over Christmas. I shopped for lavish new underwear; beribboned basques and silk knickers were his favourites. I primped and preened myself in readiness for seeing him. I'd also been working out like crazy and was thinner than I had ever been. I wanted his approval of my fitter self. Prior to his visit, his contact was frequent and loving, though it felt as though something was different this time. He sounded calm, content and appeared to be completely invested in me. His words made me feel loved and cherished, so much so that I wiped the cruelty of his desertion from my mind. I thought that perhaps our relationship was on a different, more stable plane.

But then he'd called on December 11th and, as I sat in the buttery smelling coffee shop in Bounds Green, I listened in disbelief as the words poured relentlessly from his mouth. He might as well have gripped me around the neck and slammed me up against the wall. That was the moment he broke me. That moment, my world crashed around me and I plummeted out of sight into a giant sinkhole.

With the action replay of that moment streaming in front of my mind's eye, it was as though I had been held under the water and was drowning. I breathed in, sharply bolting upright and sending a tsunami of water crashing over the end of the bath. My shrivelled fingers grasped onto the cold edges of the enamel tub and I glared hatefully at the insipid green and peach coloured tiles, which clung to the walls with the help of grey and pitted grout. I'd been at Tregellas less than 12 hours and already I was being hurled backwards into my life with Nat.

Chapter 9
SEPTEMBER 2018

After my initial disappointment with my new home, which hadn't improved despite a reasonable effort with some lively coloured throws and the regular burning of white sage, the first three months or so at Tregellas turned out to be surprisingly pleasing. Mrs Enys had built up a successful business of small homesteads that were booked back to back, and one of her USPs was a corral of ponies that would take visitors out on treks across the rolling, lettuce-green hills. The place was continuously filled with visitors and day-trippers alike, and although they generated vast amounts of work, it was easy and enjoyable.

Like a thriving baby, I had a good routine and felt as though I had settled well into my working life. Even Mrs Enys had mellowed slightly in her approach to me. She acknowledged me at least and would say good morning when our paths crossed, although she was always the consummate professional and still refused to engage in idle chit-chat.

Tall, strong looking and almost androgynous with handsome features and incredibly short hair, she appeared a formidable character. Whilst there was work to be done she was cold, direct and focused with staff, and she wasn't much warmer to paying guests, especially when they stopped her from making progress in her busy day by mollycoddling the dogs, who were constantly at her side. She was a hard worker, of that there was no doubt. As well as managing the staff and overseeing the animals and homesteads, she did all the books and administration for the place. But for all of her ferocity, Mrs Enys definitely had a soft spot for the cute and the cuddly, even if she proclaimed the cats, chickens and pygmy goats that roamed the farmstead, making everyone else's business their own, were all part of the plan to lure paying parents to her door.

I'd discovered that the dishevelled drunk guy who'd given me directions to the farm was another of life's confounding sorts. His name was Adam and he seemed to turn up whenever I was making an idiot of myself. Like the time one of the laundry bags I was carrying burst open, spilling sheets onto the yard, which had just been hosed down. And another when a goose took a dim view of me for walking past her as she pecked at tiny specks of grain that had blown across the yard. Such was her fury she'd flapped and beaten her wings, screeching at me so ferociously that I remained trapped behind a wheelbarrow until Adam saw her off. Each time, he stepped into the breach and sorted things out. One afternoon, as we passed each other in the yard, he asked me to be on the lookout for a tin of tartan paint, which I duly did. Each time I went into the workshop or the laundry, I'd poke about to see if I could find any. The next time we bumped into each other, a week or so later, I told him I hadn't found it, which made him laugh loudly. He had to explain there was no such thing as tartan paint. When I thought about it, I went rosehip red with embarrassment.

Other than an obscure sense of fun, I'd learned nothing about him save for his name, which I got from the group of young girls who also worked at the farm. They managed the ponies and small animals and were the life and soul of the place. They were the ones who undoubtedly influenced guests to return year after year. There were five of them, although if you overheard any teatime chats you could be forgiven for thinking there were twice as many. Sam, who ran the team, was as fierce and as feisty as Mrs Enys. She ran a tight ship, but when the spirit moved her, she allowed her team, like the horses, to go wild. She was blonde and round with a ruddy complexion. Larger than life, she could drink as much beer as the next man and frequently did. Though I was not invited to join their enclave, the girls craved my company on a one-to-one basis and seemed to see me as some kind of older sister figure, asking me for advice and telling me their woes. I didn't want to be wanted by them and I certainly didn't want to share my story, so I did my best to ignore them and was pleased that collectively they were reluctant to include me in their after work antics.

In my free time, I relished the endless, simple pleasures Welcombe afforded. I had spent the summer months making the effort to be kind to myself, as I tried to repair my broken body and weary mind. Now, finally, I was beginning to feel the benefit of the investment I was making in myself. Mya had pretty much left after our arrival, leaving me to figure things out for myself. I didn't miss her. Eating and sleeping well were clearly paying dividends; my sun-kissed hair shone, I had muscles again and my skin reflected the benefits of the sunshine and the copious amounts of crystal clear fresh air that had become the focus of my attention.

After my bath on the first morning at Welcombe, I walked to the sea along a pebbly, well-trodden yet narrow track. It followed a delightful stream through a lightly wooded combe, which brought me out at the bottom of the unmade road. I stood on top of a grassy embankment, leaned into the onshore breeze and stared out towards the horizon, as the gentle swell of the ocean revealed itself to me. There it was in all its glory, stretching as far as the eye could see. It was all-consuming and I basked in its strength and beauty. Following this glorious moment of meditation, I had been filled with gratitude. I'd repeated the walk every day of the intervening months and had never failed to be awestruck by the beauty of the place. When the tide was in, the waves gently caressed or else beat the life out of the ancient beach – there seemed to be no middle ground. And when it was out, the surface of the ocean flickered and danced, as the waves sketched out the horizon.

The beach was littered with magnificent, stony eruptions that burst through the sand across the bay. They were strange rock formations of mud and sand that, over millions of years, had been compressed and squished into strips of stone that lay in long rows of jagged rock, puncturing the sand at varying heights. It was as though the creator of the universe had manifested a pile of giant razor shells and then tossed them on their sides around the bay. They had a purple hue to them and were strangely beautiful, but I had learned from local folklore they were treacherous beasts that had cost the lives of many, as they gorged upon cargo ships, discharging the contents of their holds into the hands of the wreckers who had lured them ashore.

Come rain or shine, each afternoon I would walk about five miles, which was no mean feat due to the tightly packed contours of the hills surrounding Tregellas. I explored the coastal path, which I grew to know like the back of my hand. When I was more relaxed and at peace with myself, I would take the open and scenic path towards Hartland, but if I needed a challenge, I opted for the invigorating trail towards Morwenstow. It was a good long walk with steep climbs up treacherous steps and a jagged footpath that led to the original Hawker's hut – a wooden cave with a bench and a rickety door built from driftwood that nestled into the cliff top. I found it a joyful and emotive space within which to sit and reflect, as I watched the sea waltz below.

Regardless of the route I took, every step of the way was a meditation. I was mindful of the crunch of my shoes, the feel of the elements as they caressed my body and the roar of the wind or the sea. I would chat animatedly with the universe and, just as I had promised myself, I shared with the cliffs and the wholesome air my darkest, innermost secrets. These were the honest ones that revealed me to be selfish, jealous and lustful, but my ugliness was lost in the wilderness. The words I spoke and the tears I cried were carried away into the wind and, although alone, I felt safe. I noticed that the more I chatted, the more mantra I repeated, the more the beauty in my surroundings was revealed to me. All manner of plants and animals presented themselves in my reality. I felt a connection to their vulnerability and their determination to thrive and be beautiful in that environment. I took a message of reassurance from their presence that I was in the right place and heading on the right path for a free and abundant life.

Despite all of the goodness that surrounded me, Nathaniel still invaded my thoughts, but the intensity of his presence – and absence – had lessened. Thoughts of him would pop into my head as I went about my duties, but I mostly managed to push these interruptions far from my mind. However, when he came to visit at night it was a different story. The sense and the feel of him would linger large in my mind, as I imagined myself wrapped around him. The remoteness between us crushed my spirit and in the manner of an indolent ulcer, it was something which would never quite heal.

In the evenings, I read, catching up on the classics, such as *Little Women* and *Wuthering Heights*. It was with Heathcliff in my heart and the book in a soft cotton bag that I decided to set out on a walk one afternoon in September. The weather was just beginning to turn, and there was that complex mixture of cool mornings and evenings, where peaks of heat in the day made it hard to decide what to wear. I was in yoga trousers, a vest and a thin cotton hoodie, but, thinking it might get chilly, I delved into the bag of scarves I'd jammed at the back of the small wardrobe, searching for something light to put around my shoulders. The first one I pulled out was a long, teal-coloured silk scarf.

Nat had bought it for me, and this one had special meaning, because the gift came after an absence of three weeks. He'd been furious with me because I'd used his mobile phone number and email address on an order for some satin sheets. He'd always wanted some, so by way of a surprise, I'd put his contact details in the tracking information.

'Why would you do that to me? What kind of a fucking idiot are you?' he had shouted down the phone. He then hung up, leaving me no time to explain that I had done it to excite him, and vanished for twenty-one days. With a heavy heart, I sent the sheets back and never did get to enjoy the feel of us sliding around on them, as he had so often dreamed about. With each day of silence that passed, I felt as though he was punishing me for trying to do something nice for him. During that time, I could only hope he was sulking and that he would eventually return, but the uncertainty was crippling.

As was his wont, the first tentative email arrived explaining he was having problems with his phone, which is why he hadn't called. It infuriated me, not least because he signed the email 'best regards', but more because he said his phone wouldn't charge, and that he'd lost his contacts and wanted me to resend him my number. I was devastated he didn't know it off by heart or have it written down somewhere or backed up. He explained it was taking an age to get his contacts restored and that he was waiting for a new cable that would allow him to charge his phone. It was the usual kind of feeble excuse he favoured, and I knew it was a pack of lies. He lived by his phone; it was his lifeline for work, so it was complete crap that it kept failing so disastrously. I replied nonetheless.

After three weeks of neglect and an overnight stay, he announced he was taking me to Covent Garden for lunch. The day was crisp and bright, and I was in my element as we travelled hand in hand across London, both over and underground. I was glowing for having Nat beside me, and every now and then I would see him break into something of a smile, too. Being with him, out and about, where people could see us as a couple felt such a grown-up thing to be doing. It struck me as silly, as we'd done it plenty of times before, but following his period of desertion it felt good that he was as happy to be with me as I was to be with him.

We wandered through the bustling market and chatted incessantly, rekindling our connection. As the morning wore on, I gradually felt hoodwinked, when I began to realise that the distraction of perusing the market stalls meant he didn't have to apologise for his rudeness and that we didn't need to discuss his absence. It made me feel sad to think that once again he had silently stormed his way back into my life. Although I wanted answers, I was so happy to have the Nathaniel-shaped vacuum filled that I didn't dare challenge him about where he had been and why, once again, he had discarded me in such a ruthless way. I wasn't going to chance losing him again to his hidden world, not so soon after his return.

Rather at odds with myself, I moved away from Nat to a stall selling scarves, where I idly had a look and a feel of what the hipster stall holder girl had on display. Myriad colours lay before me, but it was a teal green scarf tucked away near the back of the table that caught my attention. Reaching through the sea of colour, I managed to pull it towards me without disrupting the rest of the display. As soon as it was in my hands, I fell in love with it, particularly the way the edges had been lovingly hand rolled by its artisan maker; the distinct colour was rich and the delicate fabric was light but warm. As it was silk, I figured it would probably be expensive and made a deal that if it was less than £40, I would buy it as a treat to myself.

'How much is this one, please?'

The hipster looked up from her phone a bit startled that anyone should be talking to her. 'Sixty-five quid.'

'Ah, OK, thanks.' It was terribly expensive. The budget was blown. On hearing the price, I smiled at the funky girl and crestfallen, gently set down the delicate, fluid fabric; there would be no scarf for me. Before I knew it, Nat was back at my side and, feeling excessively emotional and just a little tearful at the whole situation, I buried myself into his side, as he slipped his arm reassuringly around my shoulder.

We continued around the market and found ourselves in a slightly less crowded area, where we sat next to an outdoor heater and drank hot chocolate in the delicate spring sunshine, watching the street performers. Pretty soon, I was engrossed by one guy performing an intricate, captivating trick with members of the audience. I watched intently, not noticing that Nat had slipped away. He appeared at my side with a hand on my arm and a smile as large as a Cheshire cat's. He placed a tissue-paper wrapped packet tied with a ribbon on the table in front of me. I could scarcely dare to hope what lay within it and, upon opening the package, wasn't disappointed or surprised to see the beautiful teal scarf.

His olive branch served well in placating me. Everything was forgiven and there was nothing to be said, nothing to be put right. We returned to the flat and spent the rest of the weekend watching crazy old films like *Life of Brian* and *The*

Pink Panther. We lay in bed together, laughing at things that weren't funny.

―――

This was the way I received most of my treasures from Nat and, as I called the moment to mind, the agony of his absence followed by the warmth of his love was as raw and as full as it had been all that time ago. I could feel the familiar lack of certainty that accompanied his place in my life. The lava that lived in my belly began simmering slowly, churning and coiling and preparing to erupt, only this time it twisted over three or four times before becoming settled and still again. Something about my response had changed. This time, instead of intense feelings of loss, I felt shame at how careless I had been with myself. I thought about how destructive and interdependent our relationship had become and berated myself for allowing him unrestricted access to my deepest, most precious emotions. I realised that time after time, I had exposed my vulnerable self to his contemptuous and corrupted ways. I had gone through the same cycle with him, and although on each occasion I resolved never to have anything to do with him again, all it took was a few carefully worded emails from him and I was back, hanging on his every word until the next rejection. For two years, I had suppressed my doubts and insecurities about our relationship and let it consume me. No wonder there had been such a cavernous hole in my life after he had gone, our lives together had been a turbulent tango of epic proportions. I took a few steps back and sat on the edge of the bed, holding the scarf to my face, but then I quickly pulled myself together and stuffed it into my bag, as I made for the front door and the remnants of the late summer sun.

Chapter 10

I decided to take the bright and open route towards
Hartland, where the grazing sheep were happy to run to
my side but quick to bolt as soon as I stretched out a hand to
pet them. The earlier thoughts of Nat trailed along too, and
although I tried to out walk them, they kept their pace and
fuelled me as I strode along. I was breathing hard by the time I
reached the top of the hill and was surprised that I'd gone as
far as I had without really realising it. I turned and surveyed
the bay from the great height and was warmed to see a large
sliver of white sunlight cut a swathe across the centre of the
dark blue sea.

I took two 'changing breaths' and wandered off again in
search of inner calm. I focused my thoughts on *Wuthering
Heights* and wondered what the book would bring me. It was
the first time I had read it and although I was only a couple of
chapters in, I was already hooked. Someone had described it
to me as brutal, as it was about co-dependency and
dysfunctional relationships, and I wondered if this was why it
appealed to me. I suspected there was a correlation between
what lay within its pages and my relationship with Nat.

I plodded along and came across a sign to a footpath I had never walked before. I quickly decided that today would be a good day to give it a try. I had no real idea of where it would take me, but it was signposted to Gooseham, which was the right direction to take me inland and back to Tregellas Farm. I happily followed a well-used opening through some dense woods. It was darker and colder than on the cliff top, as though someone had turned down the brightness of the sun, so I took out the silk scarf and wrapped it around my shoulders. The striking, dappled light played tricks on my eyes and, as I followed the narrow path through the woods, I tried to see what lay ahead, but the dazzling sun that erupted intermittently through the trees made it difficult.

The meandering path finished abruptly at the edge of the wood, as it bordered a meadow of wild grasses that sloped gently upwards. The only thing that stood in the meadow was an ancient oak tree over on the far side, so I made my way through the long, prickly grass to sit in its refuge for a drink and a read. By the time I got to the tree, I was hot again. I slipped out of my scarf and hung it on one of the low branches, before walking around the gnarly trunk and exploring the rough ancient bark with my hands in admiration of the tree's great age and sagacity. Then I took off my hoodie and lay it on the floor to sit on.

I sat for a while glancing around and sipping the fresh cool water in my bottle. I was tired and knew that after a short read my eyelids would begin to weigh heavily and that a catnap would undoubtedly be on the cards. It was then that I noticed Adam. He was repairing a fence in the middle distance and was naked to the waist, obviously too hot as he worked under the gaze of the sun. After a while, he stopped what he was doing, turned directly towards me and let the sun pour down onto his face. I quickly lay down in case he saw me staring at him, but by lifting my head an inch or two off the ground, I found I could watch as he puddled himself in the rays of the sun for some time before turning back to the task in hand. My heart beat quite fast at the thought of being caught, so I lay still for a while before slowly sitting up to take another look. Once again, he was busy working away, nailing barbed wire to the fence posts, his shoulders glistening with sweat that reflected in the lowering, but still warm sun. Now that he was engrossed in his work, I could observe him openly. He was surprisingly eye-catching and pleasing to watch.

I lay back on the ground and stared through the dancing leaves of the oak to the sky-blue canvas above. I closed my eyes and enjoyed the way the sunlight flashed on the other side of my eyelids, smiling in contentment and whispering a silent *thank you* to my universe for blessing me with this moment of tranquillity. The placid wind was warm as it moved around me and I became mindful of my surroundings and then of my body. I realised that for the first time in many, many months I felt a sense of yearning.

I was longing for the feel of Nat as he lay alongside me, his arm almost entirely around my whole body, holding me tight and pulling me in close to him as he kissed me. Instinctively, I turned onto my right side to be cuddled by my memories of him. He always lay to my left and it had become a routine for going to sleep that he would spoon me as we drifted off.

As I thought about him, I could feel his breath on the back of my neck. But, as I imagined him so close and nestling into me, I realised it was Adam's body that I wanted to be pressing up hard against me. In my mind's eye, I could see dark hair, not Nat's strawberry blond. I could see Adam's tanned, smooth skin, not Nat's pale, downy arms. The feeling of tension between my legs was beginning to grow and I instinctively put my hands between them and held myself as my imagination moved quickly along. I sighed. The fantasy that Adam was kissing my shoulder and the intensity of his smooth, gentle lips was almost tangible. His big brown hand was on my hip, and, as he slipped it forward to rub my abdomen, I was aware that it was huge and strong and covered my whole pelvis, from one hip bone to the other. I felt tiny and feminine and vibrant. As though he were alongside me, I rolled onto my back and gently began to stroke myself. My imaginary Adam was now kissing my neck and collar bone. He kissed me so gently, moving ever closer to my mouth until I instinctively opened my lips to kiss him back. I recognised the sensation of my eyes flickering. Beautiful colours surged before them and blood rushed to my feet, as a fierce contraction set me shuddering and crying out. As it engulfed me, the orgasm blessed every part of my body. I rolled into a ball and sobbed gently until I fell asleep.

When I awoke, twilight was threatening to settle in. I jumped up to put my hoodie on and cast a glimpse over to see if Adam was still at work, but there was no sign of him. I was surprised by my disappointment at his absence, and shocked and ashamed at what I had imagined about him. Nonetheless, I headed back through the woods and down towards the cliff path with a spring in my step and an unrecognisable lightness about me.

By the time I reached the bay the tide was out. The lowering sun caressed the smooth sand and I couldn't resist lingering to enjoy its wonders. I must have spent the best part of an hour playing in the sand. I built castles and ran around in giant circles drawing smiley faces in it with pieces of driftwood I found lying dashed upon the rocky outcrops.

I decided it was time to try and rid myself of Nat's spectre, so I gathered up the ingredients for a burying ritual that would help me lay to rest an 'us' that was no longer useful to me. I'd read about rituals for protection when I was sixteen, whilst working at the library as a Saturday cleaner. Thinking that I had suddenly become the chief librarian, my mum had come in demanding to see me. The fuss resulted in the police being called and me having to meet with Sweaty Brian – the library's manager for domestic staff – in his dingy office. He served me a warning, but Rona, a skeletal woman who silently swept the parquet floors, had witnessed the whole thing. After my meeting, she took me under her wing and led me to a section of the library that housed two books on spirituality and the world of Wicca. With my mother in mind, Rona pointed out three spells that she felt might be useful to me. She then wrote them out for me in large, loopy handwriting. I'd kept hold of the slip of paper ever since, even though I knew the spells by heart, but had never before used any of them. I scavenged the beach to find objects I could create associations with and then set about digging myself a deep hole in which to bury my treasures. I'd gathered an empty crab shell to symbolise the emptiness of my union with Nathaniel; a feather became a peace offering to the universe for any harm I may have done to people, such as my lovely friends, as a result of the relationship; conjoined cockleshells represented the way we had been co-dependent upon each other, and a heavy rock was there to ensure he would never, ever return. One by one, I put the items into the foot-deep hole and, as I did so, I silently and repeatedly chanted a binding spell to hold him fast.

'I bind you, Nathaniel Deighton and your power to harm me. I bind you, Nathaniel Deighton and your power to harm me. I bind you, Nathaniel Deighton and your power to harm me . . .' On and on I went until the ninth repetition, by which time I was shouting and laughing and crying with joy. Once I was confident in the way I had laid the items out, I filled the hole with sand and then danced upon it. It was a liberating and sensational thing to experience and, as I twirled around like a jewellery box ballerina, I promised myself I would no longer mourn a life that was a paradox. I'd let go of the harmful and toxic relationship with this person, who was little more than an enigma.

I flopped onto the sand and stared at the sky spinning above me. Automatically, my hand felt for the piece of dark green jade I wore on a black cord around my neck. The next thing to do was to sever our connection once and for all, so I untied the cord and slipped the precious stone into my bra to keep it safe. With great care, I recited the words of the Nine Knot Spell. 'By the knot of one, the spell's begun, by the knot of two it cometh true . . . by the knot of nine, what's done is mine.'

I tied knot after knot into the cord. Once done, I held the mystical charm in the flat of my hands. The point of the spell was to stop Nat from coming anywhere near my mind or body. The timing felt right, and I knew I would now be able to let go. The spell would work, but to ensure the connection was broken forever the cord had to be buried somewhere I would not be able to find it again. I didn't want that to be on my beach, so I tucked it back into my cotton bag for burying some place up in the woods. I felt invincible.

Chapter 11

When I left the beach, dusk was nudging the day along, and although an oatmeal-coloured sky lingered, it was pretty hard to see as I walked alongside the stream back up to Tregellas Farm. Part of me wished I had taken the unmade road, but I was feeling joyous as I cautiously picked my way over the stones and tree roots. Before long, I was at the door of Hawker's Hut, and as I dug out the iron key, I noticed my teal scarf tied to a post at the entrance. I realised very quickly that *I* hadn't collected it from the branch of the tree, but there was no one else there with me, so who would know to return it? The only other person up there was Adam. I winced at the very thought.

I untied the scarf and made my way into the hut. As I perched anxiously on the edge of the bed, I weaved it through my fingers and tried to fathom out how it had come to be tied to the front of the cottage. Even if Adam had found it hanging on the bough of the tree by chance, there was no way he would have known it belonged to me . . . unless, unless he had seen me there? I was suddenly filled with dread. Maybe he had walked past me whilst I was sleeping, or maybe he had seen me observing him. Worse still, maybe he had watched me having my private moment.

I slumped back onto the bed and hid my face in the silk. I could feel my cheeks flush with colour and as they did, I began to giggle into the soft material. I laughed and laughed until I was practically hysterical. I rolled from side to side with complete and utter embarrassment and, whilst I wanted the bed to swallow me up and bury me, I was also filled with excitement. Finally, I stopped howling and blushing and lay on the bed facing the small, ancient window, with its broken latch and its water-stained calico curtains. I huddled in, covered by the light but warm material of my scarf and feeling as happy as a clam.

The next day, I bumped into Adam at around 6 am, as I made my way across to the laundry. It was my usual time, but our paths had never crossed at that hour before. And yet, the morning after the scarf incident, there we were face to face. I faltered slightly when I saw him and was disarmed by his wide grin.

'Morning, Lil,' he said wryly.

Oh my God, he knew! Firstly, he'd never looked so animated and alive before, and secondly, he had the cheek to call me Lil!

'It's Lily, actually,' was all I could muster.

As he walked by me, he corrected himself with an unsettling edge to his voice. 'Morning, Lily Actually!' And off he waltzed as bold as brass to get on with his day.

I was livid. Whatever it was he knew or thought he knew, he was going to taunt me with it, and if I allowed it to, it would bother me intensely. And so it did. I allowed it to ruin my whole day, as it played on my mind with every task I carried out. I picked apart every moment of the previous day and the preceding weeks to try and figure out what on earth was going on. Perhaps he said morning to me every day, but as I was always so preoccupied, maybe I hadn't noticed. Surely, I would have told him before now if I had heard him call me Lil?

A whole week passed. Adam's work schedule had obviously altered, as I saw him more frequently, and whenever I did his countenance was cheerful and his demeanour playful. He was a totally new person and called me Lily Actually without fail.

It frustrated me that I still had no clear idea as to how my scarf had been safely returned to me, but the biggest frustration of all was that I had begun to look forward to bumping into Adam, and I noticed how disappointed I felt when I didn't. Before I left for the laundry building in the morning, I found myself brushing my hair and plaiting it neatly instead of just scraping it back into a lank ponytail. I also made an effort to look as though I had given thought to my outfit, rather than just grabbing old yoga pants or tracksuit bottoms. Our eyes would sometimes meet as we moved around the farm, and he would gently tip his head towards me, as if knowing his interaction would unsettle me. Meanwhile, I would look hurriedly away. I found that I blushed furiously whenever I saw him, and whilst I hated it, I realised I had become intrigued by the man, and I began to seek him out.

I even went back to the field on a couple of occasions, but his work on the fence was obviously complete as he was never there. Try as I might, I couldn't find out where he went when he left the farm buildings. There were a couple of times when I saw him heading down the lane towards the farm with his ancient bicycle at his side, his staggering gait revealing another long afternoon at the Old Smithy Inn. This irritated me, and although I felt judgemental of the man for squandering his days, just as my mother had, I could see that his life in this secluded spot was dull. His whole world appeared to revolve around work, so I imagined getting drunk was his only means of escape.

Chapter 12

As a form of catharsis, I had taken to writing long and abusive letters to Nat. I had no intention of ever sending them but writing the words down and seeing them on paper made me feel so much better. The stark outline of ink on paper was unyielding and braver than I, and the letters shouted, "That was not OK" to my absent audience.

I had moved onwards through the grief cycle and was now dealing with anger. It gladdened my heart to feel the shift from the all-consuming, navel-gazing fixations of the last few months, to the projection of my life's potential. I was still hurt and thought of Nat and our relationship often, but I was confident I no longer wanted him to be part of my life. By writing down my condemnation of him, I believed I would begin to live by my words and claw back a degree of dignity. It was as though I were making a contract with myself and, although early days, I could feel myself growing within my own skin and connecting to new values of integrity, self-worth and confidence, which made me feel comfortable and peaceful within.

My interest in Adam had also grown. In fact, I had developed a bit of a crush on him, or rather on the idea of him, because I still didn't really know him. He seemed such a mystery, appearing here and there, with no apparent routine to his life. I hadn't a clue what he did on the farm and the harder I tried to find him, the less I saw of him. After the tartan paint episode, I never knew if he was being serious or not, so a pleasant chat could quickly turn into something awkward; not helped by the mini crush or the fact that I was paralysed by the scarf-shaped elephant in the room. I still had no idea of how much Adam did or didn't know. The whole 'private moment' thing bothered me hugely, and it felt as though it would one day rear its ugly head.

Adam was a challenge for me, but he was also a distraction and I was intrigued by his indistinct presence and the clumsiness that surrounded us. However, just the fact that he was of any interest to me at all suggested that this was all good and wholesome stuff. I was doing 'normal' things; this was what life and relationships should be like. Nevertheless, there were times when I felt vulnerable and my mood could change on a sixpence, from tranquillity to tears and back within a matter of hours. If a simple thought of Nat or a reminder of my sense of loss slunk up on me unawares, it was enough to spark an unsettling reaction. His dominating presence was a force to be reckoned with and when that dark miasma was adjoined to me, I resorted to my old ways and had to work hard to free myself from their grasp. It wasn't something that was conscious, or that I had much control over. This was a carnal, innate response that aroused a series of harmful behaviours, such as depriving myself of sleep and food and relentlessly exercising. Walking and running for miles on end, pushing myself harder and harder, forcing myself to run or walk up the 'hill of death', as I propelled myself towards oblivion. Each mile, each step became an endless tussle for supremacy between body and brain. I was uncomfortable as I ran, but I ignored the endless pain and my body's silent screams.

The remarkable thing for me about this time, though, was that although still powerless, I could recognise what was happening to me. Mya was nowhere to be found and as my ancient responses leapt to the fore, I took control and limited their harm. I noticed how easily distracted I was by the positive rather than the negative influences that came from my surroundings. I was changing along with the seasons. The transformation in weather and its variance as summer transitioned to autumn reflected my personal growth; both of us were growing bold then receding a little, as we made our entrance into the world and wrestled to be absolute.

It was a windy autumn, making it a time of excitement and wonderment for me, and by the end of October, the elements were working furiously on turning the bay into a maelstrom of noise and new olfactory sensations. The seaside air smelt briny and of decaying ocean flora and fauna. Although pungent on most days, it was a smell I had come to love and cherish, as I associated it with being my truest and happiest self and with mischievous moments of pleasure.

The sea frequently had a foam topping, which blew off the ocean and across the bay. Puff balls of spume littered the beach and dusted the rocky outcrops with dollops of cream. I spent ages wandering around just picking them up and letting the wild wind take them off to wherever they were destined to be. I would meditate for hours on the sea's persistence. For centuries, it had performed the same task, year in, year out. I admired its tenacity to continue to come and go. I wondered if I had ever seen the same drop of sea on more than one occasion, and I became fascinated by the noise and the strength and the endless toiling of the water as it relentlessly ground against the land. I would go home soaked with sticky saltwater and sand would creep its way into nooks and crannies, before spilling out of my underwear onto the bathroom floor as I prepared to sink into a warming bath. During my seaside forays, I would reluctantly have to tear myself away from my new playground, as failing light or an icy wind stole the beach for its own and drove me back to my hut. Being on the beach always left me feeling fortified, as the wondrousness of the elements were strong enough to take control of my brain and emotions, eradicating any negative and consuming thoughts.

One of the families who had stayed at the farm over the summer had kindly left me a kite to fly. I think they took pity on me, as I sat on the rocks hankering for a go. I'd smiled earnestly as their youngsters had played, whilst envy nibbled away inside. I hadn't realised they had seen me peeking so intently at the kite as it swooped around the bay. It was the canopy kind and stripes of bright, primary colours merged and blurred as it darted across the sky. Like its previous owners, I took to flying it on the beach, but the gusty summer backdrop had been replaced by the roar of the sea and a crashing wind that could be deafening. I felt exhilarated, as I concentrated on keeping my polyester friend airborne. The feel of it tugging against me made me laugh out loud. One minute it would be surging skyward and the next yanking me towards the pounding waves. I would scream in fake terror as it threatened to drag me across the unforgiving rocks, as the wind whistled through the tight lines, making them sing like a Celtic harp. Watching the kite felt like a form of meditation, as the bright, shiny fabric stretched and pulled, deflated, then roared away again. I loved the sensation of being buffeted by the relentless streams of air as the kite waxed and waned.

One afternoon, after the kite had just spectacularly crashed and I was walking across the shore to retrieve it from the rocks, winding the lines as I went, I noticed Adam heading away from Tregellas and up the cliff path towards Morwenstow. It was already three in the afternoon, so wherever he was going he couldn't be going far, as the sun would begin to drop into the ocean in around an hour's time. He was always so furtive and moved around in a quiet, circumspect way. I hadn't seen him in a number of days, and as I watched him head off along the coast path, my interest in him rocketed.

I scrabbled over the rocks, letting their barnacled surfaces dig into my soft hands. I wanted to try and catch up with Adam to see where he was heading off to, and I was conscious of rushing and taking chances on the rough, sloping shards of ancient rock. I found where the kite had crashed, retrieved it from its watery grave and stuffed it and the lines into my backpack, which in itself was telling, as I usually paid the greatest attention to how I packed it away.

Soon, I was hurrying my way back across the top of the rocks, nimbly traversing the barnacled outcrops. I continued to take more chances than perhaps I should have, but I made good progress and was soon back on the beach. I broke into a run and headed across the wet sand, back towards the steps that would take me onto a track that joined up with the coast path. As I neared the end of the bay, the sand took on a softer form. Mostly untouched by the sea, it was fine and dry and difficult to run on, so instead I decided to walk along the ridge of a rock that was about a foot high. Although I had a reasonable width upon which to walk across, I had to turn slightly sideways to manoeuvre across the rock's ragged top. I side-stepped my way along as fast as I dared and, as I made my last step, I noticed that the lace of my left trainer had come undone and was caught in a crevice. My body and left leg were already in motion for the next step. Inertia had the better of me and, as the rock held the lace secure, I rapidly stopped moving and fell off the ridge. The unforgiving anchor held my left foot fast and, as I tumbled downwards, it was yanked inwards until I heard my leg snap with a resounding crack. I fell hard onto the sand, winding myself in the process and hitting the side of my head on a small rock. Momentarily I lay still, shocked and uncertain as to what hurt the most.

Chapter 13

I put my hand to the crown of my head as it smarted. Although it was bleeding quite a lot, it didn't seem to be gushing. I noticed I had scuffs and scrapes on my hands, which must have occurred as they raked against the protruding barnacles on the shards of rock I had fallen from. My ankle hurt and by the time I managed to sit up, the swelling had started. It throbbed like mad and, as the pressure built around it, felt as though it were burning. All I could do was sit and watch it puff up to the size of a cricket ball.

'Ow. Ow. Owyyyy ow ow ow owwwww. It hurts! It really, really hurts!' I yelled into the wild air. I checked out my bloody hands and broken ankle and began crying the grizzling bawl of a two-year-old.

I unhooked my shoelace and somehow managed to stand up. I attempted to walk, but as I put my foot to the floor, I could feel a sharp, digging pain in the side of my ankle. I wondered how the hell I was going to get off the beach and back to the farm. I had no phone and no way of calling for help – not that there was anyone to call anyway, but there was no way I was going to manage alone.

I sat back down and began to shuffle myself backwards, digging my right heel into the sand and trying to scoot myself along towards the steps. But the sand was too forgiving, and it relinquished under the pressure of my foot. I made little progress and felt helpless and suddenly afraid that the sea would return with a vengeance to consume me, despite the fact it was a retreating ebb tide.

I looked around to see if I could see Adam returning along the path, but there was no sign of him or anyone. There was definitely no way I could get back to Tregellas. The only thing I could think of doing was to take out my kite and wrap it around my shoulders, not only to keep me warm, but I also hoped the bright colours would draw attention to me sitting uselessly on the floor. If I could just make myself visible and make it obvious I was in trouble to anyone coming down the coastal path, then I would have some hope of getting off the beach.

I changed direction and inched my way on my bottom into the centre of the beach; it was slow and agonising work and also counterintuitive, as I was heading towards the sea, but it meant that I could be seen from the cliff top paths. I was crying pretty much continually and swearing loudly, as the pain and frustration of the situation took its hold, but at least my head had stopped bleeding. My fraught state wasn't helped by the fact that the sun was beginning its descent for the day and the chances of anyone walking this stretch was getting ever more remote. I realised that although Adam had taken the scenic route to the Old Smithy, he might not come back along that path at all.

I was slowly and painfully continuing my shuffle backwards when I heard someone approach. I twisted around as best I could and saw Adam.

'Hello, Lily Actually! You OK?'

'What the hell? Do I look OK, you moron?'

And with that I burst into tears again and repeated the story of what had happened to me in such a whiney, high-pitched voice that Adam took a step back, as though he might catch some infectious disease should he get too close to me. When I finished spewing my tirade, he asked if I needed some help.

'I don't bloody believe you!' I yelled at him. 'Of course I need some help. I think I've broken my ankle and I can't walk, which is why I'm sitting here on my arse, wrapped up in a sodding kite!'

'OK, OK, I couldn't work out what you said, what with the crying and stuff.'

He bent down in front of me and looked over my leg. 'I think you may have broken your ankle, Actually.' There was a devilish gleam in those big black eyes and as he held my gaze for longer than was necessary, he melted something inside me. For the first time, I felt his inner warmth reaching out.

'Come on, let's see if we can get you home,' he said softly.

He helped me up and bent over slightly, back towards me, indicating he would give me a piggyback home. I clambered on as best I could, and he hoicked me up and tucked me in by pulling me into his hips. My head rested on his shoulder, my nose against his neck. He smelled salty, of honest work, and his hair was surprisingly soft.

As he moved off, however, my leg jiggled, sending shockwaves of pain up through my body. 'Arggghhhhh, oh my God, stop!' I yelled almost involuntarily. 'It's too jiggly, it's making my foot wobble, arhhgh, Jeeeeeezus, stop, you can't carry me like this, stop!'

Adam deposited me back on the ground. I sat panting and gasping, nauseated by the experience.

'Well, how do you think I'm going to get you back to the farm?' He was irritated and right; I couldn't see how he was even going to get me as far as the road.

'I don't know, Adam, I don't know, but it hurts when it jiggles, and I can't take the pain.'

I still sounded like a small child and pretty much felt like one. Adam wasn't exactly a knight in shining armour, but he was there and trying to help, and that's all I could wish for, but I didn't expect to have to think, too. I wanted him to make it all better, to get me somewhere safe and to get me out of pain.

'Hang on,' he yelled and scooted off towards the caves at the back of the beach. When he came back, he had with him an assortment of driftwood. He took out his penknife and began to whittle the odd pieces into more manageable sizes.

'Right, give me the kite.'

'What for? Why do you want my kite?'

'I can make a splint for your leg using the kite and the wood, then I'll be able to give you a piggyback to the farm. And it won't hurt. Simple as.' He smiled again.

'You can't do that,' I spat at him. 'You can't cut my kite. I won't let you chop it up!'

'OK, Actually, so what do you propose? We sit here until it heals, perhaps? Would you like me to summon a rescue helicopter for you, or the coastguard? My car is too wide for the road and yours would bounce you around way too much. What would you like me to do, because I have no idea what else can be done? It's your call, lady.'

I shrugged hopelessly, as I realised there was no other sensible option.

'How about the lines?' I said meekly. 'Could you use the lines to tie the wood around my ankle instead? I can get them replaced more easily.'

'They'll do just fine, as I have another idea, but I still need the kite – don't worry, though, I won't chop it into little pieces.' He helped me out of the backpack and then wrapped the kite around my injured leg, creating a supportive and soothing bandage. He did it quite tight so that it was firm but comfortable. He then placed the driftwood splints in a kind of cage fashion around my leg and ankle, before tying them tightly with lengths of kite line. Finally, he took my backpack and inserted my splinted leg into the bag, tightening the straps and cords to keep the whole thing together.

'There,' he said, looking satisfied with himself. I had to admit that it felt much better and more comfortable and, once I was up on his back, Adam was able to carry me along the track by the side of the stream and back to Tregellas.

When we arrived, instead of taking me to Hawker's Hut, he cut across the yard.

'Where are we going, where are you taking me?'

'To my place . . . you need to go to hospital, and I need to change before I take you, so we'll go to mine and then on to A&E.'

'But why? Why do I have to go to hospital now? Can't I go and just put some ice on it and see how it is in the morning? Can't we leave it for now? Can't I just rest and recover and think about it later? Can't . . ?'

'Shut up, will you! Crikey, just calm down a bit!' He was rankled and his displeasure made its presence felt as it radiated through his body to mine. His hold on me tightened, as though I might get away if he didn't keep me fast.

'You need to go to hospital today because, as you have pointed out, you have probably broken your ankle and it requires medical attention!'

And that was all he said on the matter. I shut up and let him carry me to his hut, Morwenna Mowhay.

Chapter 14

I had no preconceived idea of what Adam's place might be like, but it certainly wasn't what I would have imagined had I tried to conjure it up. It was like a beautifully arranged treasure trove of colour and texture, and it was immaculate and clean despite every spare inch of room being covered. Adam carried me over to a small sofa, where he released me from his grasp before putting to one side a pile of papers from the stump of tree he used as a low coffee table and rolling it across the small room towards me. He grabbed a cushion that looked handmade, gently lifted my sore leg and rested it on the makeshift footstool.

'I need a quick shower and change,' he said, and with that he turned and walked into the small kitchen area, returning with a brandy.

'Thank you, Adam. I do appreciate your help; I think I was just a bit shocked back there, y'know?'

'Hmmm, yes, I know, Actually.' And there it was again, the glimmer of warmth that percolated away somewhere beneath that mop of dark hair.

I took a sip of the brandy, which under normal circumstances I would have thought revolting, but its heat was more than welcome. I sat back, weirdly comforted by the throbbing in my leg; it felt secure and safe and so did I. Tendrils of brandy tiptoed around my body and, as the drink took effect, I began to look around me. The room carried the most incredible energy and it smelled fragrant and fresh, as though someone had wafted something citrusy or spicy through it just before our arrival. Despite the mass of knick-knacks in such a small place, there was a sense of peace and tranquillity.

Adam had two prehistoric armchairs and the two-seater sofa I was sitting on, but they had been lovingly recovered in beautiful swatches of a deep purple, velvet-like fabric. Scattered on them were seven cushions made of solid colour on one side and a patchwork of matching scraps on the other. Each was the colours of the chakras, so they blended beautifully against the purple and had clearly been well made by someone gifted in crafting and needlework, much in the same loving way my scarf had been made.

There were no curtains at the large patio doors, but the remnants of old, rope fishing nets had been artfully draped around them. Hanging from the same pole were pieces of sea-battered glass in myriad colours that would doubtlessly catch the afternoon sun and imbue the little haven with a hint of colour, as it made its way across the western sky.

One wall was filled floor-to-ceiling with ancient books that were clearly treasured but well read, the kind you might find in a second-hand bookshop, but there was no vellichor – no musty smell emanating from them – just an air of intrigue that made me want to read the spines, to see which characters Adam had chosen to share his personal space with.

To add to the curious collection, the most extraordinary

framed pencil drawings were hanging on the walls: images of the sea, of flora and fauna and of local buildings, too. Some were miniature in size and others were large, complex compilations of items that should never be together, yet somehow worked in their intricacy. The centrepiece was a fantasy illustration consisting of a large plant with serrated, leathery leaves that puckered up as they tucked neatly behind pink and white flowers. The leaves grew outwards instead of up and, as they did so, they turned into the waves of the ocean. Above a tumultuous sea at the front of the picture was a calm horizon and shell-pink sky. I wanted to see beyond the mount, around and behind the image. Dotted about the sketch were fairy-like creatures; their outfits were puffball tutus or caveman-type smocks made from sea foam. Some danced little jigs and some huddled around a tiny fire; one was fishing and two bashful forms sheltered under the giant leaves of the plant, one having her hair brushed with what looked like a sea urchin. The figures were corporeal and breathed life into the drawing, but I wondered why the artist had painstakingly painted tiny, enchanting characters into such a chaotic scene. It was a fascinating, beguiling piece of work.

Elsewhere, dozens of carved pieces of driftwood and works of art made with seashells and seed pods hung from the ceiling and probably made the most calming of sounds, should the wind be allowed to blow through the hut. The building was similar in layout to mine, with a bedsit arrangement for the kitchen and lounge, but I'd heard Adam go up the stairs to use his bathroom, so it was obviously different on the upper floor. I could barely hear any noise at all from up there, and I wondered if in actual fact Adam had abandoned me.

On the floor next to me was a pile of rocks and stones, and I idly picked up a couple of the smaller ones so I could look at them more closely. Each was exquisite in its own way. Unlike the ordinary pebbles you might find on the beach, these seemed to have some deeper property that radiated as I held them in the palm of my hand, just like the stone from Uncle Tom's garden. None of what I was seeing made any sense to me, as Adam didn't seem the profound type. Instead, I saw him as rather rough and ready, as someone who had little to contribute, and yet he had created this sublime sanctuary. I suddenly felt panicked. Supposing this had been created by someone else? It had never occurred to me that Adam might have a woman in his life. Clearly, I had been hugely judgemental of his whole being not to have even considered this, but it was a real probability.

As I was stuck in my seat, I couldn't get up to poke around and see if there were any signs of a woman living in the hut, but I guessed it was entirely possible. I felt stupid that I hadn't thought of it before now. After all, he was a fit looking man, so why wouldn't he have someone to share his life with? I felt rejected by my own hand and inwardly chastised myself for being so stupid to assume that he was available. I slugged back the remaining brandy, but as it hit the back of my throat it set off the most horrendous spasm and I choked. For a few moments, I couldn't cough, and I couldn't breathe in nor out. I just sat gaping-mouthed until eventually the uncontrollable coughing started.

'You OK, Actually?' Adam called down.

I couldn't answer, and within seconds he had bounded down the stairs and appeared at my side. Taking me firmly by the shoulders, he yanked me out of the sofa, bending me double before patting me between the shoulder blades.

'Did you eat something; was it just drink?'

I nodded, which didn't really help much, as he had asked two questions, but I was able to point towards the brandy glass on the sofa.

'OK, this will pass. Now, it might sound completely mad, but don't worry about trying to breathe, it's just a spasm.'

He continued the back slaps and rubbed firmly between my shoulders, trying to reassure me while I gasped for breath. 'Good girl. Just keep calm, you'll be fine.'

Although I was gulping furiously between coughs, I couldn't swallow the saliva that had accumulated in my mouth. I was retching and dribbling all over the stone floor, while Adam continued in his encouraging way.

'Excellent, you're fine, you're going to be OK; I bet you can usually hold your breath for way more than a minute, so this will be a piece of cake for you. Don't try too hard, just let it pass, OK?' His words made sense and as soon as I stopped fighting to breathe, the spasm in my throat eased.

'You OK? Slowly now, just take tiny breaths in and big breaths out.'

Still bending forward, I stared as hard as I could at his feet. One was bare and pink, with clean, short nails, the other was clad in a puffin-covered sock. Twisted and pulled on as far as the heel, it confirmed the speed at which Adam had leapt to my rescue.

Progressively, more and more air *was* going in and coming out, and my breathing calmed to near normal. All the while, Adam's gentle, placid voice and now needless rubbing and patting reassured me.

'See, you're fine, you're all good, Actually.'

As I stood up, I was shaking from head to foot, with tears pouring down my cheeks. This was more of a protective reflex than because I was upset. I wiped my mouth and looked sheepishly towards Adam. He could obviously see the fright and embarrassment in my face, as I could see it reflected back in his.

He then simply opened his arms and held me. As I clung to

him, I listened to the consoling lub-dub of his heart, and the rhythm it beat suggested I no longer needed to be fearful in my life. His body felt strong through the grey cotton of his t-shirt, but where my hand rested upon his hip, a small mound of fat peeked over the waistband of his jeans. The feel of him and his freshly showered smell made me believe he was a safe man to be with. I wanted more than anything to be protected by him.

It was clear neither of us wanted to break the embrace, but my ankle began raging at me and I was so uncomfortable I had to move. Holding me gently by the hands, Adam helped me to sit back down on the sofa. He raised his eyebrows, as if to ask if I was OK, and as I nodded, he scampered back up the stairs to finish getting dressed. Within a minute or two, he was back, and although I was still shaking, I had regained most of my composure.

'Well, Actually, you're quite a demanding little soul, aren't you? The things you do to get attention; you should be on the stage!'

'Well, now, aren't you funny, Adam? You're quite a soul, too, only more of the arse variety.'

I couldn't believe what I had said. I had never been so insulting to anyone in my life. Rightly so, Adam looked wounded, as he pointed to the front door with one hand and held up the car keys to me with the other, indicating he was off to sort out my transport. I was mortified; it wasn't even funny. I thumped the sofa either side of my thighs repeatedly and was still giving it a good pounding, with an audible 'aarrrraagh' thrown in, when he returned. Looking bemused, he came over to help me up.

'I'm sorry, Adam, that was really rude of me. It was a very unfunny joke; I'm not used to breaking ankles then drinking brandy and choking. Everything this afternoon has just been awful. I really am sorry.'

'No probs,' he offered dismissively, as he yanked me up onto his back once again.

He deposited me on the back seat of his pick-up and made his way out of the farm and onto the road for the drive to the minor injury unit at Stratton. It was a painful journey, but I didn't mention the discomfort and Adam remained silent throughout. I felt like such an idiot. How could I have been so rude? He had saved me twice that afternoon and I'd repaid him by being downright nasty.

When we arrived at the minor injury unit, Adam went in and got a wheelchair, before pushing me through to reception, so that I could register before being seen by the nurse. She was a plump but pretty young girl, with a heart-shaped face and a wide smile. As Adam wheeled the chair into the consulting room, she artfully weighed up the relationship by asking Adam to push his 'wife' to the side of the bed. With lightning speed, he replied that I wasn't his partner, and I could do little else than watch her flirt outrageously with him, as though I were nothing more than a piece of furniture. I don't know whether it was because I had been so rude to him, but Adam reciprocated with his tongue hanging out of his head. The nurse lavished her attention on the makeshift splint he had created, as though it were worthy of a Nobel Prize, and once she had finally uncovered my ankle – none too gently, either – she agreed that it was probably broken. However, she explained that as there were no X-ray staff on at that time of the evening, I would have to go back the next day to have it checked out further.

'Will you be on duty again tomorrow?' Adam asked the nurse with an eager expression on his face. Before she could reply, I exclaimed that I would make my own way there by taxi. I was angry and hurt and the turmoil of the day was too much to bear. I dug the heels of my hands into my eyes to wipe away a fresh waterfall of tears. Realising he had stepped over a line, Adam gently squeezed my shoulder and said that he would get Sam to bring me along.

Within 24 hours, I was in plaster, on crutches, and back at Hawker's Hut. The horror of what had happened to me was beginning to sink in. I was trapped! My life at Tregellas had been about getting around, being busy, independent and invincible, but there I was confined to a small, stinking room with my leg in the air and nothing to do.

Chapter 15
DECEMBER 2018

During the three weeks that followed the saga of my broken ankle, I barely saw a soul. Mya had been away but returned when I fell from the rocks; she lurked about and goaded me from the shadows. I spent quite a lot of time crying and sleeping, and it was down to me to be creative in how I managed the enforced incarceration. I made good use of the giant old TV, but I was beginning to tire of the sound of my own thoughts, as they bounced around the fermenting chambers of the hut.

In the hope of distracting myself, I tried to imagine it filled with white noise babbling away endlessly. I was terrified I would succumb once again to thoughts of Nat. I had been doing well in regaining my sense of self and hated the thought of sliding back. I realised I was being tested to see how resilient I had become and how much I had actually learned about myself, but all my situation seemed to highlight was the fact I was alone in the world, having ostracised myself from friends long before running away to the sea.

Unlike Adam, Mrs Enys eventually came to see me after

about a week. She rapped at the door so hard it reminded me of the times my mother had staggered home and banged on the door so drunk that she'd urinated in the street before I could open it.

'Morning, Mrs…'

She barged right in before I'd had the chance to invite her inside. I heard Mya call her a rude bitch, but I ignored her – even though I agreed with her.

Oblivious, Mrs Enys cut straight to the purpose of her visit. 'Becky will cover your work for you.'

There was no 'Hello?', 'How are you?', 'How's the foot?'

'Of course, I shall be paying her to work extra hours, so I won't be able to pay you at the same time. You understand, don't you?'

'Of course.'

'There's no "of course" about it, you dumb bitch. Tell her to fuck off and leave you alone.'

'Mya!'

'Pardon?' She looked around to see who I was talking to.

'Nothing, nothing . . . my, er, ankle will take a while to heal, but as soon as I can spend a bit more time up and about, I'm sure I'll be able to manage again.'

'Well, we'll see.' Mrs Enys sounded doubtful. 'Time will tell.'

And with that she left. She was blatantly furious with me and didn't hide her displeasure at my accident. I couldn't appreciate that she had a business to run and needed reliable staff with which to do that. So, instead of accepting that her irritation was probably due to the amount of co-opting and cajoling she'd had to do to cover me, I took her comments personally. I made myself feel as though all the self-discovery work and strengthening I had done had been worthless. I didn't expect to be paid whilst I wasn't working and that didn't bother me, but Mrs Enys's attitude towards me was upsetting.

'Why do you let her speak to you like that? For Christ's sake, Lily, stand up for yourself once in a while.'

'I do know how to look after myself, Mya!'

'You genuinely don't, Lily. You need to stop all this airy-fairy happy-clappy bollocks and get your life sorted once and for all.'

We glared at each other nose-to-nose, as we stood in the tiny entrance to Hawker's Hut. Then the pain slithered slowly up my leg and called for my attention.

As I sat in the lounge and waited for the day to pass, I realised I hated myself for being so weak and oversensitive. Once again, I bore the mantle of responsibility. I hated that I couldn't shake off this hugely assumptive view that I was the bad person at the centre of all things wrong. I hated that Mya was always right. I wept over the disastrous encounter with Mrs Enys, and I cried again later that same day, only this time with gratitude. One of the pony girls brought round a large jug of homemade vegetable and lentil soup, which Mrs Enys had made. It was clearly a peace offering and was appreciated as much as it was tasty.

I took advantage of the girl's visit and asked her to go up into the loft room and dig my laptop out of its case. Although reluctant to re-enter the 21st century, I realised it was a necessary evil. One of the things the Enys business empire did embrace was technology. All of the farm bookings were managed online, and all the buildings had their own Wi-Fi. It wasn't long before I was able to jump onto the guests' free connection. It was time to reach out to a couple of close, long-forsaken buddies. I didn't dare use any of my old email addresses, so I set myself up with a new Gmail account and said hello to my long-lost friends.

The first person I messaged was Lou. She was the one responsible for my first teenage hangover; she encouraged my outlandish, irreverent behaviour and filthy sense of humour. She had also meted out some of the sternest tongue lashings I had ever received.

We were at sixth form college together, but as we weren't doing the same lessons, we didn't speak until the final term. I'd been dangling from the climbing frame in a pub garden when my Pernod and blackcurrant had slipped from my hand and slopped over someone's white cricket jumper, which had been draped for safe keeping over the bottom rail. Lou leapt to my rescue, dragging me into the loo and soaking the thing in cold water while my giggling hysterics left me unable to breathe and in danger of peeing my pants. During the last week of the last term, we both took part in the annual *It's a Knockout* competition, which involved a few of us charging around with dustbin lids tied to our feet and climbing scaffolding wearing wellies and welder's masks. Lou hadn't fancied it at all but had been coerced into going along. As soon as she spotted me in the team, she came running over and managed to convince me that I should take her turn, too, 'For the greater good of the team!' This I had been more than happy to do. From there our friendship had grown, and before long I had become Stan Laurel to her Oliver Hardy.

Contacting Lou and the others was scary, as I wasn't sure whether they hated me for abandoning them. When Nat came into my life, I simply drifted away; partly because he didn't like me having friends and partly because my friends didn't like Nat – not that they had ever even met him. Initially, they were wildly excited about the man who had captured my imagination and put fire in my belly. In those early days, they could see I was thriving on his attention and they could tell I was happy when I spoke about the delightful things he brought to my world. But then our relationship stopped making sense to them. They didn't understand his need to be non-conformist and to come and go the way he did. In short, they were horrified at the rubbish I tolerated in return for very little. They felt I was accepting crumbs when I deserved so much more.

As Nat's behaviour became more extreme, it became easier and easier not to tell them about him and our life together, until eventually I stopped contacting them. Whilst at the time it felt as though my friends were being judgemental, I could now see that they were simply frightened for me.

I sent off a handful of chatty but wary messages and didn't have to wait too long before Lou replied with a cheery and happy message. She was as excited to hear from me as I was to get her reply and before I knew it, we were messaging each other a couple of times a day. Although I gave her scant detail, she was more than relieved to learn that Nathaniel was no longer in the picture, and she was excited about my new life. She was also full of great suggestions about what to watch on TV, and for things to read. It was as though we had never been apart. With Christmas a little over a month away, we made a plan for her to visit me in Welcombe. It was wonderful to be back in touch with her and her presence in my life again was an absolute blessing.

Two days before Christmas, I started scurrying around – as best I could – to make the place ready for Lou's arrival. I'd been put in a boot-type cast, which was much more comfortable. It was lightweight and removable, which meant I could bathe and get around more easily. I was also allowed to bear weight on my foot when it was in the cast, so for the most part, other than driving, I was reasonably mobile. Mrs Enys was happier, too, as I was once again able to do her laundry. Although she didn't say anything, the relieved smile she gave when I said I could resume some of my duties was apparent. The weather had mostly been dark and rainy, so it didn't really matter that I wasn't able to get out much, although on crisp mornings, when the wind chilled the air, I longed to be by the sea, to fill my lungs with the freezing freshness and to feel the darts of icy rain and sea against my face. I longed to shake off the pregnant pause in my transformation and feel vibrant and free again. I found I tired easily, and the palms of my hands were bruised from weeks of relying so heavily on the crutches. Whilst the boot was light, I still had quite a lot of pain and got cold quickly, as I moved so slowly about the place.

I hadn't seen Adam to talk to since the night he took me to Stratton. In some ways, I was quite pleased. I had blown whatever it was I thought we might have by being so rude to him. I chided myself regularly about my behaviour towards him, especially as he had rescued me several times since my arrival. I was stupid to have reacted so badly at the thought he had a woman, and that she may have made their home – it's not as though I'd ever seen him with anyone, but even if he did have someone it was none of my business. It was down to my own stupidity and rudeness that he had given me a wide berth, and I couldn't blame him.

I brushed away any thoughts of Adam to concentrate on preparing for the arrival of my lovely friend. I was adding the finishing touches to my plumping and fettling when there was a surprisingly timid knock at the door. With my boot foot, I reached it in record time and on sight, Lou and I flung our arms around each other and hung on for dear life. We laughed and cried and everything in between for a full minute before releasing each other and starting a tidal wave of girl speak for 'Hello', 'How are you?' and 'You look amazing'. It was wonderful to see her, and I was excited and a little hysterical at her arrival. We stood in the tiny hall with our reflections bouncing out of the mirror and making the room feel filled to capacity.

'Well, this is salubrious,' Lou said, holding her arms out, palms up, much as a priest would when speaking to his congregation. 'Interesting aroma. What is it? Eau de Bovine, Parfum de Piggy?'

'I know, I made it all by myself. Lovely, isn't it?'

'No, seriously, what the heck is it? Have you buried Nat under the floorboards or something?'

I was a bit taken aback by her harshness and she must've seen the light dim in my eyes.

'Come on, Lily, I was joking. Sorry to lower the tone before I've even got through the door.'

I couldn't blame her for mocking my situation, because I'd yet to explain it all to her, but I was still disappointed at how easy her callousness had slipped out.

'Lily? C'mon. I'm sorry. I didn't mean anything by it. I'm sorry, OK? Now, show me round your gaff.'

She placed a hand on my arm and tried to lead me through to the kitchen area, but we ended up in an awkward waltz, which was the salve we both needed.

After the grand tour, we curled up next to each other on the decrepit sofa. It was part of a bamboo conservatory lounge suite and it was lumpy and squealed in a plasticky way when anyone moved. Through the patio doors, which I'd never been able to open, we stared at the view of the stone, gable end wall of next door's barn. We winced in unison as a nearby security light flickered on and off in tune to a silent disco, as the sleeting rain dashed down.

In the way that best friends do, we sat drinking tea and ridiculing the hut. I had mostly learned to ignore the foetid smell, along with the 1980s décor and the desperately tired kitchen. Taking a no holds barred approach, Lou renamed it the Shitty Shabby Shack and scoffed at the eclectic mix of crockery and utensils, which anywhere else would have been considered chic and endearing, yet here, in this environment, seemed lazy and something of a health hazard. Each piece had chipped edges and cracked glaze.

Now, though, Lou's judgements sailed over my head. She didn't say anything I hadn't already thought and besides, I was enraptured by her; it was simply wonderful to be with my true friend again. She had cut short her platinum blonde hair into a wedge shape, which made it look thick and lustrous, and being tall and plump, she was as big physically as she was in spirit. The fringe hung low across her face and mostly covered one of her piercing blue eyes, although as she swished her head in the effort of conversation and laughter, it would peep out from behind the wild strands of hair. As usual, she had on thick but perfectly applied make-up, which made her appear younger than she had the last time I'd seen her a couple of years earlier.

Evening turned to night and tea to wine, as we talked through life. Lou had had an incredibly successful time of things. She was content with her work in research, and she was still single and happy about it. When we talked about my move to Devon, I made light of it and changed the topic of conversation when it came to Nathaniel. Lou knew I was in the frame of mind to take or leave my job, so it hadn't come as any great surprise to her that I had run away. I knew I would eventually have to tell her the real reason for my leaving London, but that undoubtedly horrible conversation could wait for now, and Lou was prepared to accept my silence.

It was a dream come true having Lou there with me, and when she made her way up to the futon bed, just the sound of her padding about in the eves above made me feel a warmth and contentment inside that had long been absent from my life. I had missed sharing my waking and sleeping moments with another, and until then, until hearing the gentle creaks as she made her bed and snuggled down for the night, I had little idea of how lonely I'd been.

———

The following morning started like reveille; Lou's bugle-call voice shattering my peace and quiet.

'Happy Christmas Eve!' she shouted, as she burst into my room with a breakfast cup of tea. I'd forgotten how much of a one-man crowd scene she could be. 'Come on, get up! I've got something for you.'

'But it's not actual Christmas today. Presents should be given tomorrow.'

'God, you're such a bloody straight-lace! Who said anything about presents? I just said I have something for you! Come on, you lazy git, it's 10 am – you should be up already.'

'Okay, okay, okay, sergeant major Moody, I'm coming. Let me get my leg on!'

I scrabbled around for my boot and, once assembled, I made my way into the lounge area. Lou had already made toast and scrambled eggs and, as we sat down on the disagreeable sofa and ate, she was smiling from ear to ear.

I was flummoxed. 'What's up with you, then, Mrs Smiley Person?' I asked her.

'Nothing!'

'Well, then, why are you smiling from ear-to-ear like a nutter? Your eggs are good, but they're not *that* good!'

'No real reason, I ju . . .'

Lou's phone started to ring. She grabbed it quickly and tapped the screen to accept the call. As she did so, I dropped my fork and clamped my hands to my mouth in surprise. There in front of me were five of my cast-aside friends laughing and screaming and waving at me from the distorted screen, all vying to catch a glimpse of their old friend, all trying to make their love and presence felt. The cacophony of sound and the blinding image of arms waving and kisses being blown was dazzling, but it was incredible to see them. I stared into excited faces trapped in the screen of the small phone, as my friends asked millions of questions, most of which Lou answered for me.

They were all so happy and full of energy. I had forgotten the vibrancy of girlfriends and how incredibly special they are in life. They must have squawked and babbled for a full fifteen minutes before one of them yelled 'gotta go' and the screen died in my hands.

I held it tightly, staring at it in wonder as it hit me what I'd done. How harmful I had been to myself by letting that love go and replacing it with a toxic and malevolent apparition of adoration. The shame I felt at being involved with Nat had driven me away from those who really did love and care for me, and my self-loathing had prevented me from being able to ask for their help and support sooner. I should have known they would never judge me for becoming embroiled in something so damaging. Instead of running away, I could have turned to them. Those who I'd thought were part of the problem were in fact part of the solution.

'Hey chickadee, why the tears?'

I couldn't speak, as the boiling liquid slowly rolled down my cheeks and dripped onto my hands. Lou did the kindest thing I have ever known, which was to just let me sit there in that moment. Silently, she cleared away our dishes and made tea whilst I remained seated, still staring into the black screen. I heard her pottering about and the chink of china, as a gentle trace of oranges and Christmas spices sailed over from the kitchen area. I heard the fan of the oven and the boiling of the kettle and the rustle of bags, the noise and scent of companionship and nurturing filling the gaping chasm inside me.

I don't know how long I sat in that space, but eventually Lou put two cups of tea on the small table next to the sofa and, without speaking, she took me by the shoulders and held me whilst I cried the deep and painful tears of the broken and damaged woman I was finally able to admit to being.

Chapter 16

Needing tissues, I broke the embrace and we sat quietly for some time, with me cradling my mug of tea and Lou patiently waiting for me to open up.

'So, we gonna make Christmas, then?' I eventually asked.

Lou failed to hide her disappointment, but I wasn't ready to face the Nat thing yet. Even after all that time I could still hear his voice. I could still hear, 'I thought you should know', as though it were him sitting next to me on the lumpy sofa.

'Paper chains, paper cut-outs, what do you want first?'

'You're joking, right? I asked you to bring Christmas, not playschool!'

I'd been hoping for something a little more stylish than handmade decorations.

'Where's your sense of adventure, woman? Now, get stuck into this while I check on my oranges.'

Lou plopped a pile of brightly coloured craft paper into my lap along with a pair of safety scissors. I obediently set about carving out wonky children holding hands and lopsided snowflakes that had clearly already begun to thaw. Meanwhile, Lou draped fake spruce garlands around the place. She added to them small stars of tinsel and tiny wee baubles that were colourful but dimmed by the greyness of the late, winter morning. Then, in readiness for the drying orange slices in the oven, she fashioned a table decoration whilst cinnamon, cloves and marmalade seeped into the nooks and crannies of my now lovely home. The distraction our respective tasks afforded us whilst we worked made me feel content, and I found myself talking.

'Y'know, I don't think I was ever very honest with you or the girls about Nat and the way we lived.'

'You don't need to say anything, Lily, don't go there if . . .'

'No, it's fine. I want to. Need to, I guess.'

I hadn't thought about what I was going to say. I hadn't thought about the courage it would take or how ashamed I would feel. 'I guess I'm just sorry, Lou. So sorry that I could have behaved in such a disloyal and hateful way.' I carried on cutting out a string of snowmen, who, by the time I had finished, appeared to be afflicted by some kind of terrible palsy. 'You all knew he was a dangerously destructive person, but I didn't. And then when I did know it, I chose to ignore the signs. I chose crumbs of affection. I chose settling for something unwholesome. I chose all this above the loyalty and love of my friends.'

I cut the heads off the snowmen.

'Lily, you fell under his spell. We wanted to help you, but it was something you had to go through yourself – you had to reach your own conclusions. I'm just so flaming relieved that you've finally got there.'

She put down the decoration she was making. 'We knew the man was a prick, but you wouldn't let us in, you wouldn't tell us anything, so we didn't know just how much of a prick he was. For crying out loud, Lily, we didn't know if we were going to hear that your dead body had been found by an early morning dog walker or something!'

Lou spat the words out, and I could tell that years of pent-up frustration was finally coming to the fore. I looked at her over the countertop. Her fringe covered the left half of her face, and the expression in her exposed eye cut me like a hot wire. I could tell she was exasperated, but kindness and love were also reflecting back at me.

She and the others had clearly been very worried about me. I felt guilty that I had caused them all so much anguish, and I could see what Lou meant about withholding information. At the time, I thought it was for the best, but I now realised that my reluctance to share left an echoey space in which they formed their own opinions of Nat.

'I'm just so bloody relieved this is all over, and so pleased that you are coming back to life. It's wonderful to see a glimmer of the Lily I fell in love with all those years ago at college; with your long gangly legs and gigantic eyes . . . and your clumsy ways.' As she spoke, she waved her craft knife in the direction of my booted foot, which rested on the table in front of me. 'You know, you haven't changed much in all these years – you're still a pain in the arse.'

I flinched and went to protest, but I could see from the gentle smile in her eyes that she was kidding.

'It is all over, isn't it? You are out of it now, aren't you?'

She squinted cautiously at me from beneath her blonde fringe. I didn't speak for a moment, as I wanted her previous words to settle like flakes of snow falling onto an already thick blanket of pure white love. I wanted them to settle and stay for a while.

'Oh God, yeah . . . it's well and truly over. I know I needed to get off his merry-go-round, but I could have done it without being crushed in the process.'

She was chopping something, and the rhythm of the knife on the board ticked like a metronome counting me in, counting down to what I needed to say.

'Nat's married to Sorrel, his so-called business partner, and he has been for years – and now she's pregnant. Well, is . . . was pregnant, I don't know which. The baby's due in December, I guess at the beginning, so he's probably a dad already.'

Lou skilfully hid any response she undoubtedly felt, as I continued to unburden myself. 'I knew about the smallholding in Oxford that he and Sorrel had, but he'd led me to believe she was just his professional partner. I think you knew that much, too?' She nodded. 'He told me he owned the land and she ran the produce business, which had started when they became lovers some years before, but the emotional side to their relationship hadn't worked out, so they'd kept the business going and he lived in one of the buildings adjacent to the house. I believed what he told me, yet it was all a pack of lies. All the time he was living in Oxford he was cosied up with Sorrel. How on earth he managed to spend so much time with me is beyond comprehension.

'When he called me to tell me about the baby, he said he was shocked and excited at the prospect of being a father. He didn't think it would ever happen for him and that at 44, it was incredible news to hear. He couldn't believe that she was about eight weeks pregnant and the thought scared him. On and on he rambled until at last he said, "I don't really know what to say, I thought you should know." That was all he could say to me, I thought you should bloody well know. What a fucker! And what's worse–' I laughed, as if anything *could* be any worse '–what's worse is that I did the maths and he fucked off to Oxford in October, leaving me high and dry and worried sick he was lying in a ditch in the filthy rain, whilst all the time he was at home, at . . . at.' Lou rushed to my side and clung onto my hand.

'Hey, lovely, come on. You didn't know, you couldn't have known any of this.'

'It's so horrid, Lou.' I pushed her off me. 'All the time he wasn't dead – he was making love to his wife, creating a life, being his funny, loving, best-version-of-himself. He was being a husband.'

I was appalled at myself. My bottom lip was no ally, as it continued to tremble. Lou took my hand and squeezed my fingers again, as I did the terribly British thing of sitting up and swallowing hard, before carrying on.

'We ended the call and I went back to my desk and worked to the end of the day. I went through the motions of making my way home as usual – bus, then tube, then walk. I was barely inside the front door when I collapsed on the floor and cried hysterically for hours. Then fucking Mya showed up, as repugnant as ever.'

'Mya? I thought that was, well, all sorted?'

'You and me both. Her reappearance made me realise how shafted I was. She came here with me but buggered off again shortly after I started work. She's been back a couple of times, just to put in her two penneth.'

I relaxed slightly, as the weight of my burden finally began to lift. 'It's been hard, y'know. I spent the first few months with Nat constantly on my mind. He was still very much with me, but I wrote nasty letters to him – not that I've ever sent any. I developed a technique for telling him to fuck off each time he popped into my head. I even worked a spell to keep him at bay, and I've been much happier ever since then.'

'Ha-ha-ha, you're still into your voodoo, then! You seriously worked a spell?'

Lou was laughing now. I don't think I'd told her anything she wasn't expecting to hear, and she was trying to deflect the intensity of the conversation. No doubt she was relieved it was over and had grasped hold of the opportunity to be humorous in order to break the tension.

'Seriously, I worked a spell – two in fact! They bloody

worked, mind you. His presence in my mind's eye has been far less frequent. Fleeting glances, perhaps, but nothing like it used to be. I checked the email account he used to use and there's been nothing, no contact. I finally feel as though I am free of him. I did the spell to get rid of him. I had to tie knots into a piece of black thread and say some words as I tied them, before putting it somewhere safe. You can bury the thread to make it permanent, but I stuffed it somewhere and lost it, so I guess that's just as good. Then I did a binding spell, where I buried some symbolic bits in the sand that would eventually be claimed by the ocean, to wash away everything we had shared. Although, oh my God, the day I did them, I had an excruciating experience. Let me just get the kettle on – I need another cuppa.'

'I'll do it, you mad old bird.' Lou looked at me wistfully. I didn't want her to speak. 'What the bloody hell are you like? You don't half choose 'em. I knew he was a bad lot from the way you described how he behaved and from the way you changed, Lil. He definitely has some kind of pathology . . . sociopath, psychopath? I'm not sure of the difference, are you?'

I had no idea, so I shrugged and shook my head at the same time.

'It's good you can see that now. I'm just sorry you had to go through so much hurt, and alone, too.'

She continued as though she had read my mind. 'You could've told us, you know? We'd never have judged you, but I guess you had to do it in your own indomitable way – you stubborn mare! You are loved, you know.'

And with that she moved to make the tea.

Chapter 17

That's what I liked about Lou, she was very uncomplicated. Even so, I knew it wasn't over by a long chalk. I knew that she would think about things and chew them over for days before mentioning my life with Nat again, but I also knew that whatever she had to offer would be helpful and would spur me on to think about how I needed to be.

'So, come on, woman, what's the next bit, what can be more disturbing than Twunt-features?' I laughed at hearing Nat referred to as Twunt again.

'Oh God, I could've died, only I'm not really sure what it is that I need to be embarrassed about!'

'Come on, then . . . mince pie?'

I nodded. 'Well, I went up to the cliff path for a walk. I'd take you up there, but . . .'

'Yeah, yeah, whatever, if there's no bus I'm not interested anyway.'

We sniggered; her appetite for exercise clearly hadn't changed.

'So, I'm up there wandering along, and I was all

preoccupied, as I'd just dug out a silk scarf that Nat had bought for me, and it had put him in mind. This was at the end of September, when it's kind of chilly one minute but boiling the next.'

Lou nodded and encouraged me to keep talking as she scoffed her mince pie.

'Well, I needed something to occupy my head, so I decided to walk away from the cliff path onto a route I hadn't taken before. Anyhow, I walked through some woods and got cold, so I wore the scarf for a bit, but then I ended up in this meadow where the heat holds fast. By the time I reached a tree to sit under, I was quite sweaty, so I took off the scarf, draped it over a branch and sat down to chill out for a bit. It turns out one of the guys who lives on the farm was working in the meadow that day, and well, he looked hot . . . as in hot, yum-yum hot, not temperature hot – although that too, as he was all glistening. He couldn't see me, so I got to enjoy the view for a while.'

'Oooh, you saucy minx! Nice to know you've got an appetite for everything local.'

'And some!' I licked my lips lasciviously. 'Well, no, not really, because he was always a bit of an ogre to me. The first time I met him he was pissed, which was always going to go against him in my book, but on this day, I was watching him while he worked in the heat of the sun and, as I lay there, I began to feel, well, shall we say a little warm under the collar, so I had a bit of a private moment!'

'Oh my God, you *did* yourself while you were outdoors – that's hilarious!'

'Don't! It gets worse than that! I nodded off after my moment and when I woke up, I packed up to leave. The man, Adam, was nowhere to be seen. I walked down to the beach, which is when I did my spell casting, and after an hour or so, I went home. But – and this is the mystery – when I got back to the cottage, my scarf was tied to a post near my front door. How did it get there before I did? The only person who was up there was Adam, so he must've returned it, but how the hell did he know it was *my* scarf? He could have come past whilst I was asleep or had my hand in my knickers and I would never have known!'

It was mortifying but funny too. Lou was laughing mercilessly at my story and, hearing the words out loud, I couldn't help but join in. The laughter was healing; it broke the power of the previous hour. It had been so wonderful to see the others on FaceTime that morning, but it felt even better to share honestly with Lou some of what had happened with Nat.

Once we'd talked that little gem to death, we had some food and put our noses outside the door. It was a glum but dry day, so we went for a short walk around the farm, where I pointed out strategic landmarks to Lou that would help her to picture what I was talking about when she returned to London. I took her to the stables to show her the steamy ponies and, as we rounded the block on our return to Hawker's Hut, we bumped into Adam.

'Hello, Lily Actually, how's the old boot?'

I wasn't sure if he was talking about me or my broken ankle. I still didn't get him, and once more, I didn't understand if he was joking or not. But my lack of understanding obviously registered with him. 'The old booted ankle – your jiggly one,' he clarified.

'Ah, it's getting on OK, thanks. The boot will come off after Christmas. It's been nearly eight weeks now – a long time! How're you?'

It was a thinly veiled way of telling him that I'd noticed how long it had been since we'd last seen each other, and I detected a slight wince as I said it. 'This is my friend, Lou, she's from London,' I added to ease the tension and diffuse my latent attack.

'Well, hello Lou from London, nice to meet you. Will you be bringing our worshipful mistress of the accident to the pub this evening? We have a bit of a night on Christmas Eve and could do with some more elves to help the party swing! You have the pixie haircut and Actually has the imp-like ears, so you'll make a fine pair.'

'Cool, definitely, I was wondering what you all do for entertainment round here. Give me your number and I'll text you if I manage to winkle her out from under her security blanket.'

'You look like a persuasive woman, but I bet even you will have your work cut out.'

'Er, excuse me, I am here, you know!' I managed to chip in.

The pair swapped numbers and made tentative plans for the evening and, as we turned and walked away, I explained that he was *the* Adam of *the* private moment. Lou let out a rather loud and animal-sounding 'phwor'. She might as well have been a Roman belching after a satisfying meal. By the time we were back at Hawker's, she was decidedly delighted, bouncing off the walls with excitement that he had been the man of the moment. I had a dreadful sense that the evening would be a humiliating affair, with Lou fully energised and in matchmaker mode, but nonetheless I agreed to go.

When we arrived at the Old Smithy Inn, Adam was already there and swigging back pints with some of the locals. He turned his head as soon as we walked into the bar and made a beeline for us across the stone flags – albeit a staggered journey.

'Ahhhh, Actually and London, my two favourite elves, what're you having?' Lou attempted to move towards the bar. 'Nope, no, no, leave it to me and I shall return with a tipple to suit.'

Lou and I looked at each other and laughed. This was going to be a long night.

We chose to sit near the fire, and I rested my tinsel-adorned booted foot up on the log basket and made myself comfortable. The inn was small, dark and raucous, with unmatched oak furniture and 1970s-styled lamps and old pictures. A copy of Tretchikoff's Chinese Girl hung haphazardly on the wall next to the inglenook fireplace. On the tables were old tea pots and ice buckets containing candles. At the bar, milk churns with cushions made ideal seats. It was not too busy, but the music was loud and those present had obviously been ensconced for some time. It was my first visit to the pub, and although it wasn't really my scene, it would do just fine for Christmas Eve celebrations. We had to wait for a good ten minutes before Adam made his way over to our table. Lou and I had watched him talking nineteen to the dozen to the young barman. As swiftly as the most professional of curtain twitchers, we switched our gaze as soon as we saw him make a move towards us.

'*Ear* we go, elves . . . get it? Here we go . . . *ear* we go. Elves have ears, big ears – God, I'm funny, my talents are wasted.'

In unison, Lou and I raised our eyebrows, as if both of us were thinking that it wasn't just his talents that were wasted, but it was quite funny so we allowed ourselves to laugh, something to do with the delivery and his sparkly eyes perhaps? This was a very different Adam to the one I knew.

'Nah, not really, just joshing with you. Now! C'mon, then. So, for you, London, I've got you your very own Awlright Cock-tail, seeings as you're all Cockney London and stuff!' He spoke with an Artful Dodger accent as he placed on the table a large tumbler of Advocaat and lemonade that had been garnished with a pork scratching on a cocktail stick and a piece of holly. Lou and I began to giggle. 'And for you, Actually, my little cherub, you can have this.' He placed on the table in front of me a baby's feeding cup filled with water, also decked with holly and a pork scratching. 'It's one of my finest Adam's Ale cocktails.' He winked and was smiling, suggesting something far more salacious than a simple glass of water, but I didn't really understand what he was laughing at. Lou had to explain that whilst Adam's Ale is a playful allusion to water, in this instance our joyous host was making a ribald reference to sex. After the innuendo had been pointed out, I couldn't contain either my vibrant blush or outburst of laughter, which was mainly due to nervousness, but was also secretly filled with hope.

He gently deflected the embarrassment of my innocence back to himself, and the look on his face quite suddenly changed from one of hilarity to that of mock offence. 'You saucy thing, you!' he gasped, with his hands at his face.

By this time, Lou and I were beside ourselves, and I relished the feeling of the laughter as it rattled through my soul. No one had ever paid such attention to detail when making me a drink before.

'Not sure what you were thinking of, you rude hussy. I just meant that for safety reasons, I have made you a water-based drink using my own recipe. Anything alcoholic and you'd be bound to hurt yourself – or someone else!

'Nahhhhhhhh, just blagging you. Barkeep, another Awlright Cock-tail for my elf, forthwith!' And with that the young barman brought over another snowball, one he had obviously prepared earlier. This was clearly all part of Adam's act, and it was so funny and so clever that I was soon enraptured by the whole ambience of the pub and the people therein. The effort Adam had gone to gave me a warm inner glow.

We spent hours laughing and talking with people I'd never met before, as well as singing carols and along to the Christmas pop songs blaring out of the stereo. We had the night of our lives and it was only when the barman declared a lock-in that Lou and I decided enough was enough. The local taxi company had pretty much based themselves at the pub and were continually collecting people and taking them home, so we didn't have to wait too long before we were on our way back to Tregellas. We sat in the back of the taxi and laughed conspiratorially like a pair of giddy teenagers. We weren't that drunk on alcohol, but the electric atmosphere had definitely affected us.

'He likes you *soooo* much,' squealed Lou, 'he is bonkers about you and he can't keep away from you. He didn't stop looking in your direction all evening! You've got him hook, line and sinker.'

'Don't be daft, Lou,' I attempted, but knowing she spoke the truth, I couldn't come up with anything to add. Instead, I slumped back into the seat of the taxi, smirking from ear to ear. I felt so much excitement inside that I thought it might burst out of my chest.

'Lily's in lur've, Lily's in lur've! Lily and Adam, sitting in a tree, k-i-s-s-i-n-g . . .' and with that, I turned to pummel Lou until the pair of us were hugging and laughing. I felt alive and happy, from the tips of my elfin ears to the sole of my old boot.

The next couple of days passed in a flash and before we knew where we were, Lou was packed and ready to go home. It had been the most wonderful Christmas either of us could ever recall having. We had lazed about on both Christmas Day and Boxing Day, grazing our way through an inordinate amount of food and dreadful festive TV. We'd sat and cried at *Love Actually*, during which Lou went to great lengths to point out that Hugh Grant's character David would be played in real life by Adam, and that he would be my saviour and we would fall hopelessly in love with each other. As I watched the story unfold, knowing every scene intimately because I'd seen the movie a billion times before, I couldn't help but wonder and hope that Adam would indeed rush in and sweep me off my feet. I still felt dreadful for being so horrid to him, but it was clear he had forgiven me and that he wanted to make amends.

It was about one in the afternoon when Lou stood up to leave. 'Hey, Lily, I have one more gift for you and please use it, you crazy tart. Don't hide here all alone; you're very much loved and we've all missed you and want you to be safe and well and sane!'

She handed me a box that was wrapped neatly in plain red paper. I took it from her and said that I would open it after she left, but she insisted I open it there and then. I tore back the paper to reveal a new smartphone. I couldn't believe what I was looking at. 'Oh, but Lou, I ca . . . I can't!'

'You can and you will and what is more, you'll stay in touch, or else you'll have me to answer to. It's only pay as you go, but you'll be able to top it up online.'

My hands were shaking as I lay the precious gift on the sofa and turned to hug my friend. I knew that she had forgiven me for banishing her and the others in my quest for happiness with Nat and, although I had been overwhelmed with shame at how I had behaved, I was now overwhelmed with love for the people in my life who really mattered. We held each other for some time before the clinch was broken and she left. I was sad she was returning to London, but whatever magic she had brought with her had settled into the well-worn grooves of my hut. I felt bathed in love and more healed than I could ever have achieved alone. When I eventually turned on the phone there were seven numbers already stored in the contacts – Lou, Danni, Manda, Saira, Jess, Mona and Adam. I clutched the phone to my chest as though it were a beloved teddy bear.

Chapter 18
JANUARY 2019

I was a little downhearted in the silence and peace that followed Lou's departure, but her healing touch remained, and I bathed in its glory. Even the fusty aroma had dissipated. New Year's Eve came and went with little attention other than messages on my phone from Lou and my old girls, and although I was disappointed not to have heard from Adam, I don't think anything could have surpassed the Christmas Eve fun and so I was content to settle for an early night, waking fresh and bright and confident in the knowledge I was starting the new year in a good place.

By the middle of January, I was boot free, and although my ankle was painful and stiff and would go horribly purple where the circulation was taking its time to repair, I was starting to get around under my own steam again. I was having regular physio, but the walking and activities I did around the farm were proving to be the most effective therapy. I still couldn't really leave its confines, as the uneven pebbles were too hard to walk on, but I was satisfied just to be able to get out into the fresh and invigorating January air.

As the days ticked by, I still hadn't seen Adam. I

pretended to myself that I was peeved with him – blaming his bravado and interest in me on the drink and festive spirit – but deep down I was actually relieved he hadn't pestered me. He had changed from the ragamuffin inebriate I'd first met on the night of my arrival to a complicated mixture of kindness, creativity and high energy. I found the very thought of him overwhelming, so I wanted to take my time, but conversely, I was itching to see him again. It was all a bit confusing. Lou, on the other hand, had different ideas and decided I should make a bold move and say hello to him rather than just dithering away in silence. So, I set about creating a text message to send to him, under Lou's supervision.

Apparently, 'Dear Adam, Happy New Year!' didn't cut the mustard. Nor did, 'Hi Adam, Lily here, HNY to you!' or 'Hey, Happy New Year! How're you doing? Lily' or even, 'Adam, hi, haven't seen you to wish you HNY, anyway, hope it's a good one.'

After 40 minutes and many versions later – most of which Lou made way too suggestive and inappropriate – we settled for:

> Hiya, how're you? HNY to you. See you around now that I'm out a bit more, Lily.

I got a response almost immediately, and when the phone buzzed into life a smile spread across my face.

> All right, thanks, Actually. How's the old boot – hmmm, I've used that one before, haven't I? Fancy a cuppa some time? I haven't been scalded or anything so far this year ;-D

I replied with adrenaline-fuelled fat fingers and had to

correct typo after typo before I could send the message. As I double-double checked it, my hands were trembling.

> Hahaha too funny! Tea would be great, thanks. Name a time and a place and, as long as it's the farm, I'll be there. Boot free, but limited capacity for wandering too far.

> You free now? I've just brewed some fresh coffee.

I thought about it for a moment. I hadn't expected him to reply so quickly, let alone want to see me. I couldn't think of any reason why not to go and panicked slightly as I replied that I would be with him in fifteen minutes. Then I flew into the bathroom to do something with my hair and make myself look presentable. I slipped into some clean jeans and a hoodie that was warm but reasonably feminine. Then, mostly terrified and spinning the narrow band on my little finger furiously, I made my way across the yard to Morwenna Mowhay and knocked at the door.

'Hey, come on in.'

Smiling his broad, warm smile, Adam held open the door to the little Aladdin's cave and welcomed me in. He'd obviously not long showered, as there was the sweet smell of shampoo and deodorant about him as I passed by, and his hair was still a little damp. I made my way into the lounge area and the conversation started to flow between us. I was nervous and looking for something to distract me from the butterflies in my tummy. I was also excited to be back in the tiny gallery, so I gravitated towards the wall that had the drawings on it and dived once again into the large picture in the centre. Adam came and stood alongside me with two mugs of steaming coffee in his hands.

'Bastard balm,' he said.

'Pardon? Is that some kind of ointment or a colloquial term for coffee?'

'No . . . no, Bastard balm, or Melittis melissophyllum, is the name of the flower in the drawing. It's a type of mint that grows up on the cliff path and its leaves remind me so much of the waves that I thought it would be a great basis for a bit of creative play. It still isn't quite right, but I'm not sure what it is that doesn't make it work for me.'

He tipped his head from right to left, pondering the image from different angles.

'You mean *you* did it? You created this picture and what, all of the others, too?' I waved my arm as though conducting an orchestra. I had no idea that Adam would be the creator of the artwork. I'd presumed he'd just collected it.

'Yes, I did them all and all of the dangly things and the furniture restoration. I just dabble really, a Jack of all trades, but I enjoy being creative and making things. No one else sees them – usually, anyhow – and, well, I just please myself.'

With that, Adam flushed a little and proffered me a mug of milky coffee. He hadn't asked me how I liked it. Meekly, I took the mug from him in acceptance. Nat flashed furiously into my mind. I knew I needed to say something or forever suffer milky coffee and the humiliation that I couldn't speak up for myself.

'Um, I usually take mine black, no sugar. I'm sorry, Adam . . . but can I . . ?'

'Oh God, so sorry, I just made it, didn't I. That's bad. Sorry, Lily, let me make you another.'

I felt embarrassed at having said something, whilst at the same time it felt good that I had been able to be honest with Adam and say what it was that I liked and wanted for a change. That one small comment boosted my confidence and made me feel as though I might be able to be true and authentic with this man. I sat with purpose on the purple sofa and when Adam returned, he sat alongside me, his body slightly turned in towards me.

We began to chat and four hours later, we had barely moved from our respective positions, except for refilling the coffee cups and for us both to slouch down into a more comfortable and relaxed position. Our thighs were touching, and I'd noticed that whilst talking, our hand gesticulations had resulted in gentle grazes and hand holding. It got late and, as I turned to say that I thought I should go, I noticed Adam looking intently at me. I looked away, but when I looked back towards him again, he had closed his eyes and was leaning forwards to kiss me. When our lips touched, I realised very quickly that he had the most incredible and soft mouth. As he gently pressed it against mine, I let out an awkward, candy-striped moan of longing for loving human contact. He tantalised me with short, marshmallowy presses, then longer, then short again. His tenderness took me by surprise, and I didn't know how to receive him. Tentatively, he began to introduce his tongue into the kisses. Barely perceptible flashes of sweetness that dashed from between his lips, meekly at first, until he was parting my own lips and exploring the boundary of my mouth. He grabbed the arms of my hoodie and used them to pull me towards him, practically lifting me off the sofa. Bit by gradual bit, our gentle kisses became ever more fervent, seeking more deeply, more lovingly from each other.

The effect Adam was having on me was absolute, but I didn't want to go much further than kissing with him. Scared by the intensity of the passion he was generating in me, I quietly started to ease away from him until I was able to sit back slightly and look at him.

His face was filled with want and he was smiling. 'Well now, Actually, you really are quite lovely.'

The thick, treacle tone of his voice made my stomach leap.

He leaned forwards once more, this time pulling me onto his lap so that he was able to run his hands over my body as we kissed. I felt pliable and feminine as he caressed me, and, as he slowly and gently worked his hands all over my torso, he soon enough found his way under my hoodie to my skin. His slightly rough hands swept and stroked me in such a way that I felt vital and fresh again. He whispered gently that he loved my breasts and for the first time in my life, I did, too. I'd always thought them small and rather insignificant, but Adam's reaction to them made me feel so beautiful that I began to realise they were part of my essence of womanhood.

A black dizziness crept over me. 'I should go, Adam.'

'Mmmm you should, as I won't be responsible for my actions if you stay much longer. I didn't go too far, did I?' he asked a little sheepishly.

'No, you were perfect, but I don't want to get too carried away, not tonight . . . that doesn't mean to say I don't want to get carried away with you, just not right now, if that's OK?'

'No, no, that's fine, I understand, but I could just about eat you all up, you're delicious and . . . well . . .' Composing himself, he stood up awkwardly and held out a hand to assist me in standing up.

'Come on, Actually, will you do me the honour of allowing me to walk you home? I promise no funny business in the milking sheds on the way, unless of course you fancy it?'

He draped his arm lightly across my shoulder as we walked through the various yards until we reached Hawker's Hut. Once the door was open, he kissed me gently on the lips.

'Can I see you again?'

I gave an assenting nod, not trusting myself to speak, as I was terrified I would invite him to spend the night, before turning and letting myself in.

Once behind the closed front door, I did several circuits of the downstairs, running as best I could with my stiff ankle. I was squealing and punching the air with glee, but eventually I calmed down enough to take out my phone and send Lou a quick text.

> Wowsers, he can kiss! We've had a lovely snog on the purple sofa and guess what, my teeny tiny boobies are magical and made him (and me) go all gooey and unnecessary! Who needs great big knockers like you have! Call me and I'll tell all xxx

Less than a minute later, Lou was on the phone demanding to know all the details of our evening. We chatted for the best part of an hour and, in the middle of our conversation, Adam sent me a goodnight message.

> Hi, Actually, I really enjoyed this evening. It was smashing. You might not look it but you're intelligent (joke), great fun to be with and very sexy, if I may say so (no joke). I wondered if you fancied coming up to the chapel in Morwenstow on Saturday? They have a book fair on. I thought you might enjoy getting out? Let me know, bed now . . . I'm quite tired X

I read the message out to Lou and as I did so, I was smiling from deep within. I couldn't believe that he liked me and that he wanted to see me again. He had invited me to do something grown up and interesting rather than a dull old dinner date. I found him intriguing and fascinating and fresh.

> Yes, please, I'd love it. Night night, lightweight x

'Oh my God, Lou, can you believe this? I thought this guy was a troglodyte wino who counted blades of grass for a living, and yet he's funny, eloquent, spiritual and creative in so

118

many ways. He seems so normal . . . do I trust him? Is he going to turn out to be like the twunt?'

The panic began to rise in my chest when I thought about the possibilities. Could he be showing me a mask? He'd already shown me two sides of his character – how the hell could I tell which one was real?

'I don't think I'm ready for this. Supposing he hurts me, supposing he turns out to be vile and dreadful like Nat? How the hell do I trust him? Do I let him in? How much do I give him? I don't know how to be, or what to think, and I'll ruin it before I even start!'

Lou was quick to reassure me that it was unlikely Adam was Nat's evil twin. She pointed out the love and attention he had paid to his home, and that it was obvious he had a soul. She was confident that he was fundamentally a good man. I began to calm down but was anxious I had read too much into his offer. I wondered what on earth he could possibly see in me, yet he'd called me funny and sexy . . . that should have given me some idea as to what he was thinking.

Eventually, I said goodnight to Lou and went to my bed. It took me hours to get to sleep and, as I lay there thinking about the feel of Adam's lips and hands, I could sense every muscle in my body soften and let go of the tension that resided there. It was only Tuesday and I had no idea how on earth I was going to remain calm and patient until Saturday.

Chapter 19

After four long days, Saturday finally arrived. I woke early and read with a coffee until about nine o'clock. Adam was coming to knock for me at eleven, so I had a couple of hours to take a leisurely bath and get ready for him. The night before, I had tried on every item of clothing I owned and stared at my flabby self in the hall mirror in disgust. Being limited by my broken ankle had decimated my fitness regimen, leaving me bloated and blubbery. Nothing fitted or felt comfortable and I had angrily stripped off one item after another and discarded it on the floor along with layers of my self-esteem. In the end, I plumped for a pair of tight-fitting bootcut jeans and a pink jumper, both of which were once figure hugging and sassy, and now, at least, were robust enough to hold firm the bits that wobbled way too easily.

Shoes, though, were a different matter. I hadn't actually worn any since the boot had come off, so as I stood there dressed and ready to go on the Saturday morning, I didn't really know what I was going to put on my feet. I certainly wasn't going to wear trainers, which is what I'd tended to live in since getting the boot off. I tried on quite a few pairs of shoes, even my green suede boat shoes, but it was way too wintery for them and they poked into the still sore bone. In the end, I dug out my cowboy boots, which were usually quite easy to get on, and with a bit of jiggery-pokery I managed to wriggle a boot onto each foot. I had no idea how the hell I was going to get them off again, but then I wouldn't need to at a book fair.

The morning was grey and a bit drizzly and chilly, though not cold. Adam collected me at about five minutes past eleven, just long enough for me to start getting palpitations and having a near nervous breakdown at the thought he wasn't coming and that it had all been a terrible misunderstanding on my part. As I came out of the door, he bent to give me a kiss, but, just as I turned to give him my cheek, we collided somewhere in the middle with a really awkward kiss, which was half on and half off the lips. It was uncomfortable and clumsy, and I think we both felt quite embarrassed. However, once in the car we began to chat and catch up on the few days that had passed since our last close encounter.

The ride to Morwenstow only took about ten minutes and we soon arrived at the ancient Anglican church. I was surprised by how many cars were already parked on the gravel embankment that stood between the church and the tearoom in the Old Rectory.

The church itself was nestled in a dip in the hillside, with steep embankments into which graves had been improbably hewn. Centred in a small copse, it was a picturesque yet melancholy place. I'd walked to it several times and on my last visit had spent some quiet time reading the ancient tombstones of the graveyard's long-dead residents. They made for fascinating reading, and I had felt mysteriously moved. At the same time, as I stood there intruding into the lives of other people, the weight of the most miserable cloud settled upon me. The murder of crows that lived in the trees that sheltered the graves added to the setting, giving it a sinister edge, and on that occasion I had left feeling cold and oddly bereft.

As Adam brought the car to a halt, I was suddenly a little anxious about revisiting the place, and was surprised at the relief I felt when I got out of the car and stepped into the graveyard with him by my side. His presence changed the energy of the place for me and although it was a dismal day, I was relieved to feel pleasantly calm and light in spirit. I noticed how we walked in step together as we made our way slowly along the gravelly footpath, both of us right leg forward at the same time, until we reached the narrow entrance to the church. The heavy door was propped open and a number of people were walking purposefully about.

Adam and I began to wander along the three large bookcases. Ancient and modern volumes, both large and small, were stacked neatly, and as we stared closely at the tomes, heads bobbing from right to left while reading the spines that stared out at us, we drifted off into our own worlds of fascination.

I picked up a small but perfectly preserved book. It didn't appear to have much about it at all, until I opened it up. Published in 1903, it had been awarded to someone in 1906 in the second grade of a local school. The paper was rough and granular and the print slightly off skew on each page. The book was called *Kitty Montgomery* and although I had no idea of the story, it was a small edition that I felt the need to own and treasure. The little gem rested comfortably in my hand as I continued my search for other literary nuggets. I picked out lots of books, instinctively raising them to my nose as I opened them. There is something so distinctive about the smell of a second-hand book, especially the older ones. I caught Adam looking at me quizzically as I sniffed the pages of an early edition of *Anna Karenina*, so I raised my eyebrows at him in a way I hope suggested that he was the weird one, not I. Then I spotted what I had been looking for, an early edition of *Jane Eyre* to go with my collection of classics. This one was a hardback edition and in good condition. It was published in 1943 and smelled oaky and musty. The pages were well thumbed, and a name pencilled onto the first page had faded over time. It was perfect for me.

I continued to browse the shelves but was satisfied that I had got what I had come for and no longer needed to scrutinise the day's offerings. We'd barely been there for twenty minutes and already I felt as though my mission was complete, although I didn't want it to be over. I was excited, impatient and wanted to pay for my treasures so that they became mine – it felt as though no matter what happened, they would always be with me.

I was desperate to pay but not wanting Adam to think I was bored and keen to leave, I surreptitiously sidled my way over to the cash desk, which was little more than an old-fashioned card table manned by a short, fat lady with jet-black hair and eyes the sparkly blue-green of a paua shell. She was perched on a chair, but as her feet barely reached the floor, she rested them on a red-brown labrador that was sleeping contentedly, not seeming to mind his burden. The smell of damp dog hung over the card table. As I stood and waited for her to complete a complex routine of fiddling with paper and arranging a tin filled with cash, I was reminded of standing at the ice cream van with Uncle Tom. The ritual we went through, the indecision – even though I always chose the same thing – and the sense of expectation and suppressed excitement held in suspended animation as the ice cream man went through the performance of creating soft, whipped masterpieces. All the time the worrying question of what to have raced around my head, and the pressure built as the van man cleaned the nozzle of the dispenser and threw his cloth into the sink before wiping his hands on his apron and nonchalantly throwing a nod to Uncle Tom, who would always let me go first with a, 'What'll you have, sweetheart?' Although I knew it was coming, I would suddenly panic. There were so many choices, too many choices: Funny Feet, Twister, Mini Milk, Feast.

'A ninety-nine, please.'

Without fail, I always chose a ninety-nine.

The little lady interrupted my thoughts. 'Want that one, dear?' She pointed to the copy of *Jane Eyre* I was hugging to my chest. I handed over the books and she nodded approvingly at my selection.

'I was just smiling at your lovely dog, he's sweet to let you rest your feet like that.'

'He's the third we've had, won't be havin' no more. One buggered off in 2008, only three he was. Next got 'it by my Dan's tractor. That was sad, he was a lovely thing, soft as a puddin' that one. Now this one's ruined. Got lumps all in 'im and on 'im.' I was impressed with her candour. 'From round 'ere are you, dear?'

I made to reply but she was off and running with tales of her fifty years in Morwenstow; of her husbands and children and the animals they shared and how hard her life had been. It was only when a Greek-nosed fusspot in a paisley jumper asked loudly if she had enough change that the eruption of chatter ceased to flow.

'I have, Mr Carmichael, thank you very much.'

Turning her head away from his stare, she tutted and rolled her eyes. 'Daft sod thinks he owns the place! Best pretend to look busy, my dear. Enjoy your reads.'

It was a lovely exchange and the memory of Uncle Tom gladdened me, lifting my spirits further. Soon enough, Adam tore himself away from the shelves and brought with him just one book to pay for. I clutched hold of the carefree feeling and brought it inside of myself; its colours, just like the aurora borealis, filled every cell and fibre of my being. Watching Adam, I noticed his movements were fluid and lithe for such a big man, and there was something heart-warming in the fact that he was coming towards me and was smiling, too. It was odd being so at ease with someone so soon. I had felt such a strong connection to Nat that I didn't think I would ever be able to separate from it, and I was scared I was imagining the ease of things with Adam. Doubts crept forward, and although I tried to quash them back down, their presence was real and dark. With my outward breath, the colourful lights I had just imagined living inside me began to disperse. Like seeds being blown from a dandelion clock, the slices of colour were released into the air and rose to settle in the nave roof high above me. The most miserable cloud descended again, and I went into a kind of daydream as Adam paid for his book and slipped it into the large pocket of his waxed jacket. Sensing a shift in my mood, he gently touched my shoulder to awaken me from my trance.

'Coffee?' he asked. I nodded my head as he guided me gently out of the church and towards the little tearoom nearby.

We crossed the gravel path in the drizzly rain, cursing that we hadn't brought a brolly with us. The pieces of stone were much larger on this piece of ground and I had to cling onto Adam's arm. I walked gingerly, scared that I might twist or wrench my ankle. With every other step, my foot quavered precariously on the summit of the rocky pyramids beneath the soles of my boots. Adam felt strong to lean upon and although we were silent, a frisson of energy passed between us.

As we reached the tearoom door, I depressed the latch, but the door failed to open.

'Come on, Actually, where's those muscles? You really can't do doors, can you?'

I laughed at the reference to my first night at Tregellas, when he had shown me the way to Hawker's Hut.

'Ha, well, I can normally, it's you – it must be the effect you have on me. I go all girly and rubbish.'

I was quite shocked by my honesty. I checked the words I had spoken, and on closer consideration realised them to be true. He did make me feel all girly and useless, and I really rather liked it. 'Come on, then, strong man, you do it!' And in one easy move, he reached across me and flicked the latch, gaining entry with no effort at all.

The tearoom was delightful, with the same style of heavy oak furniture that was in the Old Smithy Inn. Red and blue checked table linen adorned the mixture of tables, and an old settle worn smooth was positioned close to an inglenook fireplace. A number of spider plants dangled from high points, adding greenery to the charming space. An old chiming clock registered that the day had just about reached noon, give or take a few lost minutes with the passage of time. As we sat down, our chairs wobbled uncertainly on the smooth, polished stone flags. I put my two books on the table while Adam ordered our coffees and scones from the young girl who had appeared at our side. As he stood up to remove his coat, he glanced at the upside-down cover of *Kitty Montgomery*.

'Whatcha got? Anything good?'

Revitalised by his question, I told him all about the prize book and excitedly showed him my romantic *Jane Eyre* find. I was so chuffed and already felt such love for my beautiful books that I was disappointed at his distracted look and apparent lack of interest.

The young girl bought over our cups of fresh coffee served in white china, and whilst she moved them around the table and placed the bits and bobs for our scones and cream alongside, I tried to read Adam's face. He seemed distant and yet there was a wry look about him; I could tell he was calculating what to say next. I wanted the girl to stay a little longer, as I didn't want to hear what he had to say. I felt as though he was judging me and that he was going to be picky about the fact I had lost my head to a romantic tale from yesteryear. Whilst he adjusted the position of his coat, which he'd slung over the back of his chair, I busied myself with stirring my black coffee, which was futile, as the fresh ingredients were already well mixed.

I hadn't realised how ferociously I was stirring until Adam rested his hand over mine. 'All right, Actually, no need to take the glaze off! You OK?'

'Er, yes, fine, thank you. I just, well, it's just that, er, oh, well, this place and the grey rain, it's kind of disconcerting and has made me feel a little edgy, that's all. Anyhow, what did you buy? Did you find anything special?'

Adam shifted in his chair, making the wood squeak as it twisted under his body. 'Well, like you, I found a treasure, something I've been after for a while. It's quite a good find, paperback, published in 1965 and in very good condition, but it's not as good as yours.' He reached into his pocket and placed on the table an edition of *Jane Eyre* in practically mint condition.

'OMG, Adam! Bloody hell, that is so spooky. OMG, I can't believe it!'

I almost squealed as I was talking, as I was so excited and surprised. No wonder he had given me such a whimsical look. I picked up the small book and naturally smelled it before flicking through the pages. I was astounded by the coincidence, but Adam looked concerned. He clearly didn't get the whole book sniffing thing.

Eventually, he spoke. 'It's a story that's very special to me, and I'm not ashamed to say that it makes me cry every time I read it. I had a copy once, but I gave it to someone as a gift about five years ago and have been meaning to replace it ever since. Although I've found other copies of it, none of them have been right for me – until today. I didn't want a hardback version and finding an older paperback in good condition has been tough going, but here it was waiting for me.'

He looked at me in a way that suggested he was telling me that I was lucky for him. He took my hand and with a smile in his voice added, 'Thank you for coming with me today, Lily.'

Chapter 20

We drank our coffee and indulged in the cream tea and in fascinating, philosophical and funny small talk. Adam laughed when I told him about the little lady at the cash desk in the church and was amazed by how much I had managed to find out about her. Then, when the tearoom began to fill up, we made our move and picked our precarious way back across the gravelled parking area to the car.

'Who was Morwenna Mowhay, Adam? Was she someone famous from around here?'

'Sorry, who was what?' He stopped walking.

'Morwenna Mowhay? Was she famous? It's just that all the huts are named after famous local people and I wondered about your place and who it was named after?'

Adam began to giggle. Then he threw his head back and roared with laughter, until with hands grasping hold of his thighs, he was bent double. Tears poured down his cheeks and his face turned puce. I was dumbfounded and wondered what could be so funny. I certainly wasn't laughing. All I could do was stand still with my hands at my side and watch him in wonderment.

'Adam, what's funny?' I asked. He laughed. 'Adam, please?' I whined, while he laughed . . . and then laughed some more. 'Adam, tell me. Tell me what's so funny?' I poked him in the ribs, but he was beside himself.

Looking self-consciously around, I pushed him again a little harder, the faint outline of a smile upon my lips. 'Whaaaat?' I droned, 'c'mon tell me! What's so funny?' I had asked a reasonable enough question and was totally bemused by the scene playing out in front of me. I put my hand on his shoulder and shoved him again. Unable to help myself, I started to giggle, too, although I was simply laughing at Adam, who was laughing at God knows what. 'Adam! Come on, it's not that funny! Nothing can be this funny? Adam, please.' I started to pace a little and, becoming increasingly embarrassed, I stepped away from him before returning to his side as I scanned warily around. The passers-by were now staring, and some of them were even beginning to chortle. They were obviously enjoying Adam's incapacity.

He was completely beside himself. Each time he tried to stand up he laughed a little harder, and the more he laughed the more he cried: words, laughter, tears, runny nose, the lot. It was that funny it hurt me to watch. It must've taken him a full five minutes before he could stand up without a relapse, and each time he looked at me, it set him off again and he giggled a little more. I stood with my arms folded waiting for him to unlock the car so that I could get in and get home. I contemplated walking off, but even if I went along the road, I knew my ankle wouldn't cope. Eventually, Adam recovered enough to open the door for me. He then staggered towards the driver's side, where he collapsed into the seat alongside me. Breathing hard, he tried to control himself as he wiped the tears from his face in an attempt to regain his composure.

'Ah, Actually, you have made me so happy today, in so many ways, but that question has to be the best one I have ever, in my entire life, been asked. I know I'm laughing, but it is such a sweet and endearing thing, and it is a moment I shall treasure – it won't ever mean anything to anyone else, but to me it will always be the moment I became lost in you forever! There will never be anyone for me now – and you probably think I'm joking, because I'm still laughing, but you are definitely the girl for me. Without a shadow of a doubt, Lily Actually, you are the sweetest little thing alive.'

I was affronted. Although on the face of it he appeared to be saying the nicest possible things, it felt as though he was taking the piss, and I hated being ridiculed in such a way. I had no idea anymore what the hell was going on, or who I was with. Was the *real* Adam the one with whom I'd just enjoyed time in the church, the one who had made me feel grown up, sexy and interesting, or was he the one that appeared from time to time to be an idiot and, quite simply, rude?

I couldn't cope with multifaceted, multidimensional people like Adam. I didn't know how to be with them, how to understand them. I had enough trouble understanding people who were consistent, but this change of pace and character was beyond me. I didn't understand how people could be the same person and yet be a mixture of all kinds of traits: funny, cruel, intense, indifferent, loving, hateful. All those contradictions, all those masks they wore. It seemed as though I spent my life trying to figure out which version of the person I was with, so that I could be the right fit with them.

'Well, are you going to share the joke, or are you going to carry on enjoying it at my expense?' I glared at him, disliking him and his fit of the giggles.

'Oh, Lily, you're so adorable. Morwenna Mowhay is nothing, it means nothing; it's not a person, famous or otherwise. It's a made-up combination of words. A mowhay is a barn in which the 'mow' or hay is stored. My barn was always just called the mowhay, which is what it was originally, but I didn't like it, so I added Morwenna – the patron saint of Morwenstow – and that is how it has stayed! I'm not laughing at your expense, honest, I just lost control. You know what that's like? It's just that you were so innocent in asking that it made your question funny, so, so funny. I can see exactly why you asked, you weren't to know.'

He grasped my hand and quieted the furious ring spinning.

'It's a fucking hay barn!?' I spouted. I was beginning to see where he was coming from. He squeezed my hand again.

'Yes, Lily, it's a hay barn. A hay barn with a little bit of saint thrown in for good measure. I'm hoping her virtuousness might rub off on me!'

I began to giggle, this time in complete understanding. I put my index finger between my teeth, as though I were some kind of 1930s glamour model, bit hard into the middle of the nail and squinted. I felt quite silly, but looking at the loving look in Adam's eye, I certainly didn't feel stupid.

'Well, I'm pleased I asked now. At least I have made you smile today.'

'Smile! I thought I was going to have a heart attack!' He reached out and put his hand on the back of my head before gently tousling my hair.

Chapter 21

We drove back to Tregellas in silence, but it was peaceable and there was a comfortable ambience in the car. From the corner of my eye, I could see that Adam was stifling a laugh. I wanted to chuckle, too, but I held it back. I didn't want him to know that I was as happy as he was that I had made such an idiot of myself. The short journey was like something out of a bad comedy, where I would turn to look at him and catch him watching me, and he would quickly turn his head to focus on the road. Then, as I glanced away, I would feel his gaze return and he would surreptitiously regard me. It was a giant game of visual ping-pong choreographed to the beat of pouring rain, suppressed giggles and the distant sound of the indie music playing on the stereo. I contentedly watched the falling dribbles of water, as they were pulverised by the intermittent windscreen wipers and sent on their way into the universe.

As we pulled into the entrance to the lane where Adam and I had first met on that dark night of my arrival, he broke the silence.

'Wine, Actually?'

'Seriously? It's only one-fifteen in the afternoon, that's a bit early for a drink, isn't it?'

'Is it? I don't know?' He sounded a bit peevish. 'I just thought it would be a nice way to wind up the day. No worries if you're not up for it, I'll take you back to Hawker's'.

'Sorry, no, I didn't mean anything by it, it's kinda too late for lunchtime and too early for evening. It took me by surprise, that's all.'

I felt panicky again and wondered where this was going. I quickly figured that at this rate, he would drop me off and then vanish in a mood for the next couple of months. This was, after all, how men behaved – I was simply waiting for abandonment.

'Wine would be great. It's fine, sorry, I'm such a conformist. Lou's always telling me off for it. I'm not used to being spontaneous and going with the flow.' I sat forward and tried to make eye contact with him. 'Wine, let's do wine!'

'Are you sure? I don't want to force you or anything. Don't do something you're not comfortable with. I can take you back to yours and it will be fine, honest.'

I reached my hand out and placed it on his forearm. 'Seriously, Adam, wine will be lovely, thank you. You'll have to forgive me – I'm not well practised at enjoying myself!'

With that, we made straight for Morwenna, which pleased me as my hut was a tip. Whilst Adam poured a glass of wine, I found myself revisiting his beautiful works of art.

'Here, Maverick, get on the outside of this! It's a fine Terre di Faiano.' The perky Adam had returned. He handed me a bowl-shaped glass filled with dark maroon wine, then took a deep gulp from his own glass, held it in his mouth and sighed deeply as he swallowed the silken liquid. He sat on the sofa and signalled for me to join him, before savouring another large mouthful, clearly enjoying the flavour and the effect it was having on him. The pleasure he was deriving from the wine disconcerted me. I remembered how drunk he was at our first encounter, and all the alcohol he consumed on Christmas Eve. I couldn't help but question him about it. 'Adam, do you have a problem with alcohol?'

He stopped what he was doing and glared at me, clearly offended. He looked at the glass, looked back at me, then got up and poured what was left of it down the sink.

'No, I don't have a problem with alcohol. I enjoy a beer or three with my mates and a classy glass of red wine at home, because I appreciate the taste, the colour and the art of the process, which is why I drink it!'

He almost slammed the glass down on the counter, then he took a pint glass and filled it with water and some ice from the freezer, before huffing down heavily into the seat next to me. 'Happy now?'

'I am *so* sorry, Adam, it's just that the first time we met you were legless and then you were pie-eyed in the pub on Christmas Eve. What with drinking now and seeing how much the wine affected you when you drank it, it was as though you were loving it, as though you were a slave to its flavour.'

Adam got up and walked to the patio doors. I carried on speaking to his back. 'I just couldn't help but wonder. It's something that makes me nervous and afraid, it's just a thing I have. I'm sorry, I can see I've offended you. I wasn't judging you, I just needed to know that you're . . . that you're all right, if that makes sense?'

The question hung heavy in the air between us, and a stony silence rang out. Eventually, after what seemed like an age, he turned to face me, anger etching unflattering lines around his mouth. 'If you've had some kind of bad experience, then I'm sorry for you!' he shouted. 'But you have no right to question my behaviour, to try to change me or to condition your responses to me in line with what you think is right. This is who I am, and if you don't like it, then go!'

I was completely shocked by his outburst and felt a little afraid. I couldn't think of a retort. How could I respond to what he had just said? I knew exactly why I had reacted in such a way. If I told him then I'd end up telling him everything, and I wasn't ready to share any of it with him yet. He'd judge me, see how sordid and flawed I was and then dump me in a flash. Although by not sharing with him, I could sense I was about to start sabotaging things. It was as though I was on some kind of mission to prove myself right that Adam was, to all intents and purposes, no better than Nat, just in a different way.

Not knowing what else to do, I moved to put my glass down on the small table and made to get up and leave. I was shaking. The wine betrayed me as it quivered in the glass and, as I stood up, Adam crossed the small room and reached out for my arm. He pleaded with me not to go with sad, watchful eyes. We were silent at first, but then started apologising to each other at the same time. The tension was broken, but neither of us knew what to say next, so we sat quietly once more to let things settle.

'You nearly bloody killed me that first night, when you opened your car door and knocked me over,' he ventured.

I giggled. 'Ha, you can talk. I nearly had a stroke when I sat up and saw you gawking in the window at me! Though I couldn't believe it when I glanced down and saw you all scrambled up in your bike. I didn't know whether you were going to chop me into little pieces and stuff me into some kind of weird, Cornish, Sweeny Todd-type pasty!'

'Hmmm, well, I'm no fan of pies, but I am still dying to devour you.' And with that he leaned over and kissed me gently on the mouth.

We smooched like a pair of teenagers at a school dance.

Once again, we explored those gentle pecks with moist and giving lips until we had reacquainted ourselves with each other. He sat down and pulled me towards him and onto his lap, holding onto me tightly as he began to explore my body. He managed to slip a hand under my top and then bit-by-bit worked it into the top of my jeans. I could only allow myself to reciprocate by stroking his body through his clothes. I was desperate and yet terrified to touch him. He pulled his t-shirt over his head and then proceeded to pull my top off, too. After removing my bra, our top halves were naked as we pressed them together. He moved himself in such a way that our nipples touched, and the sensation of that silken skin on skin was almost too much for me to withstand. Adam got up and helped me to my feet, before taking my hand and leading me up the stairs to his bedroom.

Unlike downstairs, his bedroom was practically bare. An old, iron-framed double bed, which was as high as it was wide, was positioned centrally against the back wall of the bright little room. A colourful throw had been tossed across the mattress and this, along with the matching curtains and a small picture, were the only splashes of colour in the dove-grey room. Even the small wardrobe and chest of drawers had been painted in a similar colour, making them almost disappear into the walls, so they did not dominate the room. We stood by the side of the bed and began to kiss again, as Adam undid my jeans. I was scared. I hadn't been touched by anyone for months, so I quickly pulled away before his fingers reached between my thighs.

'I, er, let me take my boots off,' I managed to stammer.

I sat on the edge of the bed and removed the right boot, but the left one was more problematic. I couldn't get my foot into the right position to slide it over my still misshapen ankle. I struggled with it until Adam, on bended knee, gently worked at it until my foot was free. I noticed the top of his jeans were unbuttoned, as he gently pushed me back onto the bed, kissing my neck and breasts as he lay on top of me. Pressing against my belly, our hips found purchase and we began to grind together in a slow and balletic motion. We kissed in time with our hip movements, which would rise and decline in tempo, almost like the waves of the sea coming and going.

'I have a condom. Can I?' Adam was bashful in his question and I was so lost in the moment that I had little understanding of what he was inferring. I'd assumed he was going to make love to me and I found the fact that he'd asked endearing.

'That's fine,' I heard myself say, and with that he dug into the front pockets of his discarded jeans and threw one condom on the bed whilst ripping open the packaging of the other. Nat had always refused to use protection, despite my desire to be cautious, so even this small measure of consideration was remarkably touching.

———

'Look at us!' Adam suddenly exclaimed. Peeking down, I could see the most beautiful and sensual act of love taking place. Initially too shy to watch, I closed my eyes, but the image remained until it was replaced with familiar, dancing colours and tummy-dropping sensations, as orgasms swept our bodies. He covered us both with the throw and we lay there enjoying the rhythmic sound of our breathing until it softened into a light and gentle sleep.

Some while later, we were awakened by a sharp rap at the door. Adam jumped up and quickly reached for his jeans. The front door opened, and someone came in just as he had managed to get one leg in his trousers. He quickly called out that he wouldn't be a second. I looked at him questioningly, but he held his finger to his lips, so I said nothing. Once in his trousers, he grabbed his t-shirt and made his way down the stairs. I listened intently and could hear Mrs Enys; she was chiding Adam and talking to him in her usual commanding voice, although I couldn't make out what she was saying. I was pretty terrified at the thought of her being in his home whilst I was naked upstairs in his bed, and I prayed that she didn't demand to search the place. I was frozen and barely dared to breathe, and yet I was torn between the idea of hiding under the cover or grabbing my clothes and getting dressed. I heard the pair make their way to the front door and as they said a warm cheerio, Adam called her mum.

He bounded up the stairs like a puppy. 'Sorry about that!'

'Did you just call Mrs Enys mum?' I asked, as I propped myself up on my elbows.

'Yup, old Mrs Tweedy is my mother, don't you know?'

I roared with laughter. 'OMG, that's who she reminds me of – now I see it! I've spent seven months trying to figure out who the hell it was she reminded me of and that's it! Mrs Tweedy from *Chicken Run*! So, that's how she knew I arrived late on my first night – *you* told her!'

He dived under the cover beside me and wrestled me into just the right position so that he could snuggle me in close. We laughed in great guffaws.

'I am the son of the Tweedys, who are quite mental and just like the characters in the cartoon! She's bonkers, fierce and controlling, but I do love her in my own way, and we get on, well, most of the time, as long as we have space from each other and except for when she brings me over a game pie. I don't have the heart to tell her I'm not a fan of game, it's much too meaty for my delicate palate. I think she feeds it to me because it's one of Dad's favourites.'

'Why don't you just tell her? Surely she wouldn't mind? I didn't realise you have a dad?'

'Far be it for me to compare myself to our old friend, Jesus, but I do in fact have a father!' I laughed and punched Adam on the chest, blushing a little while he continued his story. He knew what I meant and for once didn't tear me apart in his mischievous way. 'He doesn't live here; he's got advanced MS and lives in a care home in Bideford, which is why she interviewed you there.'

'Ah, so that was her business that day, she just told me she had another meeting to attend. It didn't bother me, though, I just wanted the hell out of London. So, how long have you been here?'

'I moved back to Welcombe about five years ago. I'd been working in Cheshire as a sales director, but the relationship I was in broke down and I was a bit of a mess. I lost my job because my partner, Rachael, was pretty influential in my field and she bad mouthed me until it was impossible for me to work there any longer.

'Bloody heck, that must've been tough?'

'Well, it was and it wasn't. Mum was just getting the holiday letting part of the business up and running when Dad had a crisis, so I said I would come and help out and just never left. It suits me. I don't get paid much, but I don't have any overheads, so what I earn goes straight in the bank. I love having the time to just be me and do what I want – like be creative or read. Rachael beat me down for it and I'm happy to have found it again.' He stroked me as he stared at the ceiling. 'I don't miss the mercenary world of business, it was full of crooks and bullshitters. I'm much happier here, but old Tweedy doesn't like it, as I'm not using the degree she paid for. She won't ever let me forget it and reminds me at every opportunity that the London School of Economics has her life savings. It suited her for me to come and help out, but I don't think she expected me to stay – and now she can't get rid of me.'

'What happened in your relationship? Why did Rachael do that to you – if you don't mind me asking?'

'You can ask, it's fine.' He squeezed me a little in reassurance. 'It was all a bit crazy to be honest. She fell pregnant quite early on in our relationship, but sadly she lost the baby at about twenty weeks. She struggled quite a lot with depression for a while and I supported her as best I could. I know I was a bit rubbish, but I was sad, too. I wasn't allowed to grieve – it was all about her.'

'It must've been as dreadful for you as it was for her.' I was fumbling in the dark, having no experience of lost babies.

'It was. We were lucky in some respects, though, as we both had good jobs and were able to take a number of holidays. She started to brighten up, and while we were away on one trip, we tried to rekindle our physical relationship, which had been in a weird suspended animation for about eighteen months. We hadn't spoken of any problems, we just avoided being awake in bed at the same time. When it did happen, it was tame – no fireworks or whizz-bang – and at the next attempt, she just said to me that she didn't want to make love, which was fine, but what she meant was that she never wanted to make love with me again. She launched herself into her work as though she were a woman possessed. So, for the last four years of our relationship, there was no sex, well, there wasn't much of anything. I was humiliated and lonely, so I fell into a flirty, dirty relationship with a colleague. Rachael found out and kicked me out. It was very public, and I felt thoroughly ashamed of my actions and still feel quite guilty about what I did, but there you are, you can't change the past.'

The phrase 'flirty, dirty' caught me off guard; I realised I bore that label with Nathaniel. I wondered what Adam would think of me if he knew I had been someone's grubby secret.

'I can't imagine why anyone wouldn't want to have sex

with you. You're delightful and you made me feel absolutely amazing; it was beautiful, Adam.'

'You're beautiful! I love it when you smile, but you tend to look kinda sombre.' There was a split second of silence where Adam considered what he had said, but then with a grin he pulled me in close. 'I suppose that's what makes it more special when you do.'

'Are you serious? I don't smile?' I rolled over so that I was flat on my back, but in doing so I pushed Adam away from me. I was upset that he didn't think I smiled often, as I certainly felt smiley when I was around him. I raised my left hand above my head and fiddled anxiously with a strand of hair. 'Of course I smile. I'm a much happier person now. You're right, though, I was sad when I first came here.' I was talking to the ceiling, avoiding Adam's gaze. He was now propped up on his right elbow fixedly looking over me; he said nothing. The sound of my own breath was deafening, but I didn't know what to say next. I didn't know how much to tell him and how much to hold back.

'I know you've been hurt, it is written all over you. Your whole demeanour seems tender and raw. I worry about you and know you'll tell me your story when you are ready to, when you can trust me. That takes time, but I'm a patient man and will never intentionally do anything to hurt you, I *promise*. I just want to pick you up and protect you and let you know that everything will be all right in the end. It really will be, Lily.'

I continued to stare at the ceiling but did stop fussing with my hair, as I reached out with my left hand and rested it on his breast.

'You know so much about me already, without me having to tell you anything, but I will tell you the details one day. I *have* been hurt, in the cruellest of ways, right from my very beginning in life. My mum let me down and then last year, I

142

was deeply hurt by someone who was monstrous. He took advantage of me and then destroyed me, leaving me heartbroken. But I'm mending, honest I am, I just need patience, and I'll get there.' I swung my gaze, as I was finally strong enough to make eye contact with him again. 'I *will* get there!'

Reaching up to him, I kissed him hard on the mouth, before pulling him back down so that we were snuggled once again. Then, with him spooning me and holding me tight, sleep once more took hold of us both.

February was cold and bright, and Adam and I spent hours in the late winter sunshine walking, flying the kite and getting up to mischief. The farm was still relatively quiet and although there was work to be done, we'd get up early to complete our chores so that we could spend time out and about together and making love. I was filled with a confidence and happiness that I'd never experienced in my life before, and I quite literally felt like a new woman. The shadow the demonic Nat had cast over my life, though mostly forgotten, imperceptible and essentially dormant, was still hovering, waiting patiently in the darkness for its moment to intrude once again, and yet it was such a perfect time. Adam was thoughtful and funny, and it was hard not to be carried along in the wondrousness of it all.

Secretly, he was as much a kid as I was, and although he ruthlessly took the Mickey out of my childish traits, he was gentle and never over-stepped the mark. That said, we were fiercely competitive and created obstacle courses and held a mini Olympics on the beach, complete with running races and a long jump over the river that streamed down from the

Welcombe Mouth coombe. I'm sure half the time he allowed me to win, but I didn't care about that, it was just incredible to be with someone who cared enough about me that they wanted to please me. It didn't always end fairly and there were several impromptu wrestling matches that ended up with either one or both of us being dunked unceremoniously in the sea. When we weren't out and about horse playing, we would sit together in Morwenna and read tracts of books to each other. Sometimes, he would make up stories and tell them to me whilst I rested my head on his lap. More often than not they would make me cry, as they were so touching and heartfelt. He was incredibly imaginative and creative. Other times, he would draw whilst I read to him, but he was impervious to what I was saying and would often fail to notice I had stopped reading, as he was that engrossed in what he was doing.

I still spent time back at Hawker's, as we didn't want Tweedy to know we had become so close, and for the most part we got away with it. She continued to pop in at Adam's with a variety of pies and sweetmeats, but by happenstance, this was mostly when I was out or upstairs. When on the couple of occasions she popped by when Adam and I were sitting reading to each other, she didn't hold back on her disparaging looks, but then that was the nature of her disposition at the best of times, so it was hard to tell what she thought about us spending time together. She tried grilling Adam, but he remained tight lipped. Fortunately, she hadn't caught us in any compromising positions. Used to living freely, it took a great deal of work on my part to convince Adam that, for the sake of our privacy, he should start locking his front door.

Our weeks together flew by and we settled comfortably into a shared life. I still had another three months before my contract came to an end. My year would soon be up and I didn't want to face the possibility that Mrs Enys may no longer need me, so I kept a low profile and avoided her, in order to defer the time and space in which she'd have the chance to raise the matter with me. I didn't know if Adam would want me to stay, or if *I* wanted to stay even (although the thought of leaving made me panic), so I shoved the responsibility of sensible conversations and decision making to the back of my head and decided to cross that bridge when I came to it.

We were still in the habit of getting work done early, and late one morning, I came back to Morwenna to make some food, but as I bent to get a pizza out of the oven I somehow managed to twist my back. By the time Adam came home for lunch I was sprawled across the floor in agony.

'All right, Actually, whatcha doin' down there?'

'I'm checking out your ceiling, as it seems to be a bit wonky! What the hell do you think I'm doing?'

'Hey, come on, I only asked. What's up?'

Adam squatted down beside me and, seeing that I was unhappy and clearly in pain, he picked up my wrist and pretended to take my pulse.

'I'm Doctor Big Knob and I'm here to help. Now, can you tell me what you've done and where it is you hurt?'

His 'laughter is the best medicine' approach began to work immediately. 'Oh, doctor, thank God you're here,' I said in my best *Carry On Doctor* voice.

'Now now, be serious. It's very important that I give you the right kind of injection, so tell me where it is that you hurt? Between your legs, perhaps? I have just the right kind of injection for that!'

'Ha, this is beginning to sound like a bad porn film!' I laughed. 'No, Doctor, I was taking a pizza out of the oven and as I bent forward my back twinged, and now it's very hurty and needs kissing better.'

'I'll be the judge of that. I think perhaps you may still need a rather large injection to really make it feel better. Now, let me feel and see where exactly it is that you hurt.'

Adam proceeded to check my breasts and gently kiss my abdomen, but as I wriggled to enjoy it better my back complained once again.

'No, listen, it really does hurt. My back is so uncomfortable. Have you got any deep heat or anything you can rub on it?' I pushed him away. 'Please, Adam, I'm not up to sex!'

'Come on, I'll rub you.'

He extended his hand and gently helped me off the floor. I felt something of a fraud as we walked up the stairs together, as the pain had definitely eased. Once in the bedroom, he instructed me to take off my top while he went into the bathroom. I could hear him rifling around in the cupboard and when he came back again, I was standing naked to the waist in front of the bed.

'Trousers off, too.'

He was full of quiet intention, yet tender at the same time. Once I was down to my knickers, I lay face down across the large bed and heard him remove his t-shirt.

'Right, this may not be a professional jobbie, but here goes.'

I gathered that Adam had poured something into his hands, as I heard him rubbing his palms together. Then he started to rub the oil gently into the soul of my left foot.

'Oi, it's my back that hurts, not my foot, you big numpty!'

'I know, I know, but who's giving this bloody massage? Just lay there and let me do this for you, will you? Shhhh now, shush. So . . . going anywhere nice on holiday?' He mimicked the best masseuse.

I laughed but didn't reply, as the feel of his hands and the affectionate way in which he handled me made me relax and relinquish myself to the moment. With great aptitude and with firm but gentle hands, he made his way from my feet to my legs, to my hips and then to my back, at which point he made a token effort to address the area of soreness. He stroked every inch of my skin and the fresh-cut wood aroma of the sandalwood oil took on a creamy and spicy tone, as he neared my neck and shoulders. Once he reached my neck, he moved back down to my hips and removed my knickers. He rubbed the oil over my legs and this time, as he reached my middle, he slipped his hands to the inside of my thighs, without touching me intimately.

'I want you to turn over, but before you do, I wish to blindfold you. Is that OK?'

I didn't have time to think and, as I raised my head off the bed, he was at my side with the scarf I had removed from around my neck when I got undressed. He gently placed it over my eyes and helped me to turn onto my back.

'Do you trust me?'

'Implicitly. If you do anything I don't like, I'll never let you do it again, so of course I trust you.' I tried to sound in control but was petrified at where this might be going.

Adam returned to my feet and began once again to massage me. His movements were stronger, and I felt his hands clasp around my shins as he began to work his way up my body. I was naked both physically and emotionally and, by the time he reached the top of my thighs, I was shaking uncontrollably. Still, he didn't touch me. There was a slight pause and I heard him remove his trousers before he joined me on the bed. Kneeling beside me, I could feel energy and heat radiating from him. He oiled my torso and breasts, then bent himself towards me so that I could feel him just in front of my face. But instead of kissing me he just held his mouth above mine so that I could feel his warm, sweet breath on my lips. He loved me with gentle compassion but wouldn't allow me to move nor see what he was doing. Each tender stroke, every kiss he planted on my ultra-sensitive body was all about me, and I completely surrendered my physical and emotional self to him.

My senses, heightened by my lack of sight, fuelled an intensity in me that was all-consuming. The squeaking sound of the bed as it yielded beneath us was something I'd never paid attention to before. Nor had I noticed the scent of the softener that had dried in the wind, or the feel of the light fabric covering my eyes. The very taste of him and the smell of us were all so beautiful as he continued to give to me. My body twitched and tickled and was tantalised by his love. With every passing second, with each gentle touch, he showed me the true reward of being able to receive.

Surrounded by the sticky, tangled mess of pleasure, we lay in silence for some time, the stillness between us mirroring the intensity of the passion that had just passed between us. We held each other and not a muscle moved; we were frozen in the moment. Neither of us wanted to break it. Neither of us wanted to shatter the magic that had just occurred between us, so we stayed just as we were until we woke. Even then, the silence remained. We simply unwound ourselves from each other, turned over, cuddled up and dozed until it was dark.

The love making that afternoon changed something between Adam and me. It was as though something had fallen into place and kicked out the unspoken insecurities and uncertainties that lingered in the shadows of our relationship. It was as though Nathaniel had finally been exorcised. Several hours later we re-heated the pizza and ate in bed, and at 5am the next morning, as Adam went off to work, I skulked home to Hawker's Hut like a dirty stop out.

Once indoors, I put the kettle on, dug out some clothes for work and put my long-dead mobile phone onto charge. I just had to message Lou. It had been days since I had last been in touch with her, and although she knew Adam and I were getting close, I couldn't wait to tell her about the blindfold. I flicked the power to the charger on, and as energy returned to the exhausted battery, the phone booted up and connected to the network. Whilst I made coffee, I heard it buzz two or three times with messages. Lou had been chasing me, obviously wondering where I was, but as I reached for the phone, only one of the messages was from her. There were two others, both from an unknown number.

Hi Hot Pants

And

How're you doing?

It was Nathaniel.

Chapter 23
MARCH 2019

'What the hell, Lou, how did he get my number?'

'I have no idea!' Lou didn't like my insinuation and her stern reply screeched down the phone at me. It sounded as though I was accusing her of passing my number on to Nathanial, but I wasn't, I was just freaked out, panicking and so very angry. I panted hard and tried to calm down, but I was too riled up as I paced around the tiny, mangy front room of Hawker's Hut.

'Look, I'm sorry to sound as though I'm pointing the finger, but I can't work out how he could have gotten hold of my number. I mean, it's a new bloody number! Only six people have it, and I know none of you will have given it to him. So how, tell me how he got it and what I'm supposed to think? What does he want with me after all this time? How the fuck am I going to deal with this? What do I do now? What do I say to him? How do I . . . Oh, Lou, help me, what do I do?!'

'Woooooah! Back up, lady, you *do not* do anything. You don't *do* anything other than delete the messages and block his number, and then he can't come for you. You do it and you do it now, you hear me? We can figure out the *how* once you're protected again.'

I could sense her searching for the right words, as though fingering loose change in a pocket, blindly hoping to produce the right coins, the ones that would buy me protection from myself.

'Lily, he nearly destroyed you – you know he is going to try and hook you back in. This is a fuck off-sized red flag. See the warning signs. Read your diaries, your letters. Think about how he operated, how abused you were and how desperate you have been since you have known him.'

'It's . . . I was, wasn't I?'

'Yes! And what's more, look at how happy you have been since you met Adam.'

'But why, Lou? Why is he doing this? Why has he messaged me when I'm happy, and after all this time? Maybe there isn't a baby. Maybe it's over with Sorrel. Maybe . . . Oh, Jesus, I don't know.'

'Lily. This is the hook, plain and simple. He doesn't want you and believe me, you don't want him, regardless of what your head and your heart might be telling you. So help me, I will not let you do this, even if I have to come to the back arse of nowhere again and smash your arms as well as your legs with a sledgehammer to keep you in your room and out of danger. Believe me, I will. Kathy Bates has nothing on me. I don't want you murdering yourself, Lily, because if you reply to that demon or get hooked in by him again, that is exactly what you will be doing – murdering yourself.'

I listened to what my old friend was telling me and decided she was right. I agreed that I would delete the messages and block the number.

We continued to chat for a while, but it was strained so we said our goodbyes, leaving me to carry out my promise. I was shaken, so I poured the now over-boiled coffee into my mug, grasping it, allowing it to burn the palms of my hands, as I stared almost unseeing at my phone, which was tempting me with a toxic offering. Picking it up as though it were an unexploded bomb, I added the number to my contacts and saved it as Twunt. Seeing the nickname in writing made me feel more sick than amused, but perhaps that was a good thing, too. I read his texts once again and was disturbed by the fact that whilst they made me feel anguished, I could feel the corners of my mouth turning upwards in a nervous, involuntary smile of pleasure and satisfaction that he was missing me. I duly deleted the messages and blocked Twunt from contacting me again. Then I texted Lou.

Named him as Twunt, blocked him and deleted. I love you,
Mrs Bates, sorry for doubting you x x x

It wasn't long before she replied.

Love you, too, mad and scary bird xxx

The message from Nathaniel had unnerved me, and for several days I felt out of sorts. Fortunately, I had developed a bit of a cold and was able to use that as a reason for staying holed up in my hut whilst I attempted to centre myself. It was a convenient excuse not to see Adam, as I knew that had I been in his company, I would have given something away. Although I had told him that my relationship with Nat was dysfunctional, and that I had been treated badly by him, I had never revealed the finer details for fear of driving him away because of my disgraceful, self-sacrificing behaviour.

I was also fearful, as secretly I was delighted that Nat had contacted me again. He was obviously struggling without me.

I was relieved that he was missing me, although I really didn't want anything to do with him. Diana's sage words about staying beholden to him rang in the distance as a warning bell and I found them strengthening me in my moments of weakness, moments during which I endured the painful pleasure of thinking about being with him again. I managed to calm myself down with some meditations and crystal work. After the initial shock and as time passed with no further contact from Nat, I was able to throw myself back into work.

In part, with more and more people visiting Tregellas, I almost resented the fact that life was once again returning to the farm. With an early Easter not far away, I knew time with Adam would become a treat rather than the norm, but it was also massively convenient. It gave me the perfect excuse to invent all kinds of exciting laundry-type dramas to keep me occupied, which was an intentional ploy to keep me slightly withdrawn from Adam. It felt like the sane thing to do, as my mind was still fitfully busy because of those two short messages from Nat. I still hadn't figured out how the hell he had got hold of my number, and it bothered me. Not enough to do anything about it, but enough to occupy my headspace. *Hi Hot Pants!* I couldn't believe he was using that old opener after all that had happened, after such a long and lonely silence.

Every other day or so, I chatted at length with Lou. She winkled me out of depression and, to see me through the scare, she cleverly got me talking about Adam. I told her every moment of the beautiful blindfold massage and as I spoke, I realised she had switched my focus to something that had become incredibly important in my life. My happiness and confidence slunk in the door like something the cat had dragged in, but nonetheless it was there and so, several hard weeks after 'text gate', I opened myself up once again to Adam, giving to him fully. He was none the wiser as to why I had been so sullen, and when he asked if I was all right, I blamed my remoteness on the cold virus and work, whilst he pampered me selflessly, which made me feel guilty about being dishonest with him.

Along with the arrival of spring and the changing rhythm of farm life, we found ourselves in a new stride as a couple. We met up in the late afternoons and I would spend the night with him at Morwenna; breakfast was in bed at dawn. Through living and working together in a peaceful and nourishing way, we began to reveal insights of the true person that lay within. I had failed to find the courage to tell him about my growing-up years, aside from tales of Uncle Tom and the fact that my mum was an alcoholic, or about the hideousness that was Nat. In fact, we were so absorbed in each other that previous relationships and ancient history didn't really come into it; we were happy simply being.

On Easter Sunday, we rose early, as the plan was to get our chores done quickly and set off for a picnic. The previous night, Adam had packed his drawing things and a huge feast. Tweedy had brought over some of her cheese scones which, by all accounts, were epic. I had been excited about the day since the idea was conceived, fantasising wildly and choreographing the most magical, romantic vision. In my head, the sun would be shining, Adam would be sketching, and I would be sprawled out on a blanket reading but transfixed by him; the meaning of the black type on the white page lost on me. Whenever I was with him, I was always too excited to focus, especially when he was drawing, as he was so beautiful while concentrating. We would be surrounded in a mellow sunshine that would soften all of our edges, so that our world was dreamy. We'd eat – he'd feed me – laugh, make love outdoors. It would be a scene from the greatest love story of all time. However, as night surrendered itself to daybreak, it was clear things weren't going to be like that at all. In true early April style, it had rained heavily overnight, leaving the morning dank and humid. I woke with a fear of impending doom, but after looking out the window, I attributed my mood to the inclement weather and suppressed it, shaking myself out of my moment of uncertainty.

Adam soon chivvied me up, chiding me and dragging me along with his irrepressible energy and humour. With a new lightness about me, we set off for our walk along the coastal path towards Northcott Mouth, which is where we intended to have our delicious picnic and a couple of hours of peace. Unfortunately, though, as we climbed the grassy slopes just before reaching the church at Morwenstow, a sea fret moved stealthily in, muffling the noise of the ocean and rendering us lost in a soundless, white world. The fret was substantial, tangible and unsettling. The brightness of the white mist so close to the church made it feel somehow divine, as though we had ascended more than just the grassy slope. We knew the sea was to our right, but there was no sight of it through the wet, white blanket that enveloped us. The eerie silence soon robbed us of our light heartedness. We were both perturbed by the mist's density and how quickly it had descended.

'Adam, I think we should go inland a little.'

I sounded pathetic. I was expecting to be ridiculed but he was in agreement, so we left the coastal path and headed inland on the footpath for Gooseham. This would take us on a wide loop, back in the direction of the farm but away from the inherent danger of the cliffs. We walked in silence for a mile or so and although the atmosphere was pleasant enough, the quietness left room for reflection and self-awareness, and in that silence my restless demons started to awaken, as thoughts of Nat and his recent messages wound their cloying fingers around my heart.

I had been harbouring a growing sense of unease about the texts, which, despite all the excitement of Adam, were weighing heavily upon me and making me fearful of my feelings. Attuned to those feelings, I knew what was happening to me, but even so, there was little I could do to stop the inescapable. Nat would, from afar, propel me back against the cold steel bars of his merry-go-round. The centrifugal force would pin me in tight, and as the speed of the thing increased, I would slide back into his arms.

In the past, after each dispassionate discard, I would suddenly become anxious, sensing that Nat was obsessively thinking about me. I could feel him draining me, as though he were leeching my very soul. Without exception, I'd undergone the same drain and anxiousness cycle every time. It was as though he could connect to my energy and wear me down in preparation for the next period of idealisation.

I thought I had given up on mindlessly picking over his messages, but whilst drenched in that misty shroud, my thoughts were still consumed by him. He'd called me Hot Pants, and that told me he still saw me as sexy and was being playful, so he was obviously all right. This made the messages feel even more sinister and threatening, because I knew he meant to play with me. I knew it would be harmful to be involved with him again. On the face of it, I was committed to Adam, but the call of Nathaniel was so tempting. The old me would have already replied to him with a friendly 'hello, long time no chat' message, but the new me was telling me this would be wrong. I was at a crossroads, faced with the option of slipping back into old behaviours. The bad stuff was easy – like putting on a pair of comfy slippers. I could go there and live with whatever it threw at me, because it was familiar. Or I could leap into a brave new world. Only that terrified me more, as I simply didn't know how to do it.

The rotors of a helicopter thwacked through my brain as

reminiscences and 'what ifs' tumbled and turned inside my head. In an attempt to make the brain noise stop, I began saying a mantra in my head. *'Go away, Nat, go away, Nat.'* I repeated the words at high speed a number of times, my silent voice ever more commanding. The words barrelled around in my head at a dizzying speed. I could feel cold and metallic-tasting saliva flood around my teeth, as though I was about to vomit. A chilled sweat began to break out on the back of my neck. I stopped, squatted down and took a mouthful of water. I told Adam that I felt faint but didn't tell him why. He kept his hand on my shoulder until I felt recovered enough to stand. I dismissed my discomfort, putting it down to being a bit dehydrated and overwhelmed by the humidity, before making a great effort to smile brightly as we set off again.

My insincere attempt at composure was short-lived, though, and as thoughts of Nat ground away at me, my breath came in great, aggressive bursts. The cold sweat enfolded me. As we continued along the footpath, which was surprisingly muddy and annoyingly slippery, I swung my arms in contempt as a form of distraction.

Everything irritated me. Everything made me cross and uncomfortable. Adam surged forwards, dragging me along behind him. As we skirted, unseen, the large fields of immature crops, the noise of birdsong screeched all around us at an awkward pitch that hurt my ears, whereas normally I would have stopped to listen to their joyful tunes. The mud squelching under my walking trainers frustrated me further, as it made them dirty, bothering me hugely, whereas normally I wouldn't have given a stuff. I expended a great deal of energy trying to keep out of the mire by leaping over especially soggy bits and cautiously scanning the landscape before committing each foot to the next step. I hampered progress and irritated Adam, as he had to keep stopping and waiting for me to catch up. Grumpily, he slowed his pace right down.

We marched as best we could through the heavily laden overhanging foliage, and it wasn't long before I was soaked. Adam stormed through the low, wet branches ahead of me, and time after time they pinged back and drenched me further. But I had become consumed by myself and felt as though suddenly I had no voice. I couldn't say anything to him to improve the situation. I couldn't tell him that he was being inconsiderate, that I didn't like the way he was barging his way along irrespective of how it was affecting me. I wanted to go home. I wanted to be comfortable and dry in my smelly old hut.

I knew I needed to calm down, as I could feel a monstrous panic attack skulking beneath a thin veneer of tolerance. I tried to immerse myself in the moment and I focused intently on bringing my breath to my centre – my hara – as I tried to understand how surreal and bizarre this walk had become.

In meditation, I allowed thoughts to wash in and wash out of my mind. Just like a tube train, they came into the station and stayed briefly before I sent them on their way again. The things that passed through were the absorbing, miraculous, random and mostly wonderful moments I'd experienced since living at Welcombe. Even Diana and our curious interaction on the journey to Exeter appeared. Then I was on the beach, enjoying the feeling of my sun-kissed arms, my windblown, salty hair and the smell of the beach. The myriad faces that had holidayed at Tregellas also appeared before me.

It was working, and I was definitely calming down. I began to think about how I had arrived at the 'me' I now was, and about what steps I had taken; the nurturing and personal growth I had practised through meditation and a wholesome life, to reveal my true nature. I was still zealously repeating the words 'go away, Nat', as my mind worked to quieten the tempest I was weathering. In acknowledgment of those early days, I changed the phrase to the binding mantra, *'I bind you, Nathaniel Deighton, and your power to harm me.'*

I thought back to the day on the beach, where I had cast the spells and buried the items to which I had created a tenuous yet meaningful association. Then it struck me – I hadn't buried the cord to finalise the spell. I had lost it and assumed the spell would have been finalised in the losing of it, but obviously it hadn't been, or else Nat wouldn't have tried to contact me.

Panic seized me and without any hesitation or warning, projectile vomit came splurging out of my mouth and nose, narrowly missing Adam. I retched and continued to throw up for some time, as though my toes were being pulled up through the inside of my body and out of my mouth.

'Blimey, Actually, where did all that come from. You OK?'

Adam looked at me with grave concern. I could tell that he was horrified and revolted and could only just about bear to touch me on the shoulder. He encouraged me to walk away from the stinking bushes and then handed me my water bottle so that I could rinse my mouth out. I was shaking with the effort of such a massive expulsion, and although I had vomited every single fluid ounce of my stomach's content, I continued to retch and gag.

'You OK? What's upset you like that?'

'Oh god, I'm sorry. Eww, that was so gross.' My small, inner child rose to the surface and I began to cry, as though she had wet her pants. I rapidly scrubbed at my hands and face, as if to expunge myself from the experience.

'Hey, come on, don't be sorry, you can't help being unwell. Maybe you have a bit of flu or something. Thinking about it, you had that rotten cold recently and you said yourself you've been out of sorts, so don't worry about it. I'm just pleased you haven't got a very good aim, or else I would have been wearing that little lot!'

And with that gentle 'Get Out of Jail Free' card, I had no reason to disclose the true source of my anxiety. Adam had unwittingly provided me with an excuse that I would never have been able to come up with without lying to him. He proffered me some chewing gum, which I gratefully took as he put his arm across my shoulders and pushed me forward.

Chapter 24

I was disgusted with myself. It was a revolting display. Poor Adam must have thought me repulsive, but I had no control over what was happening to me. I was trembling with every step I took. I felt as though I had consumed a whole bottle of wine and the room was spinning uncontrollably.

We must've been walking for about fifteen minutes when Adam pointed out a bridle path. 'Here, come this way, it'll take us back out onto the coastal path, but it comes out near the top of the cliff above Tregellas, which will be quite safe, and quicker, too. You need to get to bed PDQ. You still look as rough as a badger's arse to me, although a very lovely badger. And a very lovely arse, come to that'.

I gave him a reproving stare but was secretly pleased that he still wanted to flirt with me even though I must've looked feral.

The anxiety in me quelled and I felt as though the last part of the walk had done me good. Then I caught a glimpse of a familiar tree, as it came into view on the horizon. I scanned around me and recognised the field we were crossing as the one I had seen Adam working in, on that day at the end of

September. The tree in the distance was the one I'd lain under as I watched him.

I felt uncomfortable, as he stepped back and let me cross the stile that led us into the field where the tree stood. I squeezed by him and, as I did so, thought I noticed something meaningful about the look on his face. Flooded with fear, I began terrorising myself with the dilemma of the scarf. Was he trying to tell me something by bringing me this way? Was this his way of saying that he'd watched me as I touched myself? The first dreadful seed of self-doubt had been sewn. Had Adam pursued me because of that moment?

In an instant, all sense of reason deserted me. I pressed a subconscious 'destroy all' button and the nihilistic behaviours and ancient scripts that had beleaguered me for most of my life kicked in. My brain worked as quickly as a computer virus, randomly deleting data and malignantly depositing half-truths and unimaginable self-lies.

Gone was the reality of Adam and me falling in love, in its place a wildly terrifying and despicable version of actuality. If he knew I was up for a bit of physical stuff then all of this may have been simply lust on his part, a typical bloody man being guided by his cock. He had played me like the fool I was. He had hooked me and reeled me in, knowing that if he pressed the right emotional buttons, he would be able to have his way with me then cast me aside, just as Nat had done. There wasn't any great investment on his part as we were of a similar ilk. In fact, our spirituality and creative traits had made it easier for him. I bet he couldn't believe his luck. What an absolute idiot I had been to think he actually liked me.

I was marching ahead now, oblivious of the fact that Adam was trailing behind. My mind, in overdrive, made its own sense of the last seven months, of the time since Adam had plucked my scarf from the tree. I had spent hours trying to figure out what it was he saw in me and why he liked me so much, especially when we had spent most of our relationship talking at cross purposes. I wondered what he could see in me, when no other man had ever possessed an impassioned view of me. Now I understood it, now I got exactly where he was coming from. He knew. He knew about me and about my vulnerabilities, and he had preyed upon them, just like Nathaniel. He was, after all, a professional salesman; an artful dodger who had picked my pockets, found my weakness and taken advantage. And me, like a gullible pushover, had fallen for his patter. Adam had hidden himself away on that farm knowing he would struggle to meet anyone, hiding away like the coward he was. When I thought back to the man he was when I first met him, how sullen and angry he was, and then to the man he purported to be now, it was obvious to me that he had put on a mask in order to entrap me into being his plaything. Well now his mask had slipped, and for the first time I could see he was little more than an actor.

'Hang on there, old girl, you've got a second wind about you. Wait up a bit.'

By the time Adam called out for me I was at the tree. I was out of breath and could feel rage charging through my veins like a Japanese bullet train. By the time he reached me my fury had begun to bubble over. Pacing wildly and unthinking, I yelled in a loud, strong voice at the man who, until a few minutes ago, I thought loved me.

'So, had you planned this all along, then, Adam? Were you going to bring me here anyway? Who the hell do you think you are to do this to me? You knew I was hurt and had been through hell, and you took advantage of me . . . I *know*, Adam. I know it was you and I know what you saw, and I'm embarrassed, but at the end of the day I am a human being, a flawed person with needs just like the rest of humanity! How dare you take it and use it to your own end. How dare you, how dare you!'

As I screamed at him, I went to beat his chest with my fist, but he was quicker than me. He grabbed my arm and held it hard. 'I've no idea what you're talking about, but you'd better calm down and tell me what's going on here. Stop screaming at me or I'll slap some sense into you.'

His words sliced through the air and stung both of us, as though he had actually laid his great hand across my bare cheek. We were both horrified. A moment flickered, distorted then paused. I experienced it as though it were a video which lagged in transmission before I was back in real time. Incredulous, he let go of my arm and I slowly backed away in fear, whilst he remained still, in shock at his own response. My voice dropped an octave, as I slowly spoke to his frozen body.

'The scarf, Adam, I know it was you who brought the scarf to the hut. You saw me and you took advantage of me, of my needs, and this is your way of telling me what you know.

'Why couldn't you leave me alone? I was mending after being so ruined and now, once again, everything is smashed. I can't do this again, I can't be here, I can't be your, your, whatever it is!'

I was now a few feet away and as I turned to run, Adam stood with his hands out to his sides in exasperation. He let me go.

I ran and ran as hard as I could and didn't stop until I reached home, despite barging through some of the farm's guests, sending them scattering, but caring not a jot as I elbowed my way between them. Crossing the threshold of Hawker's, I crashed onto the floor, where I sobbed and sobbed as my heart broke once more. Finally, exhausted, I fell asleep in a tight ball on the cold, hard lino.

I must have woken at some point and sleepily made my way to bed, as when I awoke properly in the afternoon of the following day, I was naked and snuggled under my soft duvet.

But it was as though I had been teleported there. I had no recollection of moving to my bed, I was dehydrated and had pulled muscles in my tummy and ribs from all the crying. As I lay there, two tiny tears began a lonesome journey from the corners of my eyes to the cool, white cotton of the pillowcase. I couldn't comprehend Adam. Initially, he had been a bit of a random drunk and then, when I got to know him, nothing short of extraordinary. I had hoped and wondered about the two of us having a life together, but everything I once believed to be true had been overturned. How could it suddenly be so different?

I lay for hours just thinking about Adam's behaviour and his attitude towards me. As I picked harder and harder over the evidence, I managed to justify my accusations about his intentions. He had manipulated the whole thing and he was as evil as Nat. No, he was worse, because even though I had only alluded to it, he knew that I had been treated badly and yet he still proceeded to monopolise the situation. It was my own fault and it was obviously something I did that made men treat me like that. The following day, Lou called, and I told her all about the failed knot spell and the debacle with Adam.

'That's why Nat sent those messages, he wants me back. All because I didn't do the spell properly. If I'd finished it instead of losing it, he wouldn't have got in touch with me. I can feel him, Lou. I can feel him connected to me.'

'Come on, Lily, don't be so bloody ridiculous. You know that's not true. You're being totally irrational now.'

'Lou, you don't know what it's like. You don't know how it feels when someo–'

'Don't tell me, when someone connects to you. Can you hear yourself? Bloody heck, Lily, get a grip, will you? It's poppycock, happy-clappy balderdash bollocks. I thought you were more intelligent than this?'

I resolved never to tell her about my shamanistic ways

again. She had no idea what that energy connection felt like. She could be as dismissive as she liked, but there was no way it wasn't real. Ridiculous as it might seem to her, I had experience to back up my conjecture. Nathaniel was coming for me. I could see him as a jaguar lying in a tree, hidden from view, stretching out his menacing paws, splaying unsheathed claws and staring with hungry amber eyes at my back, as he lay patiently in wait.

'Well, we'll have to agree to disagree. I have experience to count on and I know what's happening.'

'It'll only happen if you allow it to happen, which you won't, will you!' The tone of her voice made it quite clear this was an instruction not a question.

'And what about Adam?' I threw back at her. 'He's no Prince Charming now, is he? How confusing is he! I swear he would have hit me had I hung around. How do you explain that one?'

'I can't, Lily.' Her honesty was humiliating, but she went on to rationalise what I had told her. 'Surely if Adam saw you having your private moment and enjoyed you the way he appeared to, then why would he chance spoiling it by taking you back to the tree?'

'I don't know! It just felt as though it was a bit of a wink-wink, nudge-nudge kind of a moment, and I was embarrassed by it.'

'Is that it? Because of a bit of embarrassment, you've run away from him?'

'No, it was more than that. Embarrassed is the wrong word. It was more, I don't know, more . . .'

'Shame?' Lou offered.

'Yeah, I guess so.'

'Lily, it's nothing to be ashamed of.'

'But threatening to slap someone is, you know.' She went

quiet. 'I can't be with someone who is so quick to offer violence.'

'OK, fair enough, I just want to check something, though. You're telling me that you don't want to be with someone who will bash you, but you *can* be with someone who wants to hurt you emotionally. That's very hypocritical.'

She wasn't wrong, but it hurt to hear her say the words.

'Look, I wasn't there, and I have no idea what this is all about or why things happened the way they did, but clearly something has become lost in translation. When I met Adam at Christmas, he seemed like a cool guy who thought the world of you, and I'm sure he does. Just give things time to calm down. I bet he'll explain and you two will get back on track. Give him some space and while he's figuring himself out, look after you. Don't read too much into it, just breathe and let things settle, eh?' She paused briefly before continuing in a milder tone. 'Can I ask . . . is Mya with you?'

'No. No, she isn't. No sign.'

'Good, that's good. Are you working at the mo?'

'No. I feel shit and I don't want to see anyone.'

'Well, then tell old Tweedy you have the flu again and snuggle up.'

I laughed tentatively at the thought of Mrs Tweedy, which made me start to cry again. 'Flippin' heck, Lou! What the fuck is this all about?'

'I have no idea. It just feels so unlike him.'

'So, I'm right to feel confused, then?' I asked.

'Yeah, you are, because I bloody am. Listen, if he comes and apologises the way I think he will then give him a break and let him explain, and if he doesn't, then . . .' she broke off, carefully choosing her ultimatum. 'If he doesn't then he certainly isn't the man I thought he was.'

'But why does all this have to hurt so much? I mean, how do people *do* relationships? How do they do intimacy? That

168

fucking Diana I told you about, the one on the train, told me to 'be open', so I was and now here I am balling away to you once again!'

'This is what being alive is all about. Life can be shit and it can hurt when you expose your emotions to someone, but actually, isn't it wonderful to feel these things? Isn't it wonderful to think that you are a brave and open being who can invite people in and let people go?'

She was in her motherly stride, so I let her ramble on, disbelieving every word of it. 'Imagine going through life unable to feel, unable to experience it, just living instead of being alive. It must be purgatory. Life is a wondrous thing and you're doing it. You aren't going to go to your grave having just been through the motions and settled for less than you deserve. You're a strong and resourceful woman. Look how you've managed to ignore Nat, despite what you say about him stalking you. Look how you're changing yourself and throwing off all that shit you learned as a kid, all because you want your life to be different. Please, just do what you always do. Brush yourself off, carry on growing and carry on living, in all senses of the word.'

By the time we hung up, I did feel better for having spoken with Lou, but I was still antsy and twitchy. A couple of days later, Mrs Enys dropped by to bring me some soup – clearly her default response to illness and injury – and in an out-of-character, meaningful way, she asked how I was. I sensed she wanted to ask me some more questions, as she dallied in an awkward silence before leaving me to my sickness. I guessed she was probably fact finding on Adam's behalf, as opposed to harbouring any sort of genuine interest. I warmed the soup and ate for the first time in many hours, and although it made me feel physically better, it wasn't long before I continued in my pastime of copious crying and frequent pacing around in a fraught state.

Over the coming week, Lou remained in touch, but there was little she could say to placate me. I knew it would be a while before I began to feel in control of things again. It would take time, but that was the only thing I had plenty of – I had no appetite or energy for healing anymore.

I didn't hear anything from Adam, which in some ways was good, as I wouldn't have known how to respond to him without causing further chaos. Whenever I allowed myself to think of our incredibly magical time together, I cried like a bereaved widow as she said goodbye to her husband of forty years. It must surely be over between us. I was a raging, wildcat, bonkers woman and he was a peeping Tom wife beater; surely there was no way back to our idyll?

After a long conversation with Lou one night, I lay in bed scrutinising the mystery that was my phone. How *had* Twunt got my number? Neither Lou nor I had ever worked that one out, so I started to investigate the device with no real idea of what I was searching for. I went into various menus in my email app and found I had entered my mobile number as an additional security feature. Knowing Nat's technical capabilities, I was in no doubt that somehow he had hunted me down and hacked my account. If I hadn't been so freaked out by his presence, then perhaps I wouldn't have lost control the way I did and vomited all over Adam. Perhaps then, he wouldn't have threatened to raise his hand to me. Nat, once again, had broken everything.

I decided there was nothing I could do about anything, so I concluded to sleep as much as possible until the universe delivered its plan for me. I dozed off and waited for things to happen, but it felt as though I had a ticking time bomb lodged in the chambers of my heart.

Chapter 25

For my self-imposed week of solitude, I remained within the confines of Hawker's Hut, as though in preparation for something. I partially remerged into the world when I started getting up at 4am to go about my work. I was terrified of bumping into Adam, therefore, rising early and doing what I could in the laundry meant that by the time the rest of the farm began to awaken, I was back at home.

'You start in the middle of the night now, do you? You look like shit, too, skulking around like an escaped convict.'

Mya's scathing comments greeted me after work one morning, but she wasn't wrong. I slunk around the place, my behaviour furtive and slovenly.

'You're back then, are you?' I said, gazing at the shadowy figure lurking in the hallway.

'Get you, Sherlock! Yes, I'm back. Figured you could use some help.'

'Yeah, maybe not your help, though.'

'You know, you're gonna lose your job at this rate?'

'As I said, Mya, probably not your help!'

She was uncomfortably near the truth. I was shirking my

role and had managed to palm off my cleaning duties to one of the pony girls, who welcomed the extra cash. It meant the work was done and it kept old Tweedy off my back. But though I could run, I could not hide from her all-seeing eyes.

'Course not, Lily. You don't need help to be fucked up. You're good at tormenting yourself, you're good at living in terror. You can do that all by yourself. Good luck with it, arsehole!'

Mya walked away from me, leaving the bitter taste of honesty in my mouth. I was hungry, yet I refused to eat properly, I was thirsty, yet I rarely drank, and, although exhausted, I would run for miles or pace the room to prevent myself from falling into much needed, healing sleep. I remained unwashed, uncaring and unable to cope. It felt as though my life was slipping away, as though I was crashing my way off a cliff, much as I had feared I would on the night of my arrival at Welcombe Mouth. I had a primitive horror of insanity and yet I was compelled to be ruinous; to be as damaging and neglectful as I possibly could. The unkinder I could be to myself – the more introspective, colder, hungrier – the better. My need to be uncomfortable was comforting.

In my discomfort, I stared precariously over the precipice of an enticing inner void. For the first time in my life, I realised how like my mother I was. She had a void. I don't know what caused it, but she filled it with drink, and although our weapons of choice were different, I knew I was just a pigeon's step away from joining her in the realm of the hungry ghosts.

My gigantic hollow beckoned me and became the centre of my attention. It had been dormant for some time, but that captivating chasm suddenly grew hungry and opened up inside me once again. It was an ugly space. I had spent most of my life longing with all my heart for it to be filled with true love and affection, but I knew those things would never be a gift to me. Instead, I'd filled it with token gestures and kind words, the decaying remnants of which lay scattered around, corpse-like, suspended in a place between death and rebirth. I picked through the bones, as though I were one of the Morwenstow crows. I found the cadaverous remains of my innocence, my self-worth and my dignity, which I'd chucked into the well of myself long ago. No matter, as long as that void was filled, filled with something – anything – then it wouldn't be present, it wouldn't echo with a goading sorrow. Its emptiness wouldn't be grotesque and frightening.

Much like the appearance of Munch's *The Scream*, I felt as though I were liquefying, melting into myself. My very essence would eventually pour into the void and like my mother, I would also drown. She had drowned in her own blood; I would drown in my own self.

I lived like a sewer rat, on the brink of the abyss. Mya was at her wits' end with me. She followed me about, fugue like, watching as I sat for hours deeply ensconced in my now disgusting pigsty of a home, which I would only leave to work or run. Filthy cups filled with untouched coffee lay around the place and half-eaten pieces of toast rotted on random surfaces, as though they were obscure works of contemporary art. The fusty smell was more pungent than ever and now pervaded the whole place, rather than just the bedroom. Its latent attendance had become almost reassuring, and my acknowledgment of it proved my existence. I was eating myself alive with obsession, as I slowly sabotaged all that I had created since leaving London. I spent hours pacing the place, talking to myself and driving myself insane with introspection and furious internal dialogue, which bounced between thoughts of Nathaniel, Adam and their motives.

In just a few short weeks, the muscles I had built up had withered and my newly achieved olive skin was dry and dehydrated. My hair was permanently scraped back into a colony of rat's tails, which didn't betray how sparse and dry it had become. I was often cold but would lie uncomfortably for hours on the little conservatory couch, with a thin throw to cover me and anxiety hovering inches from my face, threatening to suffocate the life out of me.

I hurtled from complete exhaustion to being frenetically energised, one minute stuck on the miserable sofa too tired to go to bed, the next working tirelessly to try and make sense of things. Mounds of papers covered just about every surface, where I had written vitriolic letters to both Nathanial and Adam, as well as reams and reams of musings about why this was happening to me. I had lists of pros and cons about being involved with both men; their characteristics, their impact on me and how I reacted to them; the long and short-term benefits that I would gain from knowing them or, worse still, from being without them.

I hoped the words I had scrawled would lead me to spot patterns in my behaviour that would teach me how I might be different in the future, how I might decipher the rules of being human. I had created lists of options about what I could do or say to both men. More than this, there were thousands of words that declared my honest but chaotic love for them. This love was visceral and came from my very core.

My life was filled with an unbearable sense of conflict. There was a juxtaposition between my relationship with Adam and then with Nathaniel. I wanted both men but deserved neither of them. They both gave so much in their own way and yet they took *so* much from me. I was paying too high a price for their presence in my life.

I would often sit on the little wooden stairs in the hall, with Mya behind me, resting back on her elbows.

'I don't get why you're so disappointed in him?' she said one day. 'He didn't exactly set out to trap you and take advantage of you. Well, I don't think so anyway.'

I stared at her hooded eyes reflecting at me from the mirror. She was being unreasonably reasonable.

'There were loads of things you liked about him,' she continued. 'It's not as if he thought, ooh, I saw Lily masturbating, I know, I'll go back and decorate my house in a way that will make her like me, just so I can get a bit of that action! C'mon, Lily.'

She had a point. 'I know. I know it sounds stupid when you say it like that.'

I loved Adam's creative flair and spiritual soul. His intelligence and humour had swept me off my feet and I mourned the intimate tenderness and compatibility that appeared to exist between us. There was so much about him *to* like, and he had easily enticed me and won my heart. His tendency to be grumpy and his use of alcohol had thrown me to start with, but the more time we spent with each other, the less I'd seen of those behaviours. There were certainly no Nathaniel-like red flags. I had just handed myself over to Adam and taken what he was offering me at face value. Until the moment under the tree, I had no idea just how much I had misread things.

'What about hitting me? How do you excuse that one, Mya?'

'Did he hit you? Did he actually lay a finger on you?'

'No, but he threatened me. At least Nathan–'

'Don't you dare!' Mya flashed at me. Her reflection blurred behind burning tears. 'He didn't need to hit you, Lily, but he beat you to within an inch of your life.'

'But I understood him! I understood his flaws and challenges. I understood how much of an effort it took to be able to function. I understood that he was complex and how much–'

'How much of a conniving, devious, cheating, destructive and corrupted dickhead he was!'

Nathaniel had had a miserable upbringing and, like me, had been neglected by his mother. He was just ten when his parents divorced and at twelve, he decided he no longer wanted to live with his mother, as his stepfather intimidated and frightened him. He told his mother he would be staying with his father and vice versa, before sofa surfing and finally squatting in a disused house. He came back to the squat one day to find a young stray cat had moved in. This made him happy and he was content with his feline company. Struggling, but probably happier than he had ever been, he lived there for about six months, until the landlord showed up one day to forcibly remove him from the property. When Nat recounted the tale to me, he cried when he recalled how the landlord had become enraged by his insistence that he would not leave the house. Although little more than a boy, he had been foolish enough to try and stand up to the rightful owner of the property. In the end, the landlord became so incensed that he kicked the cat into a wall, snapping the poor creature's neck. Nat felt responsible for its death, even though he hadn't metered out the final blow. Eventually, at 15, after living on the streets and running roughshod, he returned to his mother's home as a wild and out-of-control young man. He had no respect for the law, his mother or anyone else. But the latent fear of his stepfather remained until it manifested into reality one afternoon, when he beat him to a pulp and then raped him.

Nathaniel had issues. I got that. Clearly, he wasn't happy being human and stupidly, I had made excuses for him knowing about his miserable past, if it was even true. I could now see he was simply an artful liar. I wondered if half of what he ever told me was true. It seemed as though he'd escaped imprisonment on too many occasions, travelled too far around the world, had too many jobs and been kicked out of too many homes to fit into his years on earth. By my reckoning, he should be about 105 to have lived all the life he told me about, and he was never clear about how he had managed to pull himself out of the gutter. It was feeble of me to buy into his frailty, but why wouldn't I? It was a terrible tale and one that would make the sternest of souls feel compassion for the man. His story was bound to draw the vulnerable towards him. From there he could unleash his own punishment on them, and it would be their fault for being so gullible, absolving him of all responsibility.

———

Adam didn't get in touch. He didn't come and find me to apologise, so he obviously hated me, and I came to dislike the brutal man who had made himself known to me on Easter Day, as well as the creative and spiritual soul I had lost. But my anxious bond with those higher aspects of his character made me think the relationship had been wholesome and genuine, and so I *missed* him, too. I missed the façade of our compatibility and I ached for the feel of him. I mourned the intimacy we had shared. It had been so beautiful, so real and grown-up. I was frightened by the thought that I wanted more and more of it. I was frightened by the gentle soul who had the potential to hurt me, both in body and spirit. I'd never encountered physical harm before and I had no capacity to understand it.

Nat, on the other hand, was merciless. Not that he would stab me whilst I was laying in my bed or anything, but there was no doubting he was mentally harmful. Nevertheless, I knew how to manage being with him, regardless of how hairbrained it was. But Adam? He was an unknown quantity. He represented a clear and present danger, as he was more directly connected to the substance of my authentic self. With that connection broken, I was already beginning to lose sight of who I really was. I was forgetting already what it was that I liked, needed and believed in.

Consumed with navel-gazing, I stopped taking Lou's calls and answering her messages – and those of my old friends, too. I couldn't deal with Lou's endless probing about whether I had heard from Adam, and the more she asked, the more painful it was that he hadn't come to see me. The more she enquired about him, the more she propelled me towards Nathaniel – although I needed very little encouragement.

Chapter 26

It was inevitable that I would eventually reply to the 'Hi Hot Pants' message. As much as I was furious with Nat for getting in touch with me, I was drawn to him like a moth to a flame, and now that Adam and I had fallen out, I had no reason to stay away. Nat and I had unfinished business and I was desperate to see if the attraction and connection that we had once shared still existed. Filled with trepidation, I unblocked his number.

I was both excited and scared at the thought of being in contact with him again. It was a terrible juxtaposition and I now understood the hold that alcohol had over my mother. The fear of unscrewing the cap on the bottle, the thrill it would release and then the inevitable heartache and destruction that would pour forth.

A real terror squirmed and slithered around snakelike in my gut when I thought about the crippling anger I had clung onto for so long, and how destructive it had been. The hiss inside reminded me that Nathanial was an unprincipled, manipulative man who had reduced me to a snivelling wreck and then contributed to the destruction of my relationship with Adam. I blamed Nat for that much more than I blamed Adam.

Despite this, my abhorrent fascination was overwhelming and my mind insatiable. I conjured up countless possibilities and fantasies, as questions about his situation with Sorrel and the baby charged around my head. I spent hours analysing what might be going on for him. I relentlessly replayed our last conversation in my head. Somehow, the fear and trepidation in his voice drowned out the part where he cruelly suggested, 'I thought you should know.' Perhaps the baby had been too domestic and functional for him. Perhaps now he was ready to settle for the passion I was so eager to give him. I wondered if he would finally choose me over Sorrel and the baby, and if it was finally time for us to have a go at a proper relationship. If, however, that could never be, then at least we would be able to say goodbye to what we had and gently bring things to a close in a more rational way, to make peace and leave the mess that had been us – the mess that had been me – in the past. I desperately wanted to be able to remember 'us' and cherish our time with affection, instead of harbouring the hurtful silence that existed between us. Whatever the outcome, contacting him now would be a win-win situation. Although I knew I was in dangerous territory, it was familiar ground. It was the script that had defined me for most of my life. In my corrupted mind, abuse equalled love. I wanted that cruel love, the lure of it was compelling. I disliked how easily I had slipped into the version of Lily I thought I had left in London. I knew I *should* find a connection to the terrifying snake in my gut and then hang onto it so that I could take action to protect myself.

In spite of all my destructive tendencies, the tiniest part of me was still desperate to get onto a new path, to break free from what I knew as normal. I went back to using old coping strategies. In desperation, I constructed – but never sent –

text message after text message to Nat. I was driven by an unbearable urge to tell him how he had screwed up my life, and to get him to take some responsibility for what he had done to me. I wanted him to know how damaging he'd been, that even after all this time he was in danger of slowly destroying me. I held back, day after day resisting the temptation to message him and throughout the inexorable passing of each 24 hours, I remained strong. I gradually gained a little confidence in myself and it pleased me that I had exercised some self-restraint and hadn't actually sent any of the messages. And for each day that passed, for each day that I didn't contact either Nat or Adam, I kidded myself I was in control.

However, a week after unblocking him, Nat messaged again.

Hey, I couldn't help but text. I know how you love this time of year. Hope you're OK. Thinking of you, Nat xxx

I read the message and re-read it. I just *knew* that he had been hovering in the background, biding his time, waiting for the right moment to strike. I knew that despite his situation with Sorrel he had been thinking about me and still wanted me, that somehow his remoteness was his greatest contrivance ever. He knew that if he made me wait long enough the pain I felt when he told me about the baby would abate and he would be able to draw me in once more. Well, he wasn't going to get me that easily, I had surrendered too much already.

It was a clever text – even I could see that. There were no questions, no reason for me to reply, and yet it begged a response. It afforded me the opportunity to easily and simply take control, put in place some boundaries, get answers to some of the questions that had haunted me since we last spoke and bring the relationship to a close with the care and dignity I sought.

I copied his words onto a piece of paper and stared at them. I played with the words for hours and settled on a reply I thought would show my maturity, and that I had moved on and was not prepared to get back onto his merry-go-round.

> Hello Nathaniel. Thank you for your message, I am OK. I was surprised to hear from you. How is Sorrel? How are things progressing with the baby? I wonder how you are and what you think of your life now? What do you mean by couldn't help but get in touch? L

I retyped the words into my phone, smiling inwardly with immeasurable satisfaction in knowing full well that he would have to reply. I had already contradicted myself and my new-found values by leaving the channels of communication open. As I pressed send, I glared at the message in its little blue bubble of betrayal. Although I knew I had let Adam and Lou down, the chemical rewards that began to flow from knowing I was still wanted by Nat far outweighed the ounce of disappointment I felt at myself.

I sighed heavily and suddenly conscious, gazed around me in horror at the disarray I had created. My phone beeped with a response.

> I'm glad that you are OK, that is great news. As for me getting in touch, it is hard to say. Every day I think of us together and can't seem to get our physical connection out of my mind. Just couldn't resist.

'You naughty imp!' Mya made my heart leap as she paraded into the room. 'That's not Adam you're texting, is it? How nice of you.' The sarcasm rolled exquisitely off her tongue.

'I don't give a fuck, Mya, just go away and leave me alone.'

'I was just saying. Just pointing out the obvious in case you hadn't realised you've just baited the devil. But then you do know that, don't you?'

'Oh, c'm–'

'And what about Ad–?'

I cut her off before she could finish her sentence. 'What of him? What *of* him, Mya? He's fucked off and doesn't give a shit, or else he would have been to see me before now. I'm not wasting my energy on something that barely got started. Nat and I have history. So, butt out!'

My phone beeped once more.

I long to be back in your arms. I long for our nights of lovemaking. There, I said it. Run while you can!

My heart skipped a beat. OMG, he *did* still want me, he *did* realise that we had shared something special. I knew I hadn't imagined it! Obviously, I had allowed my sabotaging self to misrepresent the truth about us and had over-exaggerated the bad emotional stuff. I still knew he could be a bastard and that he had got his stupid wife pregnant, but maybe she had tricked him into it in an attempt to keep him to herself. She was younger than him and obviously realised he was drifting away from her, so she did all she could to trap him into staying.

The adrenaline began to surge, as neurotransmitters worked away at a frightening pace. Although I was over excited at the thought of replying, I noticed he hadn't answered my questions. I managed to wait a full 45 minutes before sending a message back, which, whilst heartfelt, also feigned an intensity I was not feeling.

I am furious with you and have never been treated so

shabbily in my life. You were cruel and thoughtless, and I am so pissed off with you! I would much prefer to be remembering the chemistry that existed between us with affection, rather than have the hurt and anger I now associate with you!

His response was immediate.

You are right – I panicked. I didn't know what to say to you and it all came out wrong. I was a total arse and for that I will be forever sorry. If there is anything I can do to begin to make it up to you I will do it. I need you in my life xxxx

You may need me, Nat, but you can't have me – er, you're married, don't forget!!! How can I be in your life knowing you're married?

Well, you were in it before!

I didn't bloody well know that you were married before – you forgot to mention it, until you called to tell me about the baby! I wouldn't have distracted you had I known. I can't believe I did that to Sorrel. I interfered with your marriage – that's pretty damn nasty in my book!

So, you're taking responsibility for someone you don't know and passing judgement on my marriage? I'm more than capable of making my own decisions, based upon sound judgement, and I am well able to look after my own affairs, thank you!

Exactly, Nat. You duped me, you duped me into having an affair with you and all the time I just thought you needed space. You broke my heart and you nearly destroyed me. The pain was nearly too much for me x

Lily, I'm sorry. I should leave you in peace. I don't want to hurt you. I understand if it's too painful, you take care of yourself. Good to chat with you, sexy pants – will always be hot for you xx

It's OK, but you have to understand this isn't easy for me. I just want to chat with you and see how you are – catch up with you, you know. Friends only? Xxx

And so it went on. Three hours later, we had danced around our period of separation. I wasn't brave enough to ask him outright about Sorrel and the baby, and he didn't volunteer anything, so I learned little about his life. He asked most of the questions and jested with me, ribbing me about not having got myself a new boyfriend. I hadn't told him about Adam, mostly because it was over as far as I was concerned. His silence had made that clear and I had resolved to never fall under someone's spell so easily again. We arranged to speak in two days' time and with that I set about restoring some order to my life. I flew through my house getting rid of the piles of rubbish and toast art. I bathed, scrubbing myself until my skin was pink and shiny, and I even cut my hair so that it appeared fuller and more presentable. It was a bit of an iffy cut, as I just tied it into a high ponytail and chopped it, but it fell in short, chunky layers that were surprisingly even and, as my hair was quite fine, it beefed it up a little. I ate well that evening, checked in with Lou, who was relieved to hear I was still in one piece although still a bit peeved that I had ignored her recent messages, and I slept in my bed, not waking until about 7 am for a change.

There was a bounce in my step as I set off for work, and

for the next two days, as I walked and took in some much-needed fresh air, I reminisced about life with Nathaniel and speculated what the future might hold. I dared to dream and dream big. I was determined to be a more dominant force this time. I wouldn't let him push me around and keep me hidden away like some exotic treasure, only to be taken out on special occasions.

Chapter 27

By the time Thursday afternoon came around, my larder was once again well stocked with wholesome food and I was feeling so much better and happier. I knew that Nathaniel was good for me, or else I wouldn't have been feeling as good as I was. All the time I had been at Tregellas, I had worked hard at making myself well and fit, but it hadn't served much of a purpose. Nat had literally been back on the scene for two days and already I was feeling so much more like my old self.

This time, things needed to be different with Nat, and I was keen to start off in the way that I wanted to continue, so I had sheets of paper stuck to my walls, on which I had created a dizzying array of words and arrows that dashed about the pages in a trail of red, black and green ink. In big red writing under 'Not Acceptable', I'd put: 'ignoring me', 'lying to me', 'leaving me for weeks on end'. Under black was: 'to have some space for being ourselves', 'to talk about Sorrel and the baby', 'to be open and honest with each other'. And under green: 'OK to ask questions and to challenge things', 'OK to say how I want things to be', 'OK for me to say how I would like my coffee'. Each point was linked to sub-headings: wellbeing, respect (including self), thoughtfulness, compromise. The outcomes I'd highlighted were reciprocity, calm living, teamwork, love. It was a map of what was both acceptable and unacceptable and it was my handbook to life, the one I felt everybody else had except me.

There was another sheet on which was a script of key phrases I wanted to use when talking to Nat. These would demonstrate how strong I had become: 'I would like', 'I need', 'I don't like'. I wanted him to know that I had my own voice. A third contained some of our most precious memories. I had used our language, the expressions that made us an 'us'. He wouldn't be able to deny our history when I reminded him of the laughter and fun we used to have together. I was ready for anything and it was all spread out in front of me for easy reference. I needed it there, as I was all too aware that I would be beguiled as soon as I heard his voice.

I had a veggie spaghetti Bolognese cooking and a glass of red wine on the go. It was a little after five and Nat said he would call at around 6.30 pm. My heart was smacking with great force against my ribs and my cheeks glowed as I dished up my meal and sat down to eat with my phone alongside me on the sofa. I put the TV on, then turned it off. I put the radio on and turned that off, too. I just couldn't concentrate on anything other than waiting for the call. I somehow managed to eat my dinner and finish my glass of wine, as I counted down the minutes until 6.30 pm. By 6.35, I began to potter about. I took my dinner plate to the kitchen area and moved the pots around a little. By 6.45, I was beginning to feel a little uncomfortable, so I decided to wash up. I knew Nat was at work and quite often in the past, at the time when he had arranged to phone me, he had been stuck in meetings and called later than planned. It wasn't that unusual for him to be late. By 7.15, I had refilled my wine glass, washed up the dishes and put away all of the cooking materials and ingredients. By 7.45, I knew I wouldn't hear from Nat, only this time I couldn't make any excuses for him. I was bitter with anger and disgust. He knew how much the call had meant to me and I had stupidly expected – after hearing that he would do anything to make things right between us – that he would 'move heaven and earth' to speak with me, but no.

Instead of devastation I felt angry and stupid but strangely resigned and strong. Perhaps this was because I knew I could stand up for myself, that it was safe to do so, that I wouldn't lose him by being strong and that I would no longer accept from him milky coffee with one sugar. I felt his failure to call was a test; this was my chance to show him that I was capable of being a whole person and was no longer the needy, clinging vine that he expected. I'd send him the message that I didn't need him, whilst all the time knowing the intention was a hook to bring him running back to me.

Four little words, 'can't make the call' was all it would have taken! You like Led Zeppelin, so try these LZ lyrics on for size! 'Heartbreaker, your time has come . . . go away, heartbreaker.' I won't be treated like this.

I pressed send then switched off my phone and set about packing up my 'mission control' papers.

The next morning, when I did turn the phone on again, there were two messages from him. He'd apparently got stuck in a flood, his phone had died and then he was caught up in a gigantic tailback on the M4, making it too late to call. He promised he would phone the next day 'come hell or high water', but he didn't call, not until the following Monday. I was out walking in the afternoon when my phone buzzed into life. I couldn't decide whether to take the call or not and waited until the last moment before answering it.

We spoke for about 45 minutes and it was like the old days, as though no time or sadness had passed between us. When I asked about the baby, he replied with his twisted wit, 'well, it's a human.' His son had been born a bit earlier than expected at the beginning of December and apparently Sorrel had 'performed amazingly'. I really didn't need to hear that, as I felt so dreadfully guilty towards her and the news exacerbated those feelings. The guilt piled higher still, as I imagined myself with an illegitimate half-sibling to this new baby on my hip; how terrible things would be had they gone that far, had they gone beyond the blueprint of an argument about names. At the end of the day, it was a moot point, as was so often the case with Nat. Things in the future were little more than a fantasy. Knowing now that he was juggling a wife during our time, it was little wonder he was unable to construct a true future with me. It was a completely fanciful idea for both of us, but for different reasons.

I was gutted that he and Sorrel had had a son, as I quickly rationalised that their bond would be a strong one. Nat had been abandoned by his father, so I figured – rightly or wrongly – that he would want to forge a strong link, as guardian and protector, with his own offspring. My brain leapt inappropriately ahead, as I tried to work out what the impact of that would be on us. Whatever he wanted, however he wanted it to be, if it made Nat happy then I would welcome his son into our world. I would cherish my role as Aunty Lily or just simply as a friend of his father. I would never expect to replace Sorrel or deign to be a stepmother, but I would love and nurture the small boy as an extension of myself.

The sound of Nat's voice made me feel soothed and contented. I hadn't had any of my props with me, but I had rehearsed them all so well that I was able to dip into them and stand firm when talking. Nat noticed, too, and asked if he was correctly noticing a more dominant Lily. Of course, he took from that a sexual perspective, but I was able to quickly rescue the conversation before it descended into too much depravity. I felt strong against him, but equally there was a warmth and a closeness there that, until now, I could only have wished for.

Chapter 28

Glowing inwardly as a result of the call, I continued with my walk along the coast path towards Morwenstow, as opposed to going via Hartland Quay. The route was more challenging and combe after combe made my legs burn as I traversed the contours, but I needed to feel that discomfort. Moreover, there was little chance of bumping into Adam, who preferred the open verges on the other side of the beach. I must have walked for about fifty minutes just mulling over and basking in the conversation with Nat when, with a rare but not totally unusual moment of connection to my phone service, two messages arrived simultaneously. One was from Nat.

Thank you, it was like old times hearing your voice again. You sound good. When are you going to come and see me? X

The other message was from Adam.

Are you OK? I've just seen you for the first time in weeks,

you're so thin. I miss you and I'm embarrassed by my
behaviour. I would never hit you. I'm so, so sorry and
confused. I hope you're OK? xxx

Over the past two weeks, I hadn't thought with any care
about Adam and the effect of the argument on him. Instead,
my thoughts had all been aggressive and hateful; it was as
though nothing before the fight had happened. Now that I
was back in touch with Nat, there was no point in rekindling
my relationship with Adam or having any lingering thoughts
about him, so I ignored his message while replying quickly to
Nat whilst I had a signal. I agreed that it was good to hear his
voice, too, but I snubbed his invitation to see him. He was
going to have to earn the right to a visit, although mentally I
was already packed and on the road.

I squatted down to think about Adam and found that I was
surprisingly sad. The more I thought about him – about his
sense of humour, the undeniable compatibility, the way he
laughed at me in that teasing yet gentle way – the more I
realised we had had a good time together. Even though in my
head I had turned him into a behemoth of an ignoble
character, he did seem to be a lovely person and was free to
love me. Now, although he hadn't actually said as much, it
sounded as though Nat was, too. After all, he had come back
for me and wanted to see me. But Adam? He pulled at my
heartstrings and it felt good to think he had been worried
about me. I was pleased but perplexed as to what I should do.

All the way home, I thought about what I might say to
Adam, constructing a response as I walked along. I stopped at
the beach to ruminate over the last couple of months; the
progress I'd made, the laughter, lovemaking, upsets and
misunderstandings with Adam. The re-emergence of Nat and
his texts and all of the drastic changes in emotion, from
devastation, through to fear and then sublime happiness. I

kicked off my shoes and attempted to put my toes in the water, which was a ridiculous thing to do, as it was still punishingly cold. Quickly changing my mind, I sat down to put my shoes back on.

'It's chilly, isn't it, Actually.'

His voice was timid and wary, but hearing it moved something in me and the moment the words arrived in my ear, I felt myself physically yield. I snapped my head round and there he was standing just a few feet away from me, looking vulnerable and ashamed. 'Can I come and sit down?'

I said nothing but motioned for him to join me. He started to chat, complimenting me on my shorter hair, but then, almost as though he had said something too personal, he laughed nervously and changed the subject. He started to talk about me breaking my ankle, what a drama it had been and how happy he was that I hadn't broken anything else since. He went on, barely pausing for breath, his words tumbling out. I don't know if it was my brain that couldn't make sense of what he was saying, or whether it was his nervousness that made them fall out of his mouth in an illogical jumble, but I couldn't hear or comprehend what he was saying. His voice was just a low murmur lost beneath the lapping of the gentle waves. I began to feel a lump harden in my throat, as confusion and longing boiled to the surface. I knew I was going to cry and the degree to which I had missed him made the moment purgatory. I turned to look at him, but the sight of his pleading eyes and his hands tearing nervously at the hem of his jeans was too much to bear. My mouth crumpled, my tears fell and I leaned in towards him. And, as he clasped me to his chest, I wished with every ounce of me that he would hold me and never let me go. How could I have stayed away from him for so long? How could I have spurned him so easily the way I had?

He held my head close to his chest and rubbed his hands

through my hair before resting his chin down on me. There we remained until the uncontrollable emotions had abated.

'You OK?' he asked and, as I pulled myself away to answer, we kissed.

At that point, there was no mistaking the feelings we had for each other. As Adam pulled me towards him, we kissed harder and more passionately than we had ever done before. In between, Adam told me he loved me. I loved him, too, but the aching lump in my throat prevented me from getting the words out, although we were so lost in each other it didn't seem to matter too much. Before long, we were on our feet and running back to the farm, laughing at nothing in particular. Hand in hand, we tripped and fell over each other as we ascended the streamside track. Without the need for words, we both knew we were heading for Morwenna and that within a few short minutes we would be making love.

We burst through the door of the tiny cottage and immediately started to undress each other. We scrabbled about, frantically discarding our tops and trying to get shoes kicked off so that we could remove trousers and get to each other. In the end, Adam had to keep his on, as the urgency wouldn't allow the time for him to get his boots off. We were kissing frantically as he picked me up and pressed me against the wooden front door. My legs were locked around his waist and once deep inside, he rocked us both back and forth until his orgasm took the wind from our lungs.

It had the most incredible effect on me, and although I didn't climax, the elation that surged through my body was greater than that of any orgasm.

'Oh god . . . I'm sorry . . . I just couldn't hang on,' Adam panted. I knotted his hair through my fingers and pulled his head back slightly. I kissed him and laughed a breathless and satisfied laugh, which he joined in with. We were left in a mess; he waddled about with his boots on and his jeans around his ankles, until he found some tissue that I could use to clean up with, and then we flaked out on the purple sofa together, Adam holding me tight. I sat across his lap, my right shoulder tucked into his armpit and my head resting gently against him. It was heaven to be snuggling in so close to him again and we breathed in unison.

'I could stay here forever, you are so comfy to cosy up to.'

'I'd like that. There was me thinking I'd have to tie you up again to get you to stay.'

We laughed at his reference to our massage moment.

'In fact, that long green scarf of yours would do nicely. I could tie you up completely with that.'

I froze. It was now or never that I needed to ask him what he saw that day under the tree. 'It was you who tied my scarf to the front of Hawker's last year, wasn't it?'

'Mmmm.'

He was beginning to doze. I shuffled, trying to wake him without being too obvious.

'Where did you find it?'

'Find what?'

'My scarf, where did you find it?'

'Er, I don't know. On the tree, I think. Don't worry about it now. Let's sleep.'

He hugged me closer still, but after ten minutes of staring at his open-mouthed sleeping and listening to his post-orgasm snoring, I had reached maximum frustration. I clumsily got up, attempting to give him a dead leg in the process, and went into the kitchen to put the coffee pot on. Then I stomped off to the loo, making as much noise as I could. I clattered around noisily in the small kitchen, but it was the aroma of fresh coffee that permeated his dreams. By the time I got back to the sofa with mugs filled to the brim, he was more or less awake.

'So, when you say on the tree, are you saying you saw me under the tree, to know it was mine?'

'What? Oh, the bloody scarf thing – I dunno, Lily, let me wake up.' He slurped the boiling hot coffee and rubbed his hands over his face. 'Why's this so important?'

'It just is, that's all. I'm just interested to know how you knew it was mine?'

'OK, well. I was crossing the stile and when I looked up, I could see you standing under the tree, putting things in a bag. By the time I got to the tree, you were gone, but your scarf was hanging on it, so being Sherlock Holmes, I deduced it must be yours. I brought it back to Hawker's and as you didn't answer the door, I left it there for you. It was nothing really. I couldn't leave it on the tree, it's nice, a nice colour.'

I was relieved. After all my worrying, it had all been very innocent and straightforward – he hadn't taken advantage of me after all. I was embarrassed, but still needed to be certain.

'So, you didn't see me lying down beforehand, then?'

'No! As I say, you were up and packing.'

He turned towards me, sensing that there was more to it. 'What's up, Lily? Is this something to do with why you got so angry on Easter Day?'

'Well, it does and it doesn't'.

I didn't really know what to say, but I had committed to an explanation.

'Adam, I'm not very good at relationships, and people and things and stuff get all jumbled up in my head and I have trouble differentiating between those who have my best interests at heart and those who are out to do me harm. The last guy, Nathaniel, he treated me so badly, but I just kept on going back for more and more abuse – emotional abuse – from him. I just couldn't help it; I couldn't tell the difference between love and harmful stuff. It was horrible and I was stupid. But with you, it seemed different. Anyhow, I thought it was – well, it is, but, well.'

I was mortified at what was coming next, but I took a deep breath and plucked up the courage to just say it how it was. It had been so much easier telling Lou, laughing with her about my 'moment', but this was Adam I had to say it to. 'I was lying under the tree watching you work in the field and suddenly, I was completely overwhelmed sexually and found myself having a very intimate moment with myself – if you get my drift?'

He nodded, but he looked mystified and uncertain as to where this was leading. 'Afterwards, I curled up and had a cry. I'm not too sure why, but it all made me very sleepy, so I dozed. When I woke up, I was thinking about making tracks to come home. I searched around for you, but you had gone. Obviously, that was when you were walking towards the stile. You were on low ground, so I couldn't see you. I finished packing up and went to the beach, and it was only when I got home and saw the scarf tied to the front of the hut that I realised I had left it behind. I knew you were the only other person up there and I wasn't sure how much you had seen. On Easter Day, I was suddenly seized with the thought that you had deliberately taken me back to the tree to ridicule me in some way. My rational self evaporated in an instant and I became really afraid that you had pursued me because I was *obviously* sex starved and vulnerable. I'm so sorry, Adam, I just didn't think. I was feeling ill and was overwhelmed by everything. I couldn't make sense of things, which is why I was yelling indiscriminately at you. I'm so sorry, for some reason I completely lost the plot.'

I was aware that during a moment of great candour, I had lied to him about not knowing the reason behind my unbalanced behaviour.

After taking in everything I had said and not said, he sat

there in stunned silence. He now knew exactly what it was I had been thinking, and I saw how wounded he was by my thoughts. I tried to make light of it, but the sparkle had dimmed from his eyes. I had clearly hurt him bad.

He pulled me towards him whilst our coffee cooled, but I could feel that the last thing he wanted to do was cuddle. He said nothing reassuring and showed no signs of understanding. Instead, he retreated behind a wall to consider what I had revealed. I didn't stay at Morwenna that night and when it came time to leave, Adam walked me back to Hawker's and kissed me gently goodnight, but we didn't arrange to see each other again, and although I desperately wished it was a given that he would seek me out the next day, I could tell he was withdrawing from me and my despicable failings.

I was drained by the events of the day and sat down to try and make sense of what was going on. I had a quick chat with Lou and told her about how Adam and I had made up. Although she was delighted at how intense our relationship was becoming, she became distant and was obviously bemused as to why I had even mentioned 'that moment' to Adam. When my phone buzzed and I saw it was Nat again, I made excuses to end the call.

> I can't get over our conversation. It was amazing, very thought provoking and illuminating. Seriously, I would love to see you. Missing you. Xx

It made me cry to think that he wanted to see me again, and I couldn't help myself as I messaged back that I missed him too and that perhaps we'd be together again at some point. I pushed the guilt of my infidelity towards Adam deep inside in an attempt to ignore it. I also knew I was deceiving Lou, and I was disappointed that I wasn't able to tell her anything about Nat. Despite the fact I desperately needed someone to share the news with, I had to figure this one out by myself. Even after all she had said, after all her reassurances, there was no way I could ask her what to do, as she would kill me. I had no idea how to handle Nat being back in my life again, nor the conflict his presence caused in my relationship with Adam.

Chapter 29

I didn't see or hear from Adam for three days and in that time, I descended into a world of texting Nat. Throughout the day, we fervently pinged each other messages that were full of repartee, humour and sexual innuendo. In fact, some were downright pornographic and involved detailed discussions about our former, very active sex life. We were highly aroused at the titillating thought of sex with each other again, but it was only intimation. Day after day, Nat badgered me to go and visit him. He was working in Bristol, which wasn't too far away, but I explained I was busy at work and there was no way I would be able to leave the farm.

On the Friday of that week, he was due to call me but gave me the heads up he was having problems with his phone. He still hadn't bought a new one, but he was such a tightwad that this came as no surprise. True to form there was no call, but at least he had considered me this time and warned me that he might not be able to ring. At about 10.30 pm that Friday night, my fate was sealed when a text from him arrived.

Missed our chat today, sorry about that X X Off to sleep

now, you are in my heart! Sweet dreams. Night night, my
sweet x x

He missed me, he was sorry, he was thinking about me. I
resolved that I would do whatever it took to go and see him.

And you are in mine, see you very soon ;-D xxx

You mean you're coming to Bristol?

Yup, when?

Tuesday will be cool bananas. Get here for lunchtime.
Can't wait to explore you with my tongue.

And there it was, the first direct reference to us having sex.
I tried to remain cool.

Ha! You don't change. You'll have to catch me first!

And so I shall

What with?

My man trap. It gets them every time.

Them? What the hell did that mean? The word 'them'
stared back at me from its blue bubble. 'It gets *them* every
time.' The phone pinged again, distracting me.

Very much solid at the thought. See you Tuesday, Hot
Pants. I'll send details Monday x

And with that, he was gone.

I read through our messages again and for the most part I was excited and happy about the words that had been used and the tender tone that Nat had taken with me. But I was also anxious over what he had said. Negative thoughts and red flags attempted to get the attention of the sensible part of my brain. I shoved them away as hard as I possibly could. Why had he said 'them'? I wondered how many people he was trying to trap. And what about the weekend? Why wasn't he going to be in touch tomorrow? Why couldn't he carry on messaging me tomorrow so that we could plan our get together? He was obviously still tightly under Sorrel's influence.

For the first time in our relationship, I jumped onto Nat and Sorrel's Facebook pages. I hadn't dared to look before. Of course, I knew Sorrel existed, but I'd managed to ignore her presence. Seeing images of her in Nathaniel's life, in his arms even, would make her real and I would become even uglier for taking what I wanted, but what wasn't rightfully mine. But now I needed to know whether she still featured in his life, and I discovered that she did. She looked different from what I expected. Instead of the plumpish Earth Mother with a linen apron and two thick plaits, I found myself smiling back at a luminous spirit. Sorrel was like a tiny Irish dancer who could easily have borne the moniker Sinead or Grainne. She was willowy but petite, with a mop of bright ginger hair and a wild crop of freckles. I was right to have been nervous about making her real, and the sense of betrayal I felt towards her was immense. There were about a dozen pictures of her, and in each of them she was either in Wellington boots or flip-flops, always in action and never without her disarming smile. She posted nothing but recipes and gardening articles, whereas Nat was an armchair politician. They commented freely on each other's posts, or at least had done until what looked like a most miserable Christmas. The pair of them were sitting in a restaurant flushed with wine and looking fed up. I wondered who had taken the snap. Try as I might, I couldn't find any pictures of their son, to the point where I wondered whether he truly existed, despite many messages of congratulations to them both at the time of his birth. I guess it was understandable that they wouldn't want him plastered all over the internet, but at the same time they seemed to be breaking modern convention by not having any of him on either of their pages. As I snooped through their profiles, I got a buzz of adrenaline that made my hands shake and my heart pound in anticipation. I held my breath and was cautious of how I moved my hand across the screen, afraid that I might like a post or accidentally send a friend request. It was as though I were on a drip and self-medicating by cyberstalking. I spent hours drilling down into their lives together but learned nothing.

The next day, I saw Adam just as I was going out in Bertie. I had to turn the engine over three or four times before it roared lumpily into life.

'That old heap still runs, then?'

I was a bit dumbfounded. There was no way that my car was an old heap! 'I'll have you know that my Bertie is the most reliable, most handsome chap in my life!'

I'd done it again! 'No, Adam, I didn't mean that, I just meant that you can hardly call him an old heap. He's beautiful and rugged, and even if he is a bit old, he *is* reliable. I mean, he always starts . . .' My voice trailed off, but my uncertainty was unnecessary because Adam was smiling and enjoying the way I had gotten myself into such a pickle.

'I love the way you tie yourself in knots, Actually! You are such a plonker.'

'I didn't think you were talking to me. I haven't heard from you and after, well, you know, I just thought. So now I think that, well, anyway!'

'That means nothing to me. I have no idea what you just said or what any of it means. Care to explain? Perhaps over a coffee, or are you off out, seeing as you just defibrillated your old man?'

I was only going shopping, so I apprehensively agreed to coffee. He joined me in the car, and as we headed out of the farm in the direction of the Old Smithy, I glimpsed Mya in my rear-view mirror gingerly shaking her head.

I hadn't been to the pub since Christmas Eve, and I was surprised at how vacuous it was without half of the local population crammed in. I found a corner table whilst Adam went and got the coffees. The landlady gave him some real stick about having a non-alcoholic drink, but he gave as good as he got. Upon his return, eyes fixed on mine, he rather candidly started to speak. 'We, or rather I, need to talk, if that's OK?'

My stomach lurched, and as I could hardly say no, I fiddled with my little finger ring in anticipation of hearing something I didn't want to, whilst also nodding for him to go ahead.

'I have to apologise to you, but at the same time I need you to know that you hurt my feelings. I'm sorry that I didn't get in touch with you after we made up on Wednesday, but I needed some time to think about where we are.' He suddenly looked a little crestfallen, and then we attempted to talk at the same time.

'It's OK, you go.' I squeezed his hand to reassure him but had no idea why he needed that compassion. He took a dry-sounding swallow and air gurgled in his throat before he began to speak.

'Telling you I love you was a huge thing for me to do, as it's not something I do lightly, and I don't give my heart easily, either. I noticed you didn't say it in return. But I didn't tell you to hear it back, I told you I love you because I do, Lily. But . . . but I *hate* to think that you think I'm some kind of animal, someone who would pursue you purely to take advantage of you.'

Adam dropped his gaze to his coffee and gave it a laconic stir. 'I know you were hurt by whatever his name is, but I'm not him and there aren't many men in the world who would behave in the way he did towards you. And I want to promise you that I will never, ever, ever treat you in such a marginal and disrespectful way; nor would I ever hit you. I feel ashamed of how those words flew from my mouth, but I didn't know how to handle you when you raged at me. You'd been so ill, and I knew there was something terribly wrong, but you were like a wildcat and completely out of control, although that will never excuse what I said. I *am* truly sorry. I don't know whether you want me or what your intentions towards me are, but please know that you are beautiful and clever and simply perfect – and I love you.'

He stopped talking and looked at me for a reaction. All I could muster was a lopsided smile as joy pulled my lips one way and the threat of tears jerked them another. I wasn't worthy of this man. I didn't deserve his love and yet I was desperate and wanted to be greedy – I wanted his love more than anything else in the world.

I couldn't speak, so I sat there glancing between him and my hands. I could feel my old friend panic rising in my chest. It was all so huge, and as I opened my mouth to take a gulp of a changing breath, his large hand covered mine and he softly squeezed my fingers to stop me fiddling.

'You don't need to say anything, just think about it. I'd really like to make a go of us, if you think it's something you would like. I can see you're a bit fazed, so just sleep on it.'

And with that he changed the subject. He seemed calm and confident as he told me about a new piece of work he wanted to create, and he was warm as we said cheerio outside the pub, kissing me lightly on my cheek. But I sensed a sadness about him as he stood alone waving me off.

———

'And?'

Mya was waiting for me, sitting as usual halfway up the wooden staircase, staring at me in the mirror.

'And what?'

'And what did he want?'

'He wanted a coffee with me.'

'And what did he say while he was having coffee with you?'

'It's none of your business.'

'But it is my business. Tell me.' Her expression challenged me. 'Say the words, Lily.'

'He said he was sorry.'

'And what else did he say?'

'He said he was sorry and that he would never treat me badly.'

'And what else?'

'He said he would never treat me badly and that he loved me.'

'And what else?'

'He said he loved me . . . that I am beautiful and clever and perfect.' Mya slunk down a step so that she was closer to me.

'And are you, Lily?'

'Course I am!' I answered flippantly. I wanted Mya to shut up, but I could tell from the look in her eyes that she wasn't going to let me off the hook. She slipped down another step.

'Seriously?' she hissed.

'OK, then, no. I'm kind of clever but I'm definitely not perfect. No one is.'

'He means you're perfect for him, dumbass.'

And then I panicked. I knew I wasn't answering her questions correctly, but I couldn't see what she was getting at. She continued bearing down on me as I floundered for answers.

'All right, all right, I'd say I'm OKish, but I'm not really those things. Not really . . .' I paused again. 'No, then. I guess the answer is no.'

By now Mya had slithered down all of the stairs, and I felt her sitting right behind me as she stared over my shoulder and into the tiny lobby's smoky mirror.

'WRONG!' She screamed the word at me. 'Wrong, wrong, wrong. When will you learn, Lily? When will you fucking learn, you fucking fuck!'

'Learn what? What are you saying? Tell me what you mean. Tell me. Mya, help me.' But – infuriated I couldn't see what she could, that Adam loved me for all the right reasons – she refused to speak with me anymore.

I spent the rest of the weekend in such a dilemma, as I didn't know what to do with myself. I'd committed to seeing Nat and now Adam wanted me to commit to him. I paced around my small hut, made more flipcharts with pros and cons, walked the coastal path and prayed and begged the universe for a sign. I had no idea what I was going to do and no way of deciding which path I should take, until I spoke with Lou on Sunday evening. I told her about Adam and his proposal to make a go of things. The joy in her voice was palpable. She was thrilled and excited and her response gave me a much-needed boost. Although I was mostly in agreement with her and could genuinely feel a surge of passion rising within me, I told her that I would think about it for a couple of days, just to be entirely sure and to be fair to Adam. What this really allowed me to do was go to Bristol and see Nat, after which I would be able to make the ultimate choice. Finally, I had a plan and it felt good. It felt as though it was the sensible solution to a tricky problem.

Chapter 30

As promised, Nat messaged me on Monday and we began to make our plans for the next day. He was working in a place called Chapel Pill and was renting a flat in a nearby housing estate. The route was straightforward enough, up towards Barnstaple and then onto the M5, which would take me straight through. I spent the day in preparation for our long overdue rendezvous by making myself beautiful. I carefully chose the clothes I was going to wear – a white shirt, dark-coloured cropped denim jeans and, of course, my green boat shoes. I wanted to recreate Diana's style, although thoughts of betraying her and her sagacity were far from my mind. I complemented the outfit with my only set of slightly lacy underwear. I didn't have time to go and buy anything more adventurous.

Nat cajoled and motivated me with a barrage of sexy and funny messages, leaving me highly aroused throughout the day. Those feelings intensified upon receipt of his final message.

Very soon now, speak in the morning. XXX

He wanted this as much as I did.

In the early hours of Tuesday morning, I sent Adam a text explaining that I had been called away to a friend who had been injured in a car accident. She was in the Bristol Royal Infirmary, but as her family were abroad, I had been asked to attend to her until they arrived. I left the same information in a note for Mrs Enys. I apologised that I wouldn't be able to do the cleaning but explained that all my other duties were up to date. Assuming Nat would want me all to himself for at least two days, I said I expected to be back on Thursday, but I would keep them posted with progress. By 8am I was on the road and by 11am I had arrived in Chapel Pill. I was way too early but I located the apartment block then drove the short distance back to the M5 junction, where there was a service station. I had a coffee before messaging Nat.

I'm here, can meet when you're ready. Can't wait for
this xx

It was some time before I got a response, but it was a good one and I was excited that Nat would meet me outside the flat in fifteen minutes. I nipped into the toilet once more, bought some mints to freshen up my mouth and headed back to Chapel Pill.

I waited in a state of high anticipation for Nat to arrive and when I saw an unfamiliar dark blue BMW pull into the car park at speed, my heart skipped a beat – it was him! It was over a year since we had last seen each other, and I couldn't quite believe we would be in each other's company again. I got out of the Beetle and waited beside it whilst he parked, and then he was walking towards me, smiling a beaming, brilliant smile with his arms gently extended.

'Heeeyy, how're you doing?' He hugged me and gave me a

peck on the cheek before gesturing with his head towards Bertie. 'Is this yours?'

'Yes, yes it's mine. He's called Bertie. I've had him nearly a year now. He was made in 1973 and I got him from a man in Exmouth. He's great fun to drive and I love the grunty noise of the engine.'

I could hear myself wittering on and forced myself to stop. I realised I was as nervous as hell.

'You look good. C'mon, I'll show you the flat.'

We crossed the car park to the apartment building, chatting animatedly about Bertie. Nat wanted to know all about him. I had to run to keep up with his stride and trotted alongside him like a faithful puppy. I had only managed a glance of him, but I could see he was tanned, a little slimmer, fresh-faced and, for once, no frown. He was dressed in his signature Hawes and Curtis classic twill suit and Oxford shoes, teamed with a pink shirt that only men with supreme confidence can carry off. The silver Vulcan fighter cufflinks I had given him peeped out from and vanished into the sleeve of his jacket, as he marched across the car park. Whatever was happening in his life was good. I felt sick and suddenly in awe of him.

The apartments were new, large and plush. As we went up to the 2nd floor, Nat asked me about my journey and told me all about the place he was working at. He'd finally got a permanent contract that paid him the money he needed and was now 'coining it in'. This meant he had some peace of mind when it came to finances and his million-pound mortgage could be paid. I didn't want to think about his home situation and decided to tread with care on that topic, but I was relieved to hear that he wasn't exhausting himself by chasing contracts up and down the country.

He opened the front door and held it ajar for me, but as soon as it was closed, he was on me. He wasn't just hungry for me, he was ravenous. He kissed me hard and full on the mouth, squashing my top lip painfully against my teeth. I worried I would end up with Rouge Coco all over them. With unbroken kisses, we moved through the entrance hall into a large lounge area, which was bright, modern and sparsely furnished. He tugged at my white blouse and with impatience abandoned the buttons, opting to yank it over my head instead. As he did so, one of my earrings became caught up and pinged off into some unknown space. With one hand he unclasped my bra and smothered his face in my breasts. He was fondling me and pulling me towards him.

I was overwhelmed by him and didn't feel turned on in the slightest. I managed to take his head in my hands and asked him to slow down, whereupon he took me by the hand and led me to the gigantic corner sofa. He stripped off his tie and shirt and both of us, naked above the waist, lay down together. He was gentler now and as he kissed me more tenderly, he pressed up against my side and began to stroke and touch me. And then he was on his feet again, removing his trousers and then mine. I had forgotten how intimidating he was. As though possessed, he glared through me and pushed me back into a semi-sitting position with my legs apart. He leaned forwards to kiss my neck and as he did so, forced his great self quickly and firmly inside me. I wasn't ready for him and the pain was excruciating. He pulled out and flipped me over onto my front, so that I was laying across the large footstool part of the sofa. He pushed into me from behind and as he plunged into me again, he gasped with pleasure. Grasping at the little flesh I had on my hips tight between his fingers, he thrust in and out, pushing harder and faster, faster and harder until he grunted like an old boar and littered the air with curses. I was breathless through his exertion and shocked at how he had consumed me. We stayed like that briefly and as he pulled himself out, he declared in a sing-song voice 'dismount', in the same old way he had always done. As ever, it sullied the moment. He pulled me towards him and kissed me a couple of times before removing his arm from around my shoulders, claiming to be too hot to cuddle.

'Sorry about that, I just needed to have you and I couldn't control myself. It's been so long. You OK? You want a drink?'

I didn't want a drink, I just wanted him to snuggle me in and hold me. He stood up and my heart sank further when I noticed the frown was back.

'Time to get dressed. Listen, I have a video conference I have to join, and I can't do it here. I hate doing this, but it won't take too long, about forty minutes, at a guess. You make yourself comfortable then I'll be back for some more fun.'

I looked at him askance.

'Hey, come on, don't be like that. I'm supposed to be working, but once I'm done, I'm all yours. I'm a big cheese, can't let my team down, they need great leadership and I can't do that from between your delightful thighs now, can I?'

I walked down to the car park with him so that I could get my overnight bag. As we arrived at the cars, he gave me a hug.

'Sorry, can't kiss you, don't know who's twitching the curtains. See you in a bit, I'll text when I'm on my way. It is *great* to see you, to have you here.'

He beamed his dashing smile at me and unlocked his car, as I stood in wonder at the side of Bertie.

Chapter 31

I returned to the apartment and ran a deep bath to sit in whilst I tried to digest what had happened. I just couldn't figure him out. He had been so uncaring and cold; it was as though all he had wanted was to have carnal sex with me, to fuck me, to fuck anyone, I just happened to be up for it. What had happened to the love making he'd led me to believe there'd be?

My phone pinged. It was Adam with a sickly sounding sympathetic message about my poor friend and her accident. It was nauseating and I ignored it. I was surprised at how weedy he came across, but at the same time my conscience pricked at me. I knew I was being the weak one.

Nat stayed away for three hours in the end. It felt as though they lasted forever. The apartment was soulless and practically empty. There were no personal effects, just a loaf of bread in a sorry state and an ancient jar of apricot preserve. The only thing that indicated any existence of life was the presence of some low-range bathroom products and a toothbrush. I suppose it made sense, as Nat only stayed there Tuesday until Thursday. I poked around in the kitchen some more and found an open bottle of white wine in the fridge, so I poured a glass and sat thinking about Nat's behaviour. I just didn't get it. This was a side to him that I hadn't really seen, although I had suspected it existed. I felt physically sore from where he had been rough with me, and as I gently held myself with my hand for comfort, it was Adam's touch that I could feel. I reached for my phone and called him.

'Hey, how're you? Are you OK?' He answered the phone quickly, as though waiting for my call.

'I'm OK, thanks, but it is harder here than I thought it would be.'

That was the truth, but not for the reason Adam would have thought, and my honesty fuelled my guilt. We chatted for several minutes and I tried to be as vague as possible with details. I think I did fairly well, until I heard Nat's key in the door. Hurriedly, I tried to bring the conversation to an end, but Adam chatted on and on until I had to interrupt,

'Listen, I have to go. They want me now.'

Nat was soon at my side. 'OK, yes, I'll let you know tomorrow. Bye now.'

I hung up.

'Oooh, naughty, Lily, that was a furtive-sounding call. Have you been telling porkies to someone?'

Nat smiled in a goading fashion and I stood with my mouth open.

'Come on, you. I don't expect you to have been on your own for the last three or four months, or however long it's been. Is he your local squeeze? Does he have a tractor? Surely, he must have, seeing as he lives in Cornwall, or wherever it is?' He pulled me towards him and hugged me, and this time it was as though he meant it.

'C'mon, fancy food? I'm starving!' And with that he grabbed me by the hand and took me out to dinner.

The food itself was pretty average, but the company was

electrifying. I had Nat's undivided attention and he was charming, funny, interested and interesting. Clearly, seeing me laugh gave him plenty of encouragement to be his funniest possible self, which he exploited to the nth degree. He told me all about his work situation and how he'd ended up in the role in Bristol. I had no confidence that he had simply aspired and achieved, and instead I wondered how he had managed to blag his way into a very senior role. He was clearly relishing every minute of the power it afforded him. After a couple of glasses of wine, I was brave and asked about the situation with Sorrel and the baby. He evaded most of the questions but when we touched on the fact that he had a boy, I unexpectedly felt adventurous. In an attempt to show him I could laugh at myself and not take *us* too seriously, I chided him gently about the arguments we used to have over baby names.

'Oh, Jesus, you're not still banging that drum, are you? What was it we used to argue over? Bob or some dodgy 1970s-sounding name.'

'It was Thomas . . . Tom actually!'

I was wounded that he'd forgotten the name that was precious to me, and that he thought I banged on about things. My response sounded bitter and thick with vitriol, but good old Nat expertly dodged the potential for challenge and immediately changed the subject. Before long, he had me laughing again about some mad money-making escapade he'd been involved in.

Things improved as the meal progressed and the humour and warmth between us continued to increase. Whether that was down to the wine or not I can't be sure, but by the time the coffee came he was being intimate and tender with me. He even bought me a red rose from a flower seller who came to the table, one of those tacky types who prey on defenceless, wining-dining husbands and lovers, squashed into the restaurant's velvety booths with their l'amour du jour.

Under the table, Nat's legs were brushing mine and above it he was holding my hand. I was entranced, as though hypnotised. Gradually, the sexual tension between us started to rise and I felt glamourous, sexy and wanted. Unable to restrain ourselves any longer, we left cash on the table and went in search of a cab, with smiles on our faces and our fingers interlinked.

Back at the apartment, we both stripped off and he went to get in the shower. 'Joining me?' he asked, and I ran excitedly towards him. Once in the bathroom, we kissed passionately. This time, he took an interest in me and was gentler, as he began to explore my mouth. He picked me up and carried me into the shower, where he soaped us both up so that our bodies were slippery as we tried to entwine ourselves. He spun me around and, clasping my breasts from behind, began to kiss the back of my neck and pull my hips back towards his, before pushing me forwards so that I was bent double in front of him. Pressing himself into me from behind, I knew there was no way I was ever going to climax. Water was running up my back and across my head and neck. As it ran up my nose, it stung as though I'd jumped into a swimming pool and the water had been forced deep into my sinuses.

'Mmmm, you're delicious. I could never resist fucking you like this.'

He grasped my butt cheeks, pinching the flesh hard between his fingers, as he slowly pulled me back and forth onto him. 'And more weight, too, something for me to hang onto. Mmmm, lovely flesh!'

On and on he went until finally satisfied, he uttered his killer 'dismount' and pulled out of me harshly, whilst attempting to wobble what little flesh I had on my butt and thighs with his hands. I endeavoured to stand but was blinded by the water where it had made my mascara run. I stumbled in the shower as I stood up, and Nat helped me to regain my balance.

'Oooh, you look like a panda. I'll leave you to wash up . . . wine?' And with that he wrapped himself in a threadbare towel and waltzed off.

Once I had cleaned up, I returned to the bedroom, where Nat was lying on top of the king-sized bed watching TV. I checked around for my drink, as I needed a large gulp of comfort.

'Is my wine in here?'

'Ah, no, didn't get that far I'm afraid. I'll have one with you, though.'

In the kitchen, I poured two drinks and was about to take them back into Nat when I was hit with an overpowering sense of sadness. I'd rapidly sobered up and at that moment in time, I despised him and was beginning to question why I was there with him at all. And was I really getting fat, too?

What the hell was I doing when I could be with Adam? Although our relationship was a bit weird, as we were always at cross purposes, at least he actually liked and cared for me. And his love making was, well, just that. He made love to me, we made love together. I could feel tears threatening but had to control them, as Nat always said it upset him to see me cry. As soon as I walked into the bedroom, though, he could see I was upset and although I tried to pass it off as water from the shower, he could tell I was lying. Surprisingly, it had a softening effect. I joined him on the bed and as we lay in each other's arms, he gently stroked my back and asked me what I would do once my contract had come to an end at Tregellas. He told me I was wasted there and that I had so much to give back to the world. He genuinely seemed to want me to re-enter society and whilst not promising anything, he intimated that it would be alongside him, by telling me that he wanted great life changes, too. Things were hard between him and

Sorrel and they had become 'functional', with everything revolving around the baby, a son with whom he was yet to bond. He was devastated that there hadn't been that love-at-first-sight moment, and since then he had struggled to parent the new child. He and Sorrel hadn't really established an intimate physical relationship since his birth, and even before the baby it had been simply a matter of 'needs must' when they had intercourse. He felt as though they wanted different things in life. Despite the newness of their family, he couldn't see what the future held for them. He explained that the business in Oxfordshire, whilst profitable, wasn't making the killing he had envisaged, and now that he was on better and regular pay, he was no longer reliant on the income from the smallholding. He still wanted to go to Spain and appeared dogged in his thoughts. We chatted gently for some time and then he made glorious, glorious love to me – the 'old' Nat was back.

We slept tangled in nakedness until the following morning, when he made love to me again before showering and getting ready for the day. I got up and made coffee and some atrocious looking toast, spread with the ancient apricot preserve, which Nat ate in his underpants and socks, hopping from one foot to the other like an anxious ballet dancer, whilst I pushed my breakfast around my plate, unable to face it. After eating and swigging back his coffee, he got dressed and picked up his overnight bag.

'What are your plans for the day, then? I'm heading back to Oxford tonight, as I have to meet someone in Reading – a possible investor for the business – and I'm on leave tomorrow. You can stay here as long as you like, just let yourself out when you're done.'

I was astounded. The bastard! I tried to reply without sounding crushed. 'I'm going back to the farm. You know, things to do and all that.'

'Ah, yes, your farmer to do, I bet! Listen, great to catch up. Sorry to 'splash and dash', as it were, but I don't want to be late for the team. You take care, yeah.'

And with that he tightly puckered up his lips and kissed me on my astonished mouth, as though I had leprosy.

He was an unspeakably cruel man and as I watched him slowly walk to his car through the apartment window, I was taken with how he moved like an old man. I was dumbfounded by how stupid I'd been to leave Adam and to think that things would work out with Nat. After all this time, after all the healing I had done and after all the effort I had put into repairing myself, it was apparent that nothing had changed. Nat had become even more contemptible. I sent a text to Adam.

> Hi, on my way back today. The family is here now, so I can leave. See you x

It was a weird sounding message. It didn't sound like me writing it, but then I didn't feel like me. I was emotionally cold and completely stumped, confused by everything about the last twenty-four hours or so. What the hell had I been thinking? Why had I not protected all that I had achieved? It was as though my life had suddenly been transposed upon a giant game of real-life snakes and ladders, and I had just descended down the biggest, most malevolent snake.

Chapter 32

The next day, I waited for Nat to text me but when nothing arrived, I excused him, knowing he was on leave. As I unpacked the abandoned overnight bag, I came across the rose he had bought for me in the restaurant. My head warned me that I should throw it away, but the memories of the meal and the warmth we had shared when he bought it for me meant my heart was the winner of that conflict. I carefully removed about eight petals and flattened them in a piece of newspaper, which I laid inside the cover of *Jane Eyre*. I threw the remainder of the rose in the bin.

'Why are you even keeping that?' Mya asked, as she skulked over by the patio doors.

'I haven't kept it all, you've just seen me chuck most of it out.'

'But you've kept some.'

'Well, yeah, but . . . why shouldn't I?'

'Because you don't need them!' She frowned at me and I could sense her frustration building.

'I might not need them, but I like them, they're good to

look at and they'll give me confidence when I'm feeling a bit crap.'

'You have everything you need inside: confidence, control, strength – all of that shit. You've done it all before, you just need to tap into it again, for Christ's sake!'

I ignored her last comment. 'But they're meaningful. You can't pretend the night didn't happen, so what's the harm?'

'Because he's a toxic twat that you have no business meddling with. The man's a tyrant.'

'You have no understanding about him, do you? Even after all this time, even after knowing all you do about him, you don't get him at all.'

I was furious with her. She stood defiantly but stayed her distance at the other end of the room.

'Last night, he told me all about his life with Sorrel and his business, so it's no wonder he behaved the way he did towards me. He's going through some big changes and he needs to be able to get on and make them happen, without distraction!'

I was shouting and my fists were clenched, as the avalanche of words poured out. 'Don't you get that it would be too difficult for him to let go of his life with her and then become emotionally tied to me so quickly? It'll take a while for him to get his thoughts straight. Who am I, or what's more, who are you to judge him when he's going through such a difficult time?'

She glowered at me but remained patient and still.

'He's changing, Mya. He's searching for something livelier, more passionate. He wants something more like our relationship, and when he's straight he will probably cut ties with her, sell the business, then maybe, just maybe – despite you, Lou and even Adam – I shall have the love and the life I want and deserve.'

'Oh, you deserve it, all right.' Her contempt was clear.

'What does *that* mean?'

'It means, Lily, that you will end up a sour old bitch with nothing and no one. That is what you deserve.'

'What the fuck. Why are you saying that?'

'OK, then, tell me. Tell me about all those seeds of doubt that are fermenting in that cesspit brain of yours. The way he kissed you goodbye, his comments about your weight, the wine, his sadistic ways. Tell me all about that.'

She faltered, knowing I wouldn't answer.

'And leaving you. Leaving you to fend for yourself once he was finished with you. He left you alone, he always leaves you alone, and you reckon abandonment is one of your biggest fears?'

'It is, and you kno–'

'What it *is* is bollocking bollocks and pig shit!' Slowly, she prowled towards me, simmering with a rage I'd never witnessed in her. 'If you're not so bothered about being left, I can go now. It's clear I'm done here. You don't need me.'

'No! But you can't, I–'

'Oh, I can, and I will. Goodbye, Lily!'

'You actually can't leave me! I know you're in here, you fucking bitch! You are in. Fucking. Here!'

I jabbed wildly with both hands at the side of my head and pulled at my hair until the pain was so great I had to stop. It was only when the crying stopped, too, that I realised the harrowing wail I had heard in the distance had actually come from within me. Tufts of hair were stuck to my sticky, teary fingers. There was no sign of Mya reflecting back at me from the patio doors, just a sad looking shell of a girl, who had the same colour hair as milk chocolate and eyes like empty pools of amber, which were far too big for her gaunt face. I was a stranger to myself.

By the weekend, I still hadn't seen Adam. He hadn't sought me out and I hadn't gone looking for him. There had also been no word from Nat and, recalling my fight with Mya and the hideousness of her very existence, I was frightened for myself. Despite all of her warnings, I was desperate to hear from Nat. I wouldn't accept that he had discarded me again or that he was already falling into his old behaviours when we hadn't even really got going again. Day after day, I carried out routines and meditations to summon contact from him. If nothing else, it was just to prove Mya wrong. Sending out silent plea after silent plea was exhausting, and all to no avail. I heard nothing. There were no Facebook or LinkedIn posts; there was nothing to say he was alive even, but I managed to keep the nightmare possibility of his actual death out of my head. Perilously, each day that slipped by eroded the heartless attitude he had displayed towards me and enhanced the few tender moments our night in Bristol had given me. I took out *Jane Eyre* and looked at the dried rose petals, but instead of bringing me closer to Nat, they reminded me of Mya's encouraging words,

'You've done it all before, you just need to tap into it again.' Tiny grains of rationale slipped into my consciousness and I began to harvest the strengths Mya had talked about, as I endeavoured to accept my situation. I realised the only thing I could hope for from any future contact with Nat was closure.

It was obvious nothing had changed with him at all. He was just as careless with my emotions as he had always been. I hated being in the same position once again, waiting around for the text or call to say he was thinking about me. I'd been duped once more but felt able to make peace with the situation. Mya was right, I did have it in me to face my fears. I brushed myself off and started all over again, only this time I had hope and experience to keep me company.

I tried to focus on all the good I had in my life, and all the good that had happened between Adam and me. I thought about what he said to me in the Old Smithy, when he revealed his feelings for me, and finally, I began to make some sense of it. I realised that what Adam was offering was all that I had ever wished for – it was him I needed to fill my void.

Remembering my promise, I called Lou and told her that I had spent the week giving a lot of thought to the Adam situation and that I was going to make a go of it with him, if he'd still have me. I didn't confess that I'd reached that conclusion by exposing myself once again to the most malignant man I'd ever met, but I think I managed to convince myself as well as her that I was about to embark on something that would bring me a great deal of joy. The next thing to do was to text Adam.

Hi, I've been thinking. Meet me under *the* tree at 7 pm. I have something for you. Don't be scared xxx

Knowing you I should be very scared, but I'll be there.

Bring your scarf, else it will feel left out, and don't break
any bones on the way Xx

His humour warmed my heart. He sounded happy,
furthermore, his words gave me a great idea and I excitedly
began to prepare for our rendezvous. Everything was in place
by 6.45, just in case Adam was early, which meant I was able
to sit and stare out across the field where I had first glimpsed
his beautiful body. So much had happened since then and
although I felt emotionally battered, I was certain that my
time had come. My recent experience with Nat had shown me
how much I had grown; it made me realise that I wasn't as
unhealed as I thought and through our being in touch again, I
knew exactly what it was that I wanted and needed. Adam's
footsteps broke my meditation, making me jump slightly.

'Mmmm, now that's a yummy old spread! Hi, you.'

And with that he bent to kiss the top of my head, before
tangling his great legs beneath him, as he attempted to sit on
the mat next to me cross-legged, mimicking my position.

'Wine?' I proposed. He nodded and licked his lips at the
fruits and cheeses I had laid out on the mat.

'May I?' he asked redundantly, as he helped himself.

We ate in companionable semi-silence, neither of us
venturing too far away from frivolous niceties and idle chit-
chat, covering the usual staples of residents at the farm and
the weather. The recent past and what lay ahead, as yet
unseen, would have to wait. Once we had eaten, I cleared
away the remains of the food and took out a tinfoil tray and
my teal scarf.

'I want you to have something, Adam.'

He laughed. 'That's very sweet of you, Actually, but green
isn't exactly my colour. I prefer purple to be honest.'

'Well, you're in luck, then, as this isn't green, it's teal.
There's a massive difference, don't you know! You know my

suede boat shoes?' He nodded in recognition. 'Now, they're green, this is a bluer, more muted colour.'

'Ooh, get you, Mrs Arty-Farty.'

I replied with my usual retort, a light punch to his shoulder. Although we were joking, he appeared serious and enquiring, as if to say, 'What the hell is this all about?'

'It's not to wear, you big doofus, it's for something else, it's for–' I felt a bit shy all of a sudden. '–Erm, well, you know me and my little hocus pocus ways?'

'Oh God! What are you going to do now?' He smiled but still looked quizzical.

'Nothing, seriously, it's all OK, it's just a bit . . . I'm just a bit embarrassed.' I felt the wine rush to my cheeks until they felt as though they were glowing.

'Hahaha, it must be *really* bad if you're embarrassed. I've never known you to be embarrassed in your life before!'

Adam reached over and cupped my ruddy cheek in his palm. 'C'mon, Actually, it's me you're talking to.'

With his gentle reassurance, I carried on. 'Well, I want you to have the scarf as a gift, a peace offering if you will. I'd like you to take it, and–' I placed it in his hands '–and I want you to take this, too.' From my bag I produced two lighters, passing one to him. 'If we each set one end of the scarf on fire and allow it to burn from end to end, it will symbolise the end of the harm it caused, and it will destroy the confusion that loiters between us, which in turn will allow room for new things to grow. A bit like when the heather on the moor burns, new life is created. It will feel as though we are acknowledging the past, but that we are laying it to rest and creating a new era in which love can grow. As the flames travel towards each other, they will bring us closer together.'

Adam's lip tremored, and I wasn't too sure whether it was because a smile was trying to escape or because he was baffled by the whole thing.

'I've thought about what you said when we had coffee last Saturday, and I want you to know that I love you, too, but I was afraid to say it. I would really, really like to continue to get to know you better, so that we can give our relationship a chance . . . if you'll still have me, that is?'

I felt wary about making eye contact with him, but I needed no further reassurance, as he smiled from ear to ear and, without saying a word, flicked his lighter into life and ignited his end of the scarf. Quickly, I followed suit and dropped the flaming silk into the foil tray. Adam put his arm across my shoulder and pulled me in tight, as we watched the flames consume the demon destroyer, paving the way for our love to shine forth.

———

Adam and I re-entered our own little world, the one that had existed pre-Easter Sunday. It felt wonderful to be back in his arms and back in our own universe of love and affection. To give and to receive was a magical gift, and it was one that we both cherished. In May, when Mrs Tweedy decided to renew my contract for another year, Adam and I agreed that it would make sense for me to live with him, which would allow Hawker's Hut to be rented out to paying guests. Tweedy was apparently most grateful. As usual, she saw it as a business transaction that suited her needs, although she did manage an eye-reaching smile when we told her the news. Being with Adam felt comfortable and peaceful and we blossomed together. It was as though we had simply slotted into each other's lives. I began to migrate my belongings from Hawker's to Morwenna, firstly filling Adam's space with toiletries, and then with books and clothes.

But despite my newfound happiness, my head and my heart were perpetually in conflict. On the face of it, I believed that I was idyllically happy with Adam, but at the same time I was terrified he would turn out to be just like Nathaniel, and I watched him constantly for signs that he was about to devalue or discard me in just the same way.

The residual shock at how dreadfully Nat had treated me in Bristol, and how he had once again discarded me, chafed and gnawed away at me. I felt humiliated and threatened by the experience, but obviously I was unable to share it. My noxious secret flowed through my veins and lingered like slumbering Cerberus, ready to awaken and attack. And, as much as I tried to constrain and control it, Adam would always bear the brunt of my swinging moods and fitful nights. That deceitful episode in Bristol consumed my waking hours, and the more I suppressed it during the day, the more it haunted my night-time forays into REM sleep, where I lived the dreams of the troubled.

One hot night, I dreamed that Lou and I, and two other friends, were travelling to Oxfordshire. We were in Bertie, but I wasn't driving. For some reason, I was asleep in the back. When I woke and sat up, I realised we were at Nat and Sorrel's smallholding. The girls didn't know it was his place, they'd just arranged for us to stay in a barn on their land for the night. Sorrel brought us a tray of wine and strawberries to quench our thirst after our long journey, but there was no sign of Nat. We sat on a large, soft blanket to take our refreshments, and despite knowing all about Sorrel and her relationship with Nat, I tried to be relaxed and present in the moment. I had my back to the drive and in the distance, I could see Adam sitting on a fence watching the four of us enjoying ourselves.

A short while later, a car pulled into the gravel drive and I glanced briefly backwards to see Nat arriving. I felt nothing. He pulled up, got out of the car and made his way over to speak with us. As I turned around fully to look at him, I was blinded by the sun, so I couldn't see his face, just the outline of his body. As he played the role of the perfect host, he gave nothing away. He mentioned there was coffee if any of us would like some and putting my hand up, I indicated that I wanted a cup. No hint of recognition passed between us. Neither of us said anything and the girls were seemingly oblivious to who he was.

I stood up and followed Nat, but as I walked away from the picnic, I checked over my shoulder to see Adam still sitting on the fence watching us. Upon stepping into the kitchen, I recognised it immediately. Nat had once told me about a cheese making venture he'd been involved in, describing the room in detail in the process. Nat set about making coffee, but Sorrel was nowhere to be seen. In the huge, dark kitchen, I stood beside a farmhouse table with eight chairs around it, tenderly stroking the grain of the worn old pine. Nat had often told me how he fantasised about stripping me off and making love to me on the table. He told me how it plagued his thoughts.

He made the coffee and placed the cup in front of me, before looking longingly at the table, and then at me. Without saying a word, he turned and walked out of the building, leaving me standing there alone.

In the way dreams leap from one scene to the next, it suddenly became night-time and I was asleep in the barn. Lou and the other two girls were in the same room as me, and we all slept in single, white, iron-framed beds. The rough, exposed floorboards had been covered in an array of brightly coloured rugs and the large windows had been dressed with white voile, which let in the promise of a new day. I was drifting dreamily in my small bed and although I hadn't heard him enter the barn, Nat came in and got into bed with me. He snuggled in tight behind me, spooning me as he used to and then mumbling in my ear. He was whispering so gently that I couldn't make sense of what he was saying. He then clambered out of bed and left the barn. Intrigued, I followed him out shortly afterwards, only to find he had disappeared.

It was a summer dawn and there was a heavy dew on the grass. Although daybreak had arrived, the sun wasn't yet up. In the dream, I could see myself standing on the wet grass with my legs apart and my arms flopped at my sides, hands open and my slightly raised palms turned outwards, as if in despair. I was still wearing my pyjamas and appeared desolate. I sank to my knees and Lou appeared at my side. She gently grasped me by the shoulders and lifted me until I was about able to stand. She guided me towards the barn, wanting me to go inside, to be protected, to get dry. I could feel her unconditional love guiding me. I conceded, not consciously, to follow and, as I moved, I glanced up. I could see Adam still sitting on the fence, still watching the scene play out in front of him. All he did was observe and allow it to happen. I woke up screaming and terrified.

'Hey, hey, hey, Lily!' Adam yelled at me. I was breathless, sobbing and shaking, and sweat was pouring off me. Adam was up on his knees and he was trying to get hold of me as I flailed around.

'Why didn't you do anything, you bastard? How could you just sit and watch? Why didn't you rescue me? You could have made it all OK. You could have saved me. You let him destroy me. How could you just sit and watch him destroy me?'

I was hysterical, and the more Adam tried to get near me, the more I screamed at him and thrashed my arms around. My language was rancorous.

'Lily . . . Lily . . . LILY! Come on, now.'

'But it's too late, you came too late, Adam.'

'No, I didn't, it was a dream. Come here, please.' He reached over to pull me towards him, but I shrank away.

'Why did you let him have me? Why did you let me go?'

'I didn't let you go, Lily, come on, calm down. You're safe, it's OK, I'm here now.'

'I'm not safe. I'm not safe at all!'

'Shhhhhsh. Really, I didn't let you go anywhere, sweetheart. It's OK, it's OK. Here . . . look at me, here . . .'

He clasped my jaw in his hand and turned my face towards his, forcing me to make eye contact with him. 'Come on, now, it was a dream. Come here, you *are* safe now.'

I scooted up to a sitting position and hunched my knees to my chest. Resting my forearms on them, I buried my face in them and cried, as Adam knelt beside me rubbing my back. I craved a cuddle, but at the same time I couldn't stand the way his hand was rubbing my skin. I was furious with him for not coming to save me, regardless of whether it had been a dream or not. It had all been too real.

'Would you like some water or a cup of tea?'

'Tea,' I snivelled and nodded my head. Then, as Adam left our bedroom, I lay on my side and wept.

The dream spoke volumes to me. I knew I had a guilty conscience, and it was little wonder Adam hadn't saved me. Nonetheless, I was terrified I was going to have to explain what the outburst had been about. I was scared to death of reality and what life might hold.

By the time Adam came back with the drinks, I had stopped crying, but I was still trembling faintly, unnerved by the cursed dream.

'You OK? A little better now?' His sweet voice and genuine concern hit me in a wave, as a final rogue tear dripped from my chin. I nodded and he passed me my tea.

'Urgh, sugar, so now you're trying to poison me,' I managed to giggle.

'Well, you know, why would I start being nice to you after letting you down so badly? But seriously, that must've been some dream. You frightened the life out of me when you screamed. I had no idea you had such a whacking great pair of lungs!'

I snorted a snotty laugh through my nose and quickly had to wipe it with the back of my hand, but his humour was just what I needed. 'I'll get a tissue, hang on.'

'No, you stay there, I'll get it.' And with that he went ferreting around for something to blow my nose on.

'Adam, I'm sorry about that. You're not a bastard, although you were a bastard in my dream and well, I'm just terrified. Things are so lovely between us and it's not something I'm used to. Why on earth do you love me the way you do? Why do I deserve the love you give me, a love that's so wonderful? I can't believe it's true.'

He came back to bed and sat sideways onto me, stroking my hair whilst I blew my nose. 'I don't know how we got here, either. Lily Montrose in my bed, in my home, loving me. How, just HOW?'

His eyes glistened with joy as I leaned back on my pillows.

'Each morning, when I wake up, I think that my new life is all a giant dream and that you'll vanish in a puff of smoke. I have dreamed of finding you – of loving someone exactly like you – my whole life, and yet now you are here, it's as though I have a self-sabotage button that will drive you away. I simply can't believe that you're real and that you have chosen me.'

'Oh, Actually! Ya great wazzock, I–'

'I'm serious, though. Is it real? Are you a cruel trick, a figment of my imagination, or are you genuine? Are you here to stay or will you go, just like everyone else has? What have I done to deserve you if you are real? My life is littered with people who have let me down, and my last relationship was with a veritable psycho.'

Adam gave me a pained smile on hearing me use the word psycho. The gravity of my previous situation registered in a flicker across his face, as another piece of my life story puzzle chinked into place.

Clearly taken aback, it took him a second or two before he could begin speaking again. 'I don't think I can answer all of those questions, but what I can say is that I'm not going anywhere. You're as beautiful as much as you are a pain in the arse, but, as I've said before, you're perfect to me.'

'How can I be, though? I've done some horrible and selfish things.'

'You had to do what you had to do in order to survive the past. But you don't have to worry about that anymore.'

'But I've even been horrible to you.'

'And I was horrid to you, too.'

'So, why are you in my life?'

'I don't bloody know! Because we're about more than . . . than that confusion and the miscommunication stuff from the early days.'

'I don't deser–'

'Yes, you do, Lily. Come on, seriously.'

He sat forward and turned my face towards his for the second time. 'We fit together in so many ways, and all of your wonderful qualities outweigh your weirdness. I love you completely, including your slightly mad bits, and wouldn't have you any other way. Why we are in each other's lives, how long for and whether we deserve each other is a moot point. The universe has decided that we should be together, and I for one am more than happy to accept our time, no matter how long it lasts, as a gift. And I shall treasure it. I want it to last forever, and more. I never ever want to be without you, Lily.'

Adam was right and although I was still frightened and tearful, I could hear what he was saying to me and I found it reassuring. I put my mug of tea on the white nightstand beside that big, old, iron-framed bed and held him, never wanting to let him go. I loved the way he graciously accepted me holding him, rather than the other way around, which was generally the way we hugged. He was accepting my apology and at the same time letting me know that he accepted me, faults and all.

I must've held him for five minutes before he started to fidget, indicating it was time to break the cuddle. But he took me by surprise by somehow managing to pounce on top of me. Sitting astride me, he boomed loudly, 'Toast, woman, I demand toast, and plenty of it. Now get cooking!'

With that he sprung from the bed and took on an Incredible Hulk pose, before running around the bedroom wailing and beating his chest like Tarzan. I curled up into a ball and laughed and laughed. Then he grabbed my ankle and tried to pull me off of the bed, as though he were a caveman and I were his woman. He seemed to be telling me, in no uncertain terms, that he would fight to the death to keep me in his cave.

Chapter 34

As the days passed, I could feel myself flourishing, so when my phone beeped with a message from Nat about three weeks later, I was ready for him.

Hi sexy, have woken up with a stiff member after dreaming of you!!

Fuck off, Nat, leave me alone! You don't want me, so leave me alone.

Oh, you sound upset?

Yes, I am bloody upset. You treated me appallingly when I came to Bristol, and I won't put up with it. As I say, you don't want me, so let me get on with my life. Please. Go away!

I know, but things have been really crap for me. Lots going wrong – super, super busy and lots of money worries, just had to find 165k to get me a clear six months, nearly destroyed me. Finally, am able to see a bit of light at the end of the tunnel and would like to see you in that light. I understand if that's too much though. Still friends?

I didn't reply, as I thought it would only encourage him, but deep down inside, despite my happiness with Adam, there was still part of me that was desperate to find out more. I simply couldn't help myself. I managed to last about a week before constructing a long reply.

Hi Nat, I hope you are OK? I'm really sorry I was so touchy the last time I messaged, but I found the change in you very difficult to make sense of. Now you have explained to me the pressure you were under I completely understand. I really miss the playful you I caught a glimpse of leading up to seeing you in Bristol, and maybe I will see that side of you again one day. Adam – my 'farmer' – and I are seeing each other properly now, so I'm not sure what that means for you and me, or what plans you have in mind for the future. I hope you're OK and that your worries have lessened now. Yes, of course, friends forever xxx

Cool bananas, all a little crazy here. Lots of change going on. Text you when things calm down. Prophetically, seems as though Sorrel and I are at the end of the rainbow – though I take from your text you'd like me to back away from the physical element? It's ok if you do, it would be good to be clear. You sound like you need something different, happy any way you like. Catch you later sexy pants x

I was a bit flummoxed by his reply. Just as I had told him Adam and I were making a go of things, he was telling me that he and Sorrel were coming to an end. I didn't understand what that might mean for me. Once again, I was filled with self-doubt and I wondered if I had made the wrong choice. Nat wanted clarity from me, which was something I was uncertain I had, even for myself. I re-read my previous message and the concern in my words about his behaviour reminded me why I had chosen Adam. This emboldened me enough to send an honest reply.

> I guess seeing what I've written & thinking about it, I need to go with the bigger picture. The answer has to be yes, let's cut out the physical, but I'd like it if we can still be close as friends? xx

I felt a surge of calmness. I had finally been honest with him about Adam and I was confident in how I had responded. But there was no immediate reply and as the days passed, I began to worry that I wouldn't hear from him again. It disturbed me deeply to be so worrisome once more. Time and time again, I found myself in the same situation. Just how many more times would I go around in this anxious circle, continually pursued by the gigantic ogres that were otherwise known as Banishment and Abandonment? The anxiety around Nat's silence began to fester inside me like some kind of abominable tumour. I interpreted his silence to mean that I had hurt him and had blown my chances with him as a friend, let alone a lover. What the hell had I been thinking? I regretted wildly the fact I had told him Adam and I were now an item. I suppose I wanted him to be a little jealous, and to provoke him into fighting for me, but once more his silence was deafening. He wasn't going to choose me or come to my rescue.

I was being immensely disloyal to Adam, and I tried so hard to hide my inner turmoil, which, although it wasn't as unforgiving as it had been the last time, was nevertheless all consuming, as my mind was perpetually filled with thoughts of Nat. Managing my conflict of emotions, whilst feeling guilty about my fixation with another man, was almost crippling. Remarkably, despite this maleficent fascination, things with Adam were moving along well. He had become prolifically creative and his surreal works of art now included the most beautiful illustrations of my breasts, buttocks, eyes and lips, his miniature masterpieces etched on a backdrop of extraordinary plants, waves and woodland scenes.

His work had the most profound effect on me, and whilst I was drawn in by its beauty, I failed to see how he viewed me in such an artistic capacity. I questioned him closely about why he had portrayed my body as something so perfect and beautiful. I saw him as an alchemist, a transformer, as there was no way the reality of my form matched what he was depicting. His persona and presence in life was remarkable, and the intensity we shared seemed implausible. Even Mrs Tweedy was more accepting of me, and when she popped into Morwenna, she even began making small talk.

The idea of 'us' was a mysterious and wondrous thing. It was as though we were living in a magical dream. Here we were, a pair of like-minded souls who complemented each other. There was an old-fashioned equality that existed between us, and both of us were genuinely happy just to see the other happy. I didn't feel as though I was rescuing him, or him me. Rather we were humbly travelling side by side and living a shared and meaningful life together. I was able to be open and receptive to love, whilst Adam was able to receive the love and affection that I felt for him.

But our life together felt as tenuous as it did tremendous. It was easy and yet that made it feel as though something was missing from our relationship, and I suppose it was. There was no abuse or gut-wrenching complexities to navigate. For me, anyway. Little did Adam know how fragile and vulnerable things were. I was living a double life; I had my world with Adam and a hidden underworld with Nathaniel. Irrespective of how strong I thought I was being, I knew I was unable to be entirely honest with myself. I was scared I might acknowledge the ugly truth – that I was still secretly pleased to hear from Nat when he did message. I had no understanding that even though I didn't reply to him, he was still reinforcing a co-dependent relationship with me.

Chapter 35

In order to cope with Nat's silence, I put myself on a phone 'diet' and tried to restrict how much I checked and used it. I rarely had it out in public anyway, but I would interrogate it meticulously when alone. We were in the height of the season and although Adam was working flat out, I still had plenty of time for myself, and so I took myself out on afternoon walks, just as I had done the previous summer. Only instead of meditating and relaxing in the warm sunshine, I would go somewhere where I knew I'd have network coverage and spend ages rifling through Nat's social media profiles trying to figure out what was going on for him. His LinkedIn page was helpful to understand what his work life was like, and Facebook was becoming ever more fruitful. Snide comments and barbed remarks had replaced Nat and Sorrel's chit-chat, and I savoured their tit-for-tat comments on each other's statuses, as they publicly poked fun at each other. For me, this validated what Nat had said about things breaking down for them. I revelled in comments about him never being there, and he poked fun at her 'Earth Mother' articles. I loved it and wanted to see their misery played out for all to see. The snippier they were to each other, the better. Clearly, they were very unhappy and the unhappier they were, the happier and more confident I became in what Nat and I had shared.

Time passed by slowly, as though everything was drifting. Even the good bits with Adam began to blur around the edges, contaminated as they were by Nat's unseen presence. Then finally, I received the long-awaited message from him. He replied in his own indomitable way, as though no time at all had passed since our last text exchange. It was so typical of him, he simply carried on the conversation as though he had only just read my message.

> Well done you. Sounds like you are moving on nicely. If you ever need a Nat sausage top-up you are always welcome. Go forward and be happy. How are you and farmer Giles? I wish I was him right now. I would love to have my face buried between your legs x x

I had waited so long to hear from him, and the weight of expectation and my desire for a message had been excruciating, but his response sickened me. How could he be so rude about Adam? And to bring everything down to such a sexual level was plain offensive. I ignored the message. Three days later another arrived.

> Heart heavy, missing you. Glad the romance is going well, guessing from your silence. Would love a hug and kiss X

I ignored him again, and it was then he began his messaging onslaught. As they became more and more fanatical, I started to worry that Adam would find out about them. It wasn't really a problem to begin with, as they were so infrequent, but then he began texting at an alarming rate, sometime six or seven messages at once, despite the fact I was ignoring him.

I was concerned that Nat would make a terrible fuss and that Adam would find out how deceptive I'd been. To underpin my deception further, instead of blocking Nat, I simply changed his name to Elle in my contacts, so that Adam would just think they were from one of my girlfriends.

All the time, Nat was enticing me to reply, enquiring how I was, whether I was happy and if Adam and I were still together. Each time, I found the inner strength to resist responding. The volume and tone of the messages was overpowering. Each text espoused a different guise: a declaration of love, the desire for intimacy, filth and degradation of pornographic proportions, followed by seemingly sane and sentient prose. And finally, the dreaded silence. Had I paid more attention, I would have realised there was a pattern to his messages that reflected our life together. It was the same routine played out in quick time. Be nice, hook me in and get my interest, feign desire and need, debase and demean everything, then discard and ignore me for a while. It perfectly summed up everything that Nat and I had ever shared.

One evening at Morwenna, I was in the little kitchen area whilst Adam was reading some Anais Nin on the purple sofa. We had been laughing about his titillating temptress and humour and affection was high. I was busy preparing pizza and salad when my phone in my pocket beeped the arrival of a new message. Suspecting it was from Nat, I wasn't expressly interested and continued working until the meal was just about ready.

'Ten minutes, handsome, then you'll have to put your smutty lady friend away, as I want all of your attention.'

I was looking forward to the evening, as we hadn't had a chance to really chat for a number of days. I nipped to the loo

243

whilst the dinner finished off and as I sat down, I retrieved my phone to read the message. I was prepared for it to be from Nat, but not for the content.

> Hi Hot Pants. I hope you are well. I had to contact you again. I am fighting declaring love for you, as I do not want to hurt you. But I do love you and my heart aches for you. Forgive me for bringing it up x

How dare he? I had waited years to hear those words. I had been so hungry to hear them and now that I was settled and happy with Adam, he was finally saying them. He had pursued me for weeks with his relentless, risqué messages, but nothing before today alluded to the fact that he felt love for me. This news was completely out of the blue. He had been such an evil bastard to me over the years, and now he had finally said the unthinkable. I was furious and didn't know how to respond. Who the hell did he think he was? I practically thumped the screen as I bashed out a reply.

> Great timing, Nat, after all these years. I'll reply when I can think properly. You really know how to cause chaos; I can't believe you are saying this to me now!

His response was immediate.

> I should leave you alone, am so sorry for causing you pain. Take your time and let me know what you think. Forgive me for loving you, my love x

Needless to say, the date night with Adam was ruined by my sullen mood and I sought every opportunity to pick at him. He went back to *Delta of Venus* until the small hours, while I went to bed and sulked. I couldn't sleep, as I toyed with Nat's words. Did he *really* mean what he had sent, or was he just pulling me further into his evil world of hurt? It sounded genuine enough, but then that was Nat all over. When I was living in London, he would build me up into a frenzy from miles away and I would believe it when he said he was aching to come and see me and that he was moving heaven and earth to spend time with me, but he never came. I waited for hours, days even, to see him, and he simply never arrived. So why should I believe what he was telling me now?

I took myself into the bathroom, where I splashed freezing cold water on my face. For once, I missed the berating Mya would have given me had she been there. I tried to imagine what she would have said about my despicable duplicity. Downstairs was a man who was *with* me and genuinely giving me love. How could I falter at a few words on a screen? I realised I was angry with myself, not Nat. He had just thrown me a curve ball, but he would not get any more of me. It was a million-to-one chance that had brought Adam and me together, and I knew I would never find that kind of love again. I resolved to reply to Nat, but I needed time to think about my response so that it would be a clear message of complete closure and commitment to Adam.

Chapter 36
JULY 2019

A few evenings later, Adam and I hunkered down together on the beach, dreamily watching the waves roll in and out over the sandy beach. I was sitting between his legs, which were hitched up at the knees, and with my back to his belly we spooned, my arms tucked in and his chin on my shoulder.

'I do love this. Just being together, just watching and being. You've changed my life, Actually, you do know that, don't you?'

'Yeah, I do, and you've changed mine, too. I love you, but what is more, I love loving you.'

He squeezed me tight in agreement and we were silent once more, enjoying nature's performance, although I was aware Adam was a little tense. His breathing rate had increased, and he cleared his throat a couple of times. I didn't want to ask if anything was wrong, partly because I was frightened that he may have bad news to impart. I dreaded the thought that he had found out about Nat's messages, so I crossed my arms over his and held them with my hands. We were each locked in our own world watching the unfolding sundown.

'I love you, too, Lily . . . and I wondered if you would do me the honour of marrying me?'

I slowly digested the words and as they registered, I turned myself around in the space between his knees so that I could look him in the eye. I was smiling wildly and uncontrollably. I couldn't speak so I nodded my head furiously, as we reached for each other and gently kissed. We broke apart and our smiling eyes held us connected. Adam reached for me again and pressed his warm mouth against mine, as though he were kissing me for the first time.

Then, as the penny fully dropped, he suddenly pulled back. 'Oh! You bloody girl, the next Mrs Enys! Bloody Lily Montrose is going to be my wife!'

I was still speechless, still grinning wildly. We clung onto each other like limpets and rolled about on the sandy shore until eventually I turned and snuggled down to be spooned by him once more. Eventually, we had to leap up, as the tide had surreptitiously crept ashore around us, soaking our feet and bums.

The next morning, Adam was up early and went off to work, leaving me with a cup of morning tea. I was snuggled up in our cheerful, comfortable bed. The fresh linen was light and airy against my skin, as though it were a diaphanous dress. I felt blessed and content as I kept thinking back to the way Adam had asked me to marry him and how perfect it was to acknowledge our prospective union with the incoming tide. The reliability and perpetuity of the sea made a wonderful metaphor for our future together, and I dared to hope our marriage might be just as dependable. But the concept of a wedding was so ethereal that I had trouble grasping what being a bride or wife might look like. I

247

wondered how real it all was, so I decided to keep the proposal to myself until I could be more certain.

That day, I took my phone and, with great intention, drove down to the tearoom near the church in Morwenstow to set about writing to Nat. I had to get him out of my mind once and for all. The messages needed to stop. It was time for me to finally let go of him, freeing myself from the hold he had over me. I had received something I had waited for all my life. Adam had chosen and fought for me, perhaps now I would be able to firmly grasp the concept that we were built to last. The treacherous bond that existed between Nat and me had never been wholesome, it was constructed out of emotional turmoil; it was a tsunami of toxins that waxed and waned and ruled our time together.

At the very least I'd hoped for closure, but we hadn't even achieved that. We'd had no real conversation about the us that had once been. The Bristol night, although abominable, had, in its guise as a complete failure, served a good purpose to remind me about how deplorable Nat could be. Finally, I believed I was brave enough to sever my attachment to him. I was going to turn him gently away and set him free to get on with his life. The message was to be calm and clear, and it would be the last one.

My dear Nat, well, what an adventure we have had. It has to be over now, though, as my life has changed. I know you think Adam is laughable, although you have never met him, but he is a kind and good man. He loves me and is 'here' for me. We are making a go of our relationship and want it to succeed as a partnership. To strengthen it further we will be getting married – both of us want this, as we love each other. I need to be free to do this. I was deeply shaken by your declaration of love the other night, but it is too late for us, I am sorry to say. I really am sorry. Over the years we have known each other, I would have given my eye teeth to have heard those three little words, but they were never forthcoming, and I never thought I would hear them. We had some amazing and loving experiences together and you have given me some beautiful gifts – across many realms. I hope that with all my heart you can understand why I need to say this? I have loved what we have had, but it simply can't be – although I shall always treasure you. Keep safe and well and I hope you find eternal happiness in your ever-so-slightly crazy world. With love, L xxx

I pressed the send button and re-read the words. I hated hurting Nat and pushing him away, but I knew I had to be honest with him in order to move on. I re-read the message again, but my mind whirred and chaotic thoughts began to make their presence known. One minute it felt as though I had said too much about how I felt about him, the next I decided I had spoken too much about Adam, as though I were rubbing our happiness together into an open wound. I began to get muddled by my own words, so I hurriedly made my way out of the little teashop, and, taking my life in my hands for the first time since the night of my arrival at Tregellas, drove down the unmade road and onto the beach at Welcombe. Within about half an hour, a reply came from Nat.

Hello L. I always had the feeling you wanted to say 'I love you' to me and then did not. I know I frustrate you and I should leave you alone, and I am sorry for causing you pain. I haven't been able to fully give you what you want and need, but that is different now for me, my life is different. I'm happier in myself and freer than before, and the future is going to be brill (once upon a time it was unimaginable). I thought it had you in it, but sadly, you have moved on now. I do understand you need to do this. I so love you, Lily – I know I am being a shit now by saying that; you deserve more than I have given you and you're right, you should be free of me – I think I am toxic for you and I am distracting you from a good place. Be happy, Lily, good luck, be free xxx

The message may as well have been a spray of bullets from a gun. Every drop of confidence I had gushed out of the holes his word-bullets had made. I was so bloody confused by the man. When I sent my message, I thought he would have at least been upset and hurt by the fact *I* was rejecting him. I wanted him to be devastated. Why wasn't he weeping and wailing and distraught that I had set him free? I had wanted to reject him in order to feel better, but sounding resolute, he was now making hidden promises to me. His words suggested that had I not moved on, he would be available to me, and that I was giving up the opportunity for a brilliant future with him.

I baulked at the thought that he would go on and find a new life, too. I didn't want that. I didn't want to hear that he would be happy in a life free from Sorrel, but without me.

His message acknowledged that he had been a shit, and to know that he was punishing himself made me cry. But it was the thought that he harboured hopes and plans for us that ruined me. How could I have rejected him when all along he had love for me, which he'd had to smother because of his relationship with Sorrel? If only he could have shared this with me sooner. I clearly hadn't been supportive enough or cared enough about *his* needs. All the sorrow and heartache I had endured had been made by me and my selfish ways, because I wanted things to be 'just so'. I had lost sight of the pain he must've been in each time he'd had to let me down; each night he hadn't made it to my flat or been called away. I had imagined the most dreadful deceit on his behalf and had conjured up the malevolent and dark world in which he existed, when all along it had been because he was married. He had simply been striving to survive the pressures of his life, and I had behaved like a petulant child. I had been impatient and selfish and now that he had sorted out his finances and his dead marriage, I had turned him away in favour of someone new.

All too quickly, my phone beeped again with another message from Nat.

Hi, I am so sorry to contact you again, but I do miss you and I wanted you to know that you will always be in my heart xxx

Oh God, Nat, you will be in mine, too, but this is impossible now. I have always wanted to say I love you, but I didn't think you wanted to hear it, so I held back. I fell in love with you when we first met. I didn't know what to do with those feelings because I didn't get the chance to express them, so I got frustrated and irritated with you, and all that did was turn you off me and make you angry xx

I never meant to be angry with you, Lily, and I am sorry. I should leave you alone, I'm sorry for making you hurt. My life is so different now. I am going to live in Spain and I had a dream that you would come and share the adventure with me. I know you have found the love of your life, but I still want you as well. I am bad for being greedy. Ignore me, you should settle down with your working love. I am sorry for wanting you so much, I won't text again, promise Xx

By now, the tears were pouring so much I could barely see the screen. It was impossible to discern the truth, so I searched for his Facebook page. He had changed his cover picture to that of a Spanish colonial revival house against a brilliant azure sky. My pulse quickened. There were several political rantings and then I found what I had been searching for, just two simple words, 'Despedida Blighty'. It was true, he really was going off to Spain. My mouth dry, I searched for Sorrel. There had been no updates to her profile for many weeks, so I could tell nothing from that, although I ascertained that she was obviously too preoccupied for social media.

My pulse throbbed away at my temples and I was biting my dry lips as I stared at the screen. When he'd previously talked of his dream to move to Spain, I had always felt envious and frightened, as I never knew if he meant that his dream included me, or whether he was just telling me about *his* plans and *his* life. Even now, his language was ambiguous. I couldn't understand what he meant by freer. Did that mean they were no longer together, or was he just talking about being emotionally free at last? He was clearly going to Spain and by posting it all over his Facebook page, it was almost as though he was provoking me into action or had done it to make me feel jealous. But there it was in front of me, the truth that he was going. And then there was his loose invitation for me to join him.

Despite the warmth of the afternoon, I was shaking and cold and my tears were coming in sobs. I felt familiarly grief-stricken and once again panicky that I was losing Nat forever, which was utterly stupid of me, because that was exactly what I had been endeavouring to achieve. He still had control of the situation. Instead of walking away to happiness, another Nat-shaped sinkhole had opened up around me.

Chapter 37

It took me an age to calm down and when I felt reasonably collected, I marched up the steep track to Morwenna, leaving Bertie parked at the bottom of the road. He'd have to stay there overnight now, as there was no way I was going to walk down again later on, but I needed to wear off some of the chemicals that were surging around my body.

Fortunately, Adam wasn't there when I got home, so I poured a large glass of wine before slumping down on the purple sofa. I was furious with myself for being so hypocritical. I wanted to leave Nat behind, but I wanted to be the one doing the leaving. By setting me free, it was as though he was giving me his blessing to go, which felt like banishment. Despite a nod to a life that would be different and a declaration of his love for me, his attitude was one of sheer indifference. He had said goodbye in such a way that it didn't seem to matter to him either way if I were there or not. He didn't seem at all bothered that *I* wanted to be rid of him. There'd been no show of heartbreak or desperation on his part at my rejection. I wanted him to show me how hard it would be for him without me, and that his world had caved in just as mine had back when he'd said, 'I thought you should know', but there was nothing. No emotion, sadness, regret or even an acknowledgement of the awesome times we'd shared. There was no sign to me at all that I mattered.

The small lounge dimmed around me as the day faded into the early evening, and it was only when Adam arrived home that I realised how late it was.

'Hey, sugar, your honey is home, come 'ere, gorgeous.'

He'd obviously been at the Smithy, and as he lumbered forwards to take hold of me, I lost my patience.

'For fuck's sake, Adam, you're pissed! Look at the state of you. You can't just come back here and grapple me about like that. I'm not some kind of ruddy sex doll, ready to swing into action just because you want it!'

He staggered awkwardly backwards, as I pushed past him and stomped out of the hut, leaving the door wide open. I ran down the hill to Bertie and by the time I got to him I felt horrible. I was still angry with Adam for coming home trollied and for behaving like an arse, but because of Nat's reply, my reaction had been completely over exaggerated. I needed to get home and apologise. I dug my car keys out of my pocket and slowly drove Bertie up the unmade road, whilst shuffling ideas around my head as to what excuse I could make. Nothing I could invent seemed logical, so I figured I would wing it and see what came out once I was home. I wasn't particularly good at thinking on my feet and I couldn't decide whether now was the time to tell him about Nat. At least I could be honest and say it was over with him.

Once back at Morwenna, I could hear Adam in the bath. I climbed the stairs and followed his trail of clothes to outside the bathroom door. I found myself standing at the threshold wondering if I should go in or not. I felt a sneeze coming on and even though I did the atishoo as quietly as I could, I'd been rumbled.

'I heard you come up the stairs. You coming in or are you just going to stand there fiddling with your ring and frowning? I know that's what you're doing. I know what you're like when you're nervous. Get in here, Actually!'

True enough, my fingers were working feverishly away at the sliver of tungsten on my little finger and my brow was furrowed. Reluctantly, but relieved that he had humour and didn't sound too drunk, I made my way into the bathroom and perched on the side of the bath.

'And?' Adam asked. It was a rhetorical question, though, as he continued to speak. 'How many times do we have to have this conversation, Lily? I didn't want you for sex, I wanted to hug you. I wanted to play with you. I wanted to give you a big, drunken, slobbery hug and a kiss, because you're going to be my wife and that really excites me, even after I've had four pints with the lads up at the Smithy. Even after I've had a hard day at work . . . no, *especially* after I've had a hard day at work, because you're the softest, most tender person in the whole world to me and it feels so damn good to come home to you and dive into your presence. None of that other shit matters, but *you* do. I haven't been to the pub for weeks because I prefer to be with you, and I only went there tonight as I had to collect something from one of the lads. He kept me waiting and I had a few pints, so kill me now for being such a bad guy!'

'Adam, you shouldn't have to explain yourself to me, it's fine, honest. I reacted in a selfish way and I am really, really sorry. I was just a bit overwhelmed at your boisterousness, that's all. Mix that with being a bit tired and hormonal and it was a recipe for disaster.'

'Well, you've been really hormonal for a few weeks now, so maybe you should get yourself checked? You're definitely out of sorts. You've been fiddling with that bloody ring constantly, which is always a sign you're uptight. I swear that one of these days your finger will unscrew. Come on, Lily, where did your perky go?'

'It's fine, honest, I've just been a bit uncertain about things. You know, I feel as though I'm living someone else's life. It is all just so . . . I don't know . . . just that, it's well, so perfect. I'll get my confidence – I'm getting my confidence – I know it's coming, so bear with me, won't you? It is coming. You do feel loved, don't you?'

'I do feel loved, Actually, I can even show you how much.' Taking hold of his penis, Adam popped it out of the water and waggled it at me, which just made me laugh.

'Sorry, love, you're on your own. I'll let you have that one for free. I'll get some food on.'

And with that I kissed his damp forehead and swept out of the small bathroom, feeling ever so slightly better than I'd done ten minutes earlier, although the nagging sense of betrayal continued to chatter away in the safe box in my head. I had still failed to tell him about Nat.

I made my way across the bedroom and along the way picked up Adam's pants, socks and jeans, which I went to dump on the bed. As I did so, I noticed something bulky in one of the front pockets of his Wranglers. Without stopping to think, I reached in and pulled out a ring box. It was covered in teal-coloured velvet and had a tiny but beautifully engraved gold clasp. I turned the small treasure over in my hands, stroking the velvet and following the nap of the fabric. Intrigued at the thought it might be an engagement ring, but too terrified to open it, I quickly returned the box to the pocket and tossed the jeans onto the bed, before running down the stairs to start cooking.

I now had a new anxiety, something more tangible to tear apart. Thoughts ricocheted around my head. Was it a ring? If so, what was it like? Supposing I didn't like it? What's more, when was he going to give it to me?

Chapter 38
AUGUST 2019

Out walking back from Morwenstow one afternoon in August, I was playing the 'Why does Adam Enys love me the way he does?' record in my head. I was aware that I frequently pushed him away in my obstinacy to cope with everything myself. That was mainly due to the fact I was used to looking after myself and unless someone could do something the way I wanted and needed it to be done, I'd rather do it myself. It sounded uncharitable, but it was hard for me to put my wellbeing into the hands of others. I remember once being really poorly and finally relinquishing and asking a friend to get some shopping for me. I hadn't needed much, but I gave her specific instructions on what it was that I required. She brought the shopping round and it was only when I unpacked it that I discovered she had bought cheap supermarket eggs and not organic ones. I cried bitterly, which sounds ridiculous, but I was so frustrated that I had put my faith in her and still ended up with the wrong eggs. It became a metaphor for life, because all too often I had ended up with something I had wanted or needed, but it just wasn't right. The 'eggs' were always wrong.

I never once wondered how my minor rejections of Adam affected him and I continued to be worried sick that he wasn't right for me. I was convinced that one day I would turn around and he would have evaporated, as though he were little more than a figment of my imagination. Either that or he would become so frustrated with me that he would up and leave, just like Nat had done. My thought processes gathered steam and raged on. Supposing I got left behind? Supposing he dumped me and then went on to be happy, to live a passionate and fulfilled life, achieving peace, contentment and self-actualisation without me, just as Nat was purporting to be doing? The what ifs paralysed me, and I hated the insecurity my doubts instilled. Surely Adam needed someone confident and brimming with self-love to reflect his wonderful nature. I certainly wasn't worthy of him. Not only was I a liar and a cheat, I was also weak and scared of most things. He only wanted to marry me because he didn't know what an awful person I really was.

I was beginning to panic, as I chewed over all the reasons Adam shouldn't have anything to do with me, let alone marry me. As I descended the steep path down to Welcombe Mouth Bay, I could see on the beach far below that someone had carved into the sand gigantic letters that seemed to beam with love. An I and an A had an adorably fat heart squashed between them, as someone had declared 'I heart A'. It made me smile. It made me think about loving Adam, and the thought of someone else loving him suddenly filled me with insane jealousy. Was the A for Adam? I rapidly started to think about people in the village whose names began with an A, but I could only think of Alan, who was married, and Alfie the dog. I guessed it could be either, but I frightened myself by imagining that someone else might be in love with my man. By the time I reached the unmade road, I had broken into a jog and although facing a killer hill, I ran to meet Adam at Morwenna.

I walked in the door to the heady smell of garlic, tomatoes and basil.

'Mmmm, Mr Enys, you smell lovely. Yummy!'

'Ah, 'tis the lady of the house. Here.' He passed me a full glass of dark, red wine.

'This is nice, Adam, thank you for cooking. I wasn't expecting you until later.'

'I know, I didn't think I'd be done yet either, but here I am, cooking and pandering to your every need. Now, Mrs Sticky Knickers, bathe then come back and the food will be ready.'

'Okey dokey, what's cooking?'

I made towards the cooker and was about to take a lid off one of the saucepans when Adam leapt in front of me.

'Eh-eh, no you don't, Missy! My domain tonight! Hands off . . . although while you're there, do us a favour and chuck me a teaspoon.'

Without thinking, I opened the small drawer that was just behind me. As it cracked open, there in front of me was the teal-coloured velvet box.

'What's this?' I held it up so he could see what I was holding.

'What does it look like to you, Actually? Open it, see what's inside.'

I looked between him and the box. My heart danced and a quivering smile tweaked cautiously at my lips. I slowly lifted the lid to reveal the most beautiful emerald ring I had ever seen deeply embedded in a purple satin cushion. It was so beautifully cut that the flat surfaces refracted and yet managed to absorb the yellow light that shone from above, giving it a milky quality. The stone was set in a white gold band, with the most exquisite filigree work holding the precious gem fast. I glanced back at Adam, who was now down on one knee.

'I love you, Actually, and I want to spend the rest of my life with you. Will you *please*, *please* marry me . . . again.'

He took the box from me and taking my now visibly shaking left hand, slid the emerald ring onto my ring finger. It fitted perfectly, as though it had been made just for me. My right hand was firmly clamped across my mouth and with a surge of happiness that welled up from the centre of my very being, I managed to eke out a reply. 'Oh, Adam, yes, I'll marry you. I love you so much . . . I love my ring, too, it's beautiful.'

This proposal felt so very different from the one on the beach just a few weeks earlier. I hadn't even thought about a ring the last time, but it was perfect, so perfect, and way beyond anything I could have ever imagined.

'Only the best for you, Actually!'

'Thank you, Adam, right from the bottom of my heart, it is magnificent.'

I held my hand in front of me and admired the gem on my finger. I showed it to Adam then looked at my hand again. I was totally transfixed by it, but for once I didn't cry. I squatted down so that I was at the same height as Adam, pulled his head against my chest and held him quietly, as I secretly continued to admire the beauty of my hand with the new treasure on show.

'OMG – I love A! It was you! It was you in the sand, you were telling me, telling the world, "I love Actually!"' Laughing, I pulled his head back by his thick hair and smiling a smile that came from my very core, I kissed the treasure of a man I wanted to spend the rest of my life with.

As we ate that evening, I could barely stop looking at my beautiful ring. Adam explained how Ian from the Smithy had made the box for it. 'I was bloody terrified. When I went to see him, he had three pieces of velvet, one purple, one a mustard colour and the other teal. I didn't want purple, as that was to be the colour of the lining. Mustard . . . well, the only place for mustard is on the side of a plate, which left teal, the most terrifying colour in the world to me!'

'How come?' I spoke the words with the devil in me, knowing full well why he hated the colour. Before he had time to look up from his plate and empty his mouth, the laughter escaped my lips.

'You little cow.'

I took a big swig of wine and waved my fork in circles, goading him! 'Hey, come on, you're supposed to be loving me tonight. Anyhow, you love me because I'm funny, you told me so . . . tell me about my ring, husband to be!'

'Not much to tell really. I got the stone, I got the ring made, I put it in a box and I left it in the drawer. It's been there for days, but as you're so shy of the kitchen, you just didn't find it.'

Now he was playing with me. I grabbed my wine glass and went to sit on his lap. 'Now tell me and tell it good.'

Hitching me onto his lap and cradling me into his chest, he began again. 'OK, well, once upon a time there was the most complicated woman in the whole world.'

I wriggled, kicking my legs out as I tried to sit up, but he held me fast.

'But . . . but she was also the most sensitive and beautiful woman I had ever met. Intelligent and perceptive, she wheedled her way into my life and turned it all upside down. In a crazy way, but in the most delicious way possible, too. She had a childish and tender outlook on life and was so in tune with everything I love and live for that I decided, despite all of her bonkers ways, that she would make me the happiest man on earth if she stayed with me until I died. I don't think she will ever realise just how much I love her, I just wish she didn't think she isn't worthy of my love, that she doesn't deserve it for some reason. I wish she would have more faith in my love for her.'

He stopped talking and stroked my arm. I tried to speak

but he squeezed me and shook his head, not wanting me to say anything.

'Lily, I will do anything in the world to protect and love you forever, wherever you are and no matter what. I just hope that I can make you happy and fulfilled and that you believe in me one day.'

I clung onto him as hard as I could. There were no words for me to say, no promises to make. He knew that I would do the very best I could to eventually lay my demons to rest. He was promising me the time, the patience and the understanding to deal with my monsters. He was telling me that he had unconditional love for me. He swallowed hard, his voice tight and filled with emotion, but he carried on talking.

'Ian reckoned there was some artisan jeweller in Barnstaple who could make the ring for me, and although he sounded a bit flaky on the phone, when I went to meet with him he was just awesome. I took the stone and some sketches of what I wanted, and he quickly tweaked the design so that he would be able to get it to work. I borrowed Jenny from the pub's finger – I didn't hack it off or anything – I just measured it. Turns out she was just the right size. The stone belonged to my grandmother and she had given it, along with three other stones, to Mum, who promised one of them to me, as and when I found the girl I wanted to marry, which, my lady, just happens to be you.'

He pulled me in tighter. 'Is it OK? Do you mind that the box is teal?'

'No, Adam, not at all, it is just so beautiful. The whole thing works perfectly together . . . it hasn't really been in the drawer for days, has it?'

He laughed. 'No, of course not, doofus. I put it in there when I got home. I spent ages deliberating how I would give it to you, and this felt like the most natural way of doing it. I wanted to make it as low key as possible, nothing grandiose, just something in keeping with our lives, and it couldn't have been more perfect. Especially the message on the beach. That was the icing on the cake for me. Your timing and the tide were spot on!'

We continued to sit at the table for some hours, talking as usual about this, that and everything else. We didn't mention the actual getting married bit, but we did talk about how we envisioned our lives together. The last time I had played with the possibility of a shared life had been with Nat, and I was antsy and uncomfortable at the thought of making plans, so I gently moved the subject along until we were on safer territory. The thought of making decisions about my flat and our lives was just too big for me, and Adam sensed that but was gracious and didn't push it. Every now and then he would reach over and examine his work of art on my finger, and I would grin from ear to ear at how special and loved I felt by its presence. I could see Adam's influence in the scrolls and twirls of the white metal as they clung onto their precious cargo. He and the goldsmith had created a diminutive work of art; it was a truly magnificent piece and I was filled with gratitude and love.

Chapter 39

The next morning, Adam headed off late for work and as soon as he was out of the door, I made my way down to the bay. On the way, I sent Lou a long overdue text message.

I'm getting married!

Within minutes, she was on the phone. 'Oh my God, Lily, how did that happen? I'm guessing Adam, unless you've met someone else along the way! You were thinking about just trying a relationship the last I heard, so that's moved along a bit bloody quickly. When did he ask you, do you have a ring, is it huge?'

She was squealing down the phone in delight, and her infectious excitement set me off, too.

'Oooh, hang on a sec, too many questions. Yes, Adam, erm, what else was there?'

'When and how did he ask you?'

Lou's interrogation was full on. She wanted to know everything about how we'd got back on track and the proposal. When I told her how Adam had popped the question, and about my bespoke ring, I could hear how emotional she was just from her breathing. She was choked with love and affection for me, which made me want to reach down the line and hold her.

'You deserve so much happiness, Lily, and this sounds bloody perfect. He is showing you how much he loves you in the most personal way, and that is just what you should have. Your life has been hard, and you've been treated abominably in the past, so it's fantastic that the man has come good and corrected the error of his ways. Now, he's a fella who *does* have your best interests at heart. He clearly loves you for the phenomenal person you are, and I'm *so* chuffed for you. I can't even find the words to say how happy I am.'

'I know, it's amazing, isn't it? I'm really, really happy, Lou, and to think that Nat wants to marry me is just unbelievable.'

'Whoa, whoa . . . Nat? What do you mean by that?'

I was confused. I didn't understand why Lou was talking about Nat all of a sudden.

'What do you mean? I don't get it. I'm marrying Adam. Why bring Nat up now?'

'You said it. You said it just now, "and to think Nat wants to marry me". What the fuck are you up to?'

I couldn't breathe, I was still really confused. 'I'm not up to anything. I don't get it. I don't get what I just said. I thought I said Adam. I didn't say Nat. I'm sure I didn't say Nat?'

Panic gripped hold of me, and I began pacing around on the shale, feeling it crunch beneath my feet.

'You said Nat, Lily!'

There was a long, painful silence. I knew that Lou was probably telling the truth, but I genuinely couldn't recall saying Nat, and if I did, then she was right. What the hell was I thinking? Why had his name slipped out so easily? I knew what the next question was going to be, so I steeled myself and waited.

'How much contact have you had with him?'

I rapidly tried to formulate an answer to give her, but I could never lie to Lou. 'What? Nothing, none I mean. I haven't heard from him for ages. He did message me, but I haven't replied or anything for weeks now.'

'OK, so the last I knew you had blocked him and *couldn't* hear from him. So, what changed?'

'I unblocked him after I'd been sick all over Adam. You knew about that, the sick bit? I just went into this massive decline and holed myself up. It was as though it was starting all over again and I was terrified. I knew he'd been trying to contact me, or at least he'd been thinking about me, but I didn't do anything about it. I swear I didn't, Lou.'

'Listen, there's no point in trying to convince me. This is your bag, nothing to do with me. If you're trying to convince anyone it's yourself, and I'm sick of hearing it. I'm sick of all the excuses and lies!'

'But I'm not lying. I'm trying to tell you the truth. I'm trying to tell you that it's all over and finished with Nat. God knows why his name came out. I told him the other day that it was all over. He tried to tell me he loved me and wanted me to go to Spain with him, but I know my life is here with Adam, and I don't want anything to do with him.'

I seethed away at Nat for causing chaos at a time when Lou and I should have been embroiled in unbridled girlie wedding chat.

'Yes, I feel rejected by him. Yes, I'm angry and hurt that after all this time he declared his love for me. Yes, it will take me a while to get over this and settle down, and yes, I wish he had told me before, but he didn't! And all that has done is help me to see that I want to be with Adam!'

I had yelled this pretty much at the top of my lungs and was breathing heavily as I finished my outpouring.

Lou knew me so well that she waited briefly before helping me to climb the gallows, where I waited for the noose to tighten.

'And does Adam know that you've been in touch with Nat?'

'No, Lou, no, he doesn't,' I croaked. 'He doesn't know anything about Nat, other than the fact we had an unsatisfactory relationship. He has no idea of what that means even. He doesn't know about Bristol or the messages. He knows nothing.'

'Bristol? What about Bristol?'

I'd slipped; the short drop left me hanging.

'So, you've seen him *and* you spoke to him the other day.' She sounded exasperated.

'Oh, Lou,' I sobbed. With every word that fell from my lips, I felt as though I was destroying our friendship. 'I am *so* sorry I did such a stupid thing. I was confused. I didn't know what to do. I didn't know what to think or how to be. I tried to sort it out myself, and I didn't do it right. And it doesn't matter how many times I say this or how often I find myself in this situation, I just can't do relationships or people. I can't figure them out or understand how I need to be. So, when Adam told me he loved me, I freaked out and went to see Nat in Bristol. It was such a weird, weird night. To start with, he bowled me over and was rough and forceful with me, but then he was loving and kind. The next day, though, he just left me. I thought he was going to be around for a day or two, but he just disappeared, and I didn't hear from him for ages. Then when he did reappear, he started bombarding me with messages. I ignored them, I really did ignore them, for ages. I was really good and when Adam asked me to marry him, I took control and told Nat to get on with his life. I sent him away. He told me he loved me, and about moving to a place in

Spain. Although I admitted that I still had feelings for him, I told him it's Adam I want. Nat's gone now. It's over, finished.'

'How can you even contemplate marrying Adam? Do you really think you're being fair with him? Clearly, he loves you very much – and take note – he is *showing* you how much he loves you. Actions really do speak louder than words. You're fucking cruel, Lily. Thoughtless, careless, selfish and–'

'I know, I know, I know. You think I don't know that I am all of those things. I've been that person my whole life, and I have tried year after year to get rid of that version of me. Don't you think I hate myself for that? Do you think I want to be like that? I *am* trying. Each and every day, I try to be a worthy person, and although you won't believe me, I am getting there. Adam knows that I have baggage, and that I'm broken, but he has already told me he has enough love for me to be patient and calm, and that he will support me as I continue to grow. And I trust him. I trust that with his attention and affection, I will get there. He's told me he will always be there for me, no matter what.'

It sounded as though I was saying he would always love me, irrespective of how obnoxious I might be, as though I could pretty much do as I please and he would always be there, turning the other cheek. It wasn't what I meant at all, but in my fury and anxiety the words had tumbled out and assumed their own meaning. Lou was silent.

'Lou, Lou, are you still there?'

I heard her sniff, she was crying.

'I'm still here.'

Then silence, a long, long silence.

'I just don't know what to say, Lily. I love you so much and fear for you, but this? This is just, well . . . I don't know. You lied to me.' Her voice broke as she cried. 'I just don't know how to help you. I can't tell you what to do or what you need, but maybe you should think about getting some help, and I hate to say this, but you *really* should consider Adam in all of this. How can you marry a guy you say you love, yet you're still obsessed with someone else? And believe me, you *are* still obsessed with Nat, whether you like it or not. It's as though you're addicted to him. He gives you a fix that lasts for a while and then he disappears. Just as you are going through withdrawal and are desperate for another fix, he appears again, topping you up. You've become dependent on him and he's loving it. How can you let Nat continue to abuse you like this? All this business about Spain, what's all that about? And loving you, come on. You made it sound as though he bloody well near raped you in Bristol for Christ's sake, and that was just a couple of months ago. He is sick to do this to you, to do it to lots of people. I swear he has girls all around the country. When he's in touch with you he's ignoring them, and vice versa. I'm sorry, but he's a fucking monster! You lied to me, and to make things worse, you lied to me about a fucking monster!'

Lou's words carved great crevices through my heart, leaving me desolate. Both of us were in tears.

'I just don't know what to do.' It was more of a pathetic statement than a question, but eventually Lou answered it.

'You need to get some help, some professional help, Lily. I will always love you, but right now I can't help you. I can't stand by and see someone I love destroying themselves in the way you are. You are an intelligent, motivated and driven person in so many ways. Look at what you have done with your life, where you have pulled yourself up from, yet when it comes to this moron you have an inability to effectively break the destructive cycle. Please, please save yourself. I always said I would come back to that arse end of nowhere and smash your arms as well as your legs with a sledgehammer to keep you in your room and out of danger, but I can't, Lily, you are beyond me. I can no longer help or protect you.'

I could hear the despair in her voice, and it was painful to acknowledge. I felt guilty for lying and for putting her through so much pain. It was as though my mother was speaking to me from beyond the grave, and I was back to being that careless, thoughtless, selfish child again. I didn't know how to respond and the silence was thick and weighty, as I sat on a rock picking at a random piece of vegetation that had attached itself to the ancient, stony surface.

'I understand, Lou. I'm so sorry. I promise I'll get it sorted. I think you're right, maybe some help again. Love you muchly.'

I hung up the call and she texted her response.

Love you millions, always will. Take care xxx

Her words made me feel hopeless and full of shame. I sat for some time staring ahead into the ocean and wondering how the hell I was going to set myself straight. I was sick of the Nat versus Adam battle, but there was no one else to blame it on, it was down to my own weaknesses. Lou had made so much sense and was always right about everything. I had to trust her and the lifeline her words proffered me. I agreed that I did in fact need the help of a professional. I had years of history to unpick, and although I'd tried before, I had always stopped counselling when things became too difficult. It was no wonder I could not achieve lasting change. At the first sign of a setback, I would topple back into the pit of shame and despair. But I had to keep trying, and I had to let Lou know she was right.

Will seek help, I can't do this alone, but want to more than ever. I'm sorry for being such a pain in the arse. One day, I will be a fine, upstanding human. Please don't despair, please don't abandon me, don't leave me behind. I can and will change, but it may take some time. Thank you for being my voice of reason xxx

I know you will, you're Lily Montrose. You're already a fine human being, you just need some sense kicked into you. I will never abandon you or leave you behind, you mad fool, no matter how ugly it might get xxx

Chapter 40
SEPTEMBER 2019

I had to get back to Tregellas, as I had some work to do for Mrs Enys before the end of the day. So, I buried my phone in my pocket and ran up the stream sidetrack towards home. As I went, I thought about Adam and how he had carried me up the same track with my broken ankle. Once again conscious of how frightened I was of losing him, I latched onto the fleeting finger of jealousy that had poked me when I saw the 'I heart A' sign in the sand, which fired me up and helped me to regain my composure. I knew I couldn't live anywhere but here. It was Adam I needed to – no – that I wanted to devote my life to.

I had made this decision countless times and chided myself for being back in the same muddled state, but this time it felt different. Lou's words had been spot-on. I couldn't do this on my own and would definitely seek help. I had a complex background, which had made me the way I was, and I couldn't change it, but I could change how I was reacting to Nat. It didn't matter that he had just brushed me aside as though I was unimportant in his life. I was confident that I would be able to get over being separated from him, as I had done it before. And although it might hurt and take a long time, I would do it whilst loving and being loved by Adam.

I was running by the time I got to the top of the track; I leapt over the rocky outcrops that peppered the path and ducked under the overhanging trees. My running may have been hard, but it was effortless. With every stride, I felt light and determined. Something primeval was driving me back to Tregellas, and I was desperate to be within its safe confines.

I rushed through my afternoon chores and made it back to Morwenna in good time to make Adam a meal. I wanted it to be one made with the intention of love and adulation. I said a prayer to the universe over the ingredients and constructed a cashew and aubergine lasagne. I bathed, washed my hair and put on my skinny jeans and a camisole vest top. As Adam came through the door, I held my finger to his mouth to stop him from speaking and kissed him warmly before planting a glass of icy cold wine in his hand. Then I led him upstairs, where I signalled for him to stand still by the side of the bed. I went into the bathroom and turned on the hot tap, so that it would fill the bath very slowly. I returned to him, kissing every inch of flesh that was revealed as I stripped him off. Now and again we would take a mouthful of the icy wine, which would dribble and spill as we made love to each other. We could hear the sound of the bath running in the background, and the slow stream of water as it tinkled against the cast iron tub added the pressure of time, making the moment more intense. Our urgency rose ahead of the water level until we were spent and breathless on the old bed. Between gasps, I could hear that the tune of the water had taken on a deeper tone, which told me the bath was over half full.

'You'd better bathe, it sounds as though it's ready – and dinner is, too.' I propped myself up on my left elbow and smiled at his peaceful face. 'C'mon, Enys, bath!'

And with that I ran the knuckle of my thumb up his thigh, which I knew would make him move. He was so ticklish there, especially after having an orgasm, and sure enough he bent double, almost as though it was a reflex action. He reached out a hand to grab me, but it was futile and I escaped, screaming like a banshee as I ran to check on the water, which was fine. The bathroom was filled with steam, so I turned off the hot tap and topped it up with a little cold; it was now perfect to step into. I stripped a few whorls from the lavender plant on the windowsill and tossed the fragrant blades into the swirling water. Then, as I walked into the bedroom, I slapped Adam hard on his exposed butt cheek and told him he had ten minutes until dinner.

I was humming as he came into the small kitchen area behind me. He held up his now empty wine glass and raised his eyebrows at me, offering a top up for us both.

The meal was delicious and afterwards, we sat on the floor and read to each other. I had recently become interested in poetry and had a Mary Oliver book on the go, whilst Adam was reading a repair manual for a 1954 Little Grey Fergie tractor, which was unintentionally beautifully written. When he picked it up to read it to me, I was a bit affronted, but the words were musical and he spoke with perfect received pronunciation, which kept me laughing and interested all at the same time. He was a comedian at a superficial level, but he had a deep and beautiful soul.

As we lay in bed that night, we talked about our love and how miraculous it was that we had found each other. In that moment, I could see a projection of our lives, as though it were an old black and white movie playing out on 35mm film. I even thought of Nathaniel, but I ignored his presence and let my thoughts of him wash in and wash out, as though he were nothing more than a piece of jetsam aimlessly floating on the waves of the Celtic Sea.

Over the next three days, I received more messages from Nat, which I ignored, as they no longer had any impact. It seemed the more I ignored him the harder he tried, and the less I liked him. His messages were desperate and pleading, and my respect and need for him dwindled with every word. Then came his final text.

Hey hun. I don't blame you for not replying, but I'm done here now, last and final offer, I will stop asking. I feel so perfect when I am with you. Please know I love you, we have something special – maybe not conventional but it is genuine from my side. I can't wait to make love to you again and long for you. If you want that, too, meet me at the apartment in Bristol on Sept 28th at 11.00, because I'm driving to Alicante from there. Last chance, sexy lady, see you there or never xxx

Chapter 41

The early autumn mornings were a delight to wake up to and, as Adam was the first to rise, he would bring me a cup of tea, kiss me gently on the forehead and go off to work.

I lay there with the feel of him fresh on my brow and, as I cupped my turquoise mug of tea, I noticed the light refracting from the emerald on my left hand. It sent slices of colour splattering across the ceiling. Smiling, I pulled the white cotton throw over my shoulder and set about daydreaming. I dropped off into a restless slumber and dreamed that I took Bertie to a car showroom, where I sold him to an offensive little man with a huge belly, chewed fingernails and a dreadfully pockmarked face. He gave me the heebie-jeebies, but I sold Bertie nonetheless and bought a brand-new blue estate car. It had lots of buttons and gadgets but could at best be described as functional. I had no idea why I had cast aside my beautiful but ancient Bertie and settled for this steady-Eddie estate instead. As soon as the deal was done, I regretted it and realised I had made a mistake. Immediately, I wanted Bertie back, but the awful man wouldn't accept my offer and told me that he had already been sold.

I awoke startled and strangely low in spirit. The dream was massive, and it snuck under my skin and attached itself like a conjoined twin. As I showered, I scrubbed away at my skin as if to relieve myself of it, but the dream continued to plague me. As I dressed, I found myself pacing around the room tormenting myself with it. I listened to the news, ate my breakfast and got ready to begin my day, but all the time the dream created an itch I could not scratch.

Chapter 42

I took one last look around me, removed my engagement ring and placed it gently in its teal box, before setting it back in the same kitchen drawer Adam had put it in when he asked me to marry him. As I picked up my copy of *Jane Eyre*, the only possession I wished to keep, I said a silent sorry to him and walked out of the door.

As soon as I was on the road to Bristol, I knew instinctively that I was doing the right thing; the dream interpretation had made itself known to me. It was as though Bertie were Nat and I was settling for Adam – the blue estate car – because he was reliable and was giving me everything I needed. Life was too easy with him. Nat was flawed, but, like Bertie, exciting. I felt guilty at having walked off and left Adam, but he knew me well enough to know that I wasn't a safe bet. Despite all that he'd said, he knew in his heart I wasn't marriage material. I was doing what was best for us both. In the long run, I would save him a whole bunch of sadness and hurt.

The miles galloped away as I thrashed Bertie up the M5. I couldn't get there quickly enough. I'd placed my green suede boat shoes neatly on the passenger seat, and I rubbed gently away at the hard rubber pads on the pedals with my bare feet. Although the day was grey and overcast, I was sweating profusely. My hands were slippery on the wheel and my jeans stuck fast, yet my mouth was dry and I had the beginnings of a headache. I aimlessly drummed the little finger of my left hand against the Bakelite wheel, tapping out a mesmerising rhythm that kept me occupied as the miles ticked by. I counted down the markers. Sixty became forty, forty was soon twenty and before I knew where I was, I had reached the exit slip road. I sped off the motorway, passing the service station where I'd had coffee on my previous visit to Chapel Pill, and driving way over the speed limit to the apartment, arriving at 10.43. I'd made it just in time and, although I couldn't see Nat's BMW, I wasn't worried, as he frequently either up or downgraded his car, so I could never be sure what he was driving. Stuffing my feet into my shoes, I made my way to the flat we had spent the night in.

I hadn't messaged Nat – just like I hadn't left a note for Adam – I was on autopilot and fizzing with excitement. Nat wouldn't believe his eyes when he saw me. At last, after all the years of complex niggles, we were finally going to make a steady relationship together. I had known this all along; that this, one day, would be our destiny and that we would be together, united in happiness. I had hoped all along that eventually Nat would deliver the love and devotion I always knew he had in him.

Lou would kill me this time, but once Nat and I were settled, I would call her and explain how things had all worked out. Her words about never abandoning me or leaving me behind gave me comfort. Yes, she would be as mad as hell, but in time she would be happy for Nat and me. She could come and visit and spend the summer with us. I imagined the two of us together in the yard of the colonial house, sipping sangria while Nat worked away at the BBQ, laughing together and enjoying not only the warmth of the sunshine but also our enduring friendship. I would still get some counselling help, as I could no longer ignore the presence of so much hurt and trauma. This would make a massive difference to my relationship with Nat, and perhaps he would have some therapy, too. It would be idyllic, and I felt blessed and thrilled at the prospect.

Once inside the building, I knew roughly which direction I was headed in and instead of taking the lift, I bounded up the stairs, where I was confronted with identical apartment doors. I was suddenly uncertain about where to go. I stared into the corridor trying to figure out where I was and which way I should go, but my mind was thick, as though it was trying to churn treacle. I panicked, as I realised I didn't even know the number of the apartment I was looking for. Things looked so different from the last time I was there. I was lost. I ran down corridor after corridor searching for something, anything that was familiar, but nothing registered.

I ran down a flight of stairs and repeated the same search on that floor, too. Why the hell hadn't I paid more attention when I was with Nat that night? Why hadn't I messaged him to tell him I was on the way? Supposing he went without me because he didn't know I was here? A wave of paralysing fear swept over me, knocking the wind out of my sails. I had to get out. I had to get back down to the car park so that I could breathe and, if Nat should arrive, then he would at least find me.

I reached the exit and, as I staggered through the doors and came crashing into the fresh air, my teeth chattered and I started hyperventilating. I gulped in masses of air way too quickly and the tingling around my lips and mouth spread down to my hands, cramping them into gnarly claws. My vision blackened and narrowed, as though I were looking through the wrong end of a pair of binoculars.

I tried desperately hard to arrest the rapid breathing by holding my breath for as long as I could. One second, then perhaps two, but the feeling I was dying forced me to take half a dozen hurried breaths to compensate for the suffocation. The sound of blood gushed between my ears and around my body in time with the thump beating away in my chest. A muffled voice from a distant memory surfaced. 'Don't try too hard, just let it pass.' Soon, my pounding chest slowed to the rhythm of the soothing voice and something inside clicked. Whether it was physiological or psychological, I'm not sure, but nonetheless my body began to realise that I had more than enough oxygen and that I was safe and wasn't going to die. I was able to briefly hold my breath without feeling stifled. I carried on taking those slow, gentle breaths until eventually, after what felt like an age, my breathing began to return to near normal.

My hands were shaking. I glanced round the car park but the cars were a jumble; it felt impossible to know what to do. In my panicked state, I convinced myself that I should try once more to find the flat. I went back into the building, only this time I went up in the lift, in the hope of spotting a familiar landmark.

I stopped at the first floor and apprehensively poked my head out of the lift doors in order to try and get my bearings. It definitely wasn't that floor, but when I repeated the exercise on the second, I happened to spot a painting I recognised, and from there I was able to find my way to the correct door. As I approached it, arm raised to knock, it suddenly opened.

A young man was just heading out. 'Oh, hi, can I help you?'

I was suddenly stuck for words. I had no idea who I was talking to or why he should be at Nat's flat.

'Erm, well, I'm not sure really. I'm here for Nat – well, I'm looking for him – he's kind of expecting me. Do you know him?'

'Yes, yes, I know him, he took care of this place for me for a while. And you are?'

'I'm Lily.'

His deadpan face revealed that my name meant nothing.

'Oh, OK. So, listen. Nat's not here, he's left for Spain already, you missed him by a day. Sorrel and Tom flew out a couple of days ago and Nat drove down yesterday. He's probably not that far away from their new place now, if he's not there already, bearing in mind he drives like an F1 racer!'

The wrecking ball again, only this time it smashed into my solar plexus. I staggered backwards, as though I had been punched. I couldn't believe what I was hearing. I couldn't believe that Nat had done this to me, that he had lured me there knowing full well that he wouldn't even be in Bristol by then. It was all just a big scam to deliver one final heinous act of destruction.

'Oh God, you OK?'

The man reached out to steady me and, grasping my forearm, he stopped me from collapsing against the corridor wall. His fingers felt as though they were burning into my arm, and although he was talking away, I couldn't make any sense of what he was saying. It was as though I had my head ducked beneath the water of a packed swimming pool; the noise around me was loud and indiscernible, burbling, nonsensical. Pressure was building in my ears and my eyes burned. Everything was moving in slow motion and I felt weightless, as if I was drowning. The only thing that had registered, the thing that had done the real damage, the thing that had sliced me to the very core, was the young man casually referring to Nat's son as Tom. That was *my* name, *my* name for *our* child.

I shoved the man off and have a vague recollection of his

futile, clawing attempts to engage with me, but I staggered blindly back to the lift and somehow out of the building to Bertie.

How sick Nathaniel was, how callous and cruel to inflict this on me. I knew at last how wicked he really was. The recent messages, the declaration of love, the changes to his life, all lies to cripple me once and for all. All carried out with forethought and malice, all designed for the most dramatic devastation and all deployed to destroy me and any chance of a normal life. If he couldn't have me in the way he wanted – picking me up, putting me down, toying with me as and when he so pleased – then he didn't want anyone else to have me, and he would relish annihilating me in the process. Poor old Lily, not tough enough to play with the big boy, therefore, she can meet the same fate as the kitten: kicked hard against the wall and broken.

Once inside Bertie's small space of amniotic tranquillity, I didn't know what to do or where to go. Mya had been true to her word and abandoned me, and she was right to do so.

I was alone.

I was no one.

I had nothing.

I could be nothing more, so I picked up my book and walked.

Chapter 43
DECEMBER 2019

The last few words fell from my calm mouth and I could feel a pleading, questioning look on my face as I made eye contact with Grace, almost as though I were seeking her approval to stop talking. I felt drained, yet in some way lighter because of it. I'd been taken out of myself whilst being fully immersed in nothing but my story. It had taken hours to tell it. I had no idea where it had all come from, and although I had recounted it, it was as though it belonged to someone else. I was merely the narrator of a tale that had happened to a far off and unknown girl.

I had become hypnotised by the storytelling, and slowly my awareness began to return to the purpose of our meeting, to myself and to Grace, and to the tiny stud that sparkled in her right nostril. It was new and I liked it, as it enhanced her gentle glow. The first couple of times I had met her, I hadn't trusted her at all. In my uncertainty, I had mistaken her blushing apple cheeks and her rosebud lips as patronising in their generosity. I thought she was someone who was going to pat me on the head and ask, 'and how did that make you feel?', just like those before her. But I had been wrong. All she had asked was, 'how *are* you?'

Grace had learned all there was to know about me, inside and out. With the picks and brushes of her trade, she had excavated those dark little skeletons that I – no, we as humans – prefer not to acknowledge, the ones that are in fact part of, and essential to, our very being. She had sifted the sediment and unearthed the reason I had been found at midnight by some PCSOs, on the beach in Western-super-Mare. I was barefoot, with nothing but a bunch of keys and my copy of *Jane Eyre*. Later, I recalled a freezing cold police cell and hushed voices. Faces, some familiar, were blurred behind a curtain of kaleidoscopic colours that came with the prescription-induced sleep, and although I am now found, I am still dreadfully lost.

I'm not too sure how I ended up at the clinic, hospital, whatever it is. It is a place like no other I have ever known. Its opulence and sense of gravity gives me the feeling of brushing velvet in the wrong direction, and it is not a place I feel comfortable in. It has all the luxury of a plush hotel, but it is safeguarded by heavy doors with gleaming glass panels and touchpads that allow you to come and go, provided you have the correct fingerprint. I have a spacious suite, with a large picture window at the far end, through which I sit and stare at an expanse of stunning scenery. In the foreground, an ancient cedar tree gently rustles in the wind, and way off in the distance, the rolling hills tumble and fall over each other until they vanish over the horizon. And now, as we sit in a small counselling room, with its fascinating wallpaper of olive-green leaves and purple petals that seem to fold, dissolve and blend into one another, I realise I have come to like Grace and the intriguing pattern. I've spent three months staring at them from the plaid green sofa.

My belly growls. Hunger has returned to replace my empty starvation. The telling of my story is cathartic and healing, but I know it is just the very start of my recovery. My face is sticky with tears and there are piles of used tissues in the wastepaper basket – clearly, I have cried a great deal.

'And this?' I say, holding my arms open to the sumptuous sanctuary that surrounds us, 'how did all of this come about? I can see it must be massively expensive, but I doubt I'm paying for it?'

'I can't tell you who is paying, but I can tell you that you know your benefactors.' She tilts her head in a Princess Diana way that accompanies her probing and usually precedes a question I might struggle with. Hesitantly, she speaks. 'Do you have any questions?' I know she is heading somewhere specific, but my tired head weighs heavy and I'm unable to guess what is coming next. I shake my head.

'You're a tough and brave lady, Lily, and you deserve the love you are being shown. It is my job – no, it's my *privilege* – to help you enjoy that love.'

I nod and my dehydrated brain wobbles inside my head.

'We do still have some work to do. You realise that this is just the beginning?' Grace shifts stiffly. 'And Mya, we need to talk about Mya.'

I'm unable to answer and we briefly sit in silence.

'I know you've had help with Mya in the past, but I think it would be helpful if I could just understand a little more about her. Can I ask you a couple of questions about her?'

I shrug.

'You only ever see her reflection, is that right?'

I nod.

'But you hear her voice and you reply to her as though you're in conversation with her?'

I nod once more.

'And you haven't seen her since your argument?'

A devastating longing for the soul who has shared my lived existence for more than thirty years grips me, but I sit in a silence that Grace seems to hold in the palm of her hand, making it safe. I feel her empathy alongside me, not wanting anything from me, just giving and simply being there for me. It is comfortable and OK for there to be no words.

She looks again with her Princess Diana glance, checking I'm OK to proceed. 'It's fine, we'll come back to it . . . I do have a couple of messages for you, though, would you like them?'

I nod my consent.

'Well, Lou and the girls send you all of their love and hugs.'

I can see she registers my unease. 'It's OK, they're fine, they're just happy to know you're OK.'

She hesitates momentarily before proceeding. 'The other message didn't make any sense at all, it seemed a bit bizarre when I received it, and I was uncertain as to how I should give it to you, or whether it was even appropriate to or not, but now it makes perfect sense.'

I feel a frown creep across my brow, but she softens and there is undoubtedly a moment of joinder between us. The therapist falls away and the human Grace joins me. She smiles with great affection. 'It's from Morwenna Mowahy! Yes, I thought she was a real person, too!'

She raises her eyebrows in a conspiratorial 'I'm as thick as you' manner. I smile, but it is a fixed, false grin that comes from a place of trepidation. I want to cry, but I can't. I know that whatever she is about to say will be hard to hear. I twist the ring on my little finger, fiddling with it furiously, with the feeling that one of these days my finger will unscrew. I see the kindliness in Grace's eyes; I know that I need to and can take responsibility for my actions. I know that I must acknowledge the pain and unhappiness I have caused, and I am willing to do so. Grace takes a deep breath in and then cautiously speaks. 'Next time you're in our kitchen, do us a favour and chuck me a teaspoon, I shall always be waiting for it, Actually.'

A lump in my throat stifles me. I have never felt so small, so humble, so ashamed, so unconditionally loved. But I know that I am fine and always will be, as I hear myself whisper, 'Adam'.

Acknowledgments

My heartfelt thanks to you, Mum and Dad, you're inspiring in so many ways and there are no words to express my love and gratitude.

To Dibsy and Mia, thank you for bearing the brunt of my first draft, I hope you recover from the trauma.

Thank you, Keith, for all that you are; your encouragement and insight know no bounds. I love you dearly.

My love goes to Sarah and Morag of the Fluffy Olives, only because you'd do me some mischief if I failed to mention your invaluable friendship in my acknowledgements.

To Lynn, for giving me the name Montrose, as well as the space and time in Cornwall to finish Lily.

A special mention here to Amanda Malben for your writerly wisdom and gallons of coffee. Thank heavens for that terrible night some years ago when our friendship was forged. I appreciate you so very much.

I'd also like to thank Juliet for working with me over the years and for guiding me towards my greater self.

Finally, I want to thank Danielle for investing in Lily, and for all of your editing/publishing knowledge and expertise.

About the Author

Sarah was born in Hertfordshire, where she lived and worked for many years in the NHS. She attended Oxford Brookes University and graduated with a merit in Creative Writing.

Sarah now lives in rural Northamptonshire with her partner Keith and their dog and cats. She continues to write, paint and work as a wellbeing coach.

Merry Go Round is her first novel.

Printed in Great Britain
by Amazon

50826207R00177